TUSK JUSTICE

VICTORIA TAIT

DEDICATION

For Cassandra, Allie & Dad
for helping bring this book together

GET EXCLUSIVE MATERIAL
BY JOINING MY BOOK CLUB

If you'd like to hear from me about my books, author life, new releases and special offers, then please join my book club by visiting VictoriaTait.com. I don't send spam and you can unsubscribe at any time.

Building a relationship with my readers is one of the most exciting elements of being an author.

If you would like to receive regular updates, please visit VictoriaTait.com.

Thank you, and enjoy Tusk Justice.

KISWAHILI WORD GLOSSARY

- *Asante* Thank you
- *Boda boda* Motorbike taxi
- *Bomori* Elderly man in Kalenjin dialect
- *Chai Tea* consisting of bags or leaves boiled in a mixture of 2/3rd water and 1/3rd milk
- *Dawa* Cocktail Vodka based cocktail with lime and honey
- *Habari* Greeting used like hello but meaning 'What news?'
- *Kahawa* Coffee
- *Kanga* Colourful cotton fabric (also Swahili for guinea fowl)
- *Kikoi* Brightly coloured striped cotton fabric
- *Kikuyu* Kenyan tribe
- *Kizunguzungu* Dizziness
- *Kuni* Wood
- *Matatu* White Toyota minivan
- *Mabati* Corrugated iron sheeting, often used as a roof material
- *Mitumba* Second-hand clothes, shoes and fabric market. Literal meaning is 'bundles' derived from

the plastic wrapped packages the donated clothing arrives in

- *Msitu* Forest
- *Mzungu* European/White person
- *Nyama* Meat
- *Pole* Sorry
- *Podo* Large evergreen/coniferous tree.
- *Shamba* Farm, garden or area of cultivated land
- *Shuka* Thin, brightly coloured blanket in bright checked colours, where red is often the dominant colour. Also used as a sarong or throw
- *Sukuma wiki* Braised kale
- *Syce* A groom/someone who looks after horses
- *Tusker & Whitecap* Brands of beer brewed by East African Breweries
- *Ugali* Thick porridge made from maize

OTHER WORDS & PHRASES

- *Boot* Car trunk
- *Crisps* Chips
- *Chips* Fries
- *Court Shoe* Woman's low heeled smart shoe
- *Jerrycan* Large flat-sided metal container for storing or transporting liquids, typically petrol or water.
- *Lift* Elevator
- *NGO* Non-governmental Organisation
- *Staffroom* Break room
- *Trainers* Sneakers

STYLE, SPELLING AND PHRASEOLOGY

Mama Rose, the main character through whose eyes we view events, has a British education and background. She uses British phrases, spelling and style of words.

Kiswahili words are also used in the book and most are linked to a Glossary at the back, which briefly explains their meaning.

These words add to the richness and authenticity of the setting and characters, and I hope increase your enjoyment of Fowl Murder.

CHAPTER ONE

One elephant is killed every fifteen minutes in Africa. The dead lactating female found on Mount Kenya, with her tusks removed, was just one more statistic. Rose Hardie did not want her infant calf to become another.

R ose closed her veterinary bag, lifted her tall lanky frame and arched her back, grimacing in pain. She waggled her arthritic fingers, which were always more swollen and painful in the morning, and opened a small blue plastic cool box. Inside, the canine rabies vaccinations for her clinic stood secure and upright in their moulded styrofoam tray.

Rose was a forthright European woman in her mid-sixties, who had been born and brought up in Kenya. The long, often arduous, years were etched on her permanently tanned face, topped with frizzy white hair. Kipto, her African house girl of indeterminate age, set a cup of tea on the small wooden kitchen table, but nearly knocked it over in surprise when Rose's mobile phone rang in the still morning air.

Even without her glasses, Rose recognised the 'Y' on caller ID, which meant the caller must be Yasir, an elderly African vet based in Nairobi, the capital of Kenya, who Rose occasionally consulted. Rose, or 'Mama Rose' as she was affectionately known by the African community, was not a qualified vet, but held the official title of Veterinary Paraprofessional.

She had gained her knowledge and experience treating a variety of domestic, farm and wild animals in her local community during the past forty years.

"Habari, Mama Rose. I hope I haven't woken you, but I need your assistance." Inwardly, Rose groaned, intuitively knowing her morning plans would be disrupted. "Local women collecting firewood have spotted a young elephant wandering near the Mount Kenya entrance to the elephant corridor."

The seventeen-mile elephant corridor was constructed in 2010 to link the mountain with the wide plains of grassland to the north, and passed under the busy A2 highway.

Yasir continued, "I've been appointed by the David Sheldrick Elephant Orphanage to fly up and help with the rescue. They are asking Davina Dijan if we can land at the Gaia Conservancy airstrip, but I fear it may take us several hours to get organised.

Mount Kenya Trust rangers have been sent to locate and secure the elephant calf, but I would feel reassured if you could be on hand to treat any immediate injuries."

The rangers had found an adult female elephant's decomposing carcass five days earlier, during a routine foot patrol along the winding forest paths on the lower slopes of Mount Kenya. Their concern for a missing calf prompted a search and rescue operation and they undertook ground-level searches in the forest under rough, brown-barked, African Olive trees and coniferous Podos.

The Trust's horseback patrol hunted for the calf higher up Mount Kenya on heathland between giant pineapple-shaped groundsels. After two days with no sightings, helicopter searches began. They were conducted by Equator Air, an aviation company from Rose's small town of Nanyuki, three hours north of Nairobi. Rose was relieved the young elephant had finally been located.

She opened the boot of her battered red Land Rover Defender and placed her medical bag inside. She added plastic buckets and some shuka blankets.

As Kipto dragged a metal jerrycan full of water across the dusty ground, the morning's peace was disturbed by the roar of a motorbike engine. The sound ceased and Rose heard a young male voice shout from the far side of her entrance gate, "Habari. Can you let me in?"

The disembodied voice sounded like that of Thabiti Onyango, a twenty-year-old African youth, who Rose and her husband Craig had become friends with after his mother was killed. Kipto rushed across to unlock the gate, which was secured at night to prevent intruders, and Thabiti wheeled in his red Honda motorbike.

"Early start," he commented.

"I could same the same about you." Rose raised an eyebrow in surprise. Thabiti was not normally an early bird.

"The first light of the day is best for taking photos. I captured some great shots of the mountain as the sun rose behind it, and there is still snow on the higher peaks."

Rose was unaware of Thabiti's interest in photography, but had no time to find out more at the moment. "Make yourself useful and lift those water containers into my car."

"Where are you going?" Thabiti groaned as he heaved the first container unceremoniously into the boot of the Defender.

"Careful," chided Rose. "A young elephant has been spotted by the elephant corridor. It's on its own and thought to be the offspring of the elephant killed by poachers last week. The David Sheldrick Elephant Orphanage is undertaking a rescue operation with the help of Mount Kenya Trust rangers. They've asked me to assist."

"Can I come?" Thabiti's eyes shone with excitement in his oval face. "I could film the rescue and take some photos.

Record the mission. I know the Sheldrick Trust post video footage on their website."

Rose paused. She wasn't particularly bothered about Thabiti filming the event, but an extra pair of hands, which she could trust to do as they were told, might prove useful. She knew the rangers to be enthusiastic but excitable.

CHAPTER TWO

Rose stood on a bank of red volcanic soil, crumbly underfoot and interspersed with rocks and waxy green-leafed gum tree saplings. Her white hair was wild and dusty, and her lined face was etched with worry. She heard a cacophony of cries: a noise guaranteed to alarm the calf, she thought.

"Mama Rose, they find it." The head ranger, in his forest green shirt, trousers and peaked cap, bounced up and down excitedly on the balls of his feet.

"Tell them to be quiet," Rose admonished. "They'll scare the elephant. I won't be able to treat any injuries with adrenaline pumping through its body. And the noise will hardly assist a safe and calm rescue."

The ranger whistled and the noise subsided. Peaked-capped heads appeared from behind various thorn bushes. As the ranger strode down the bank towards his men, Thabiti reached for his phone.

"Ow!" exclaimed Thabiti and sucked the tip of his finger. He had stabbed it on the common spike-thorn bush which hid its slender spikes behind a screen of cream petals.

The small elephant appeared from behind a yellow-flowered maumanda bush, swaying on its feet. Thabiti started recording the scene with his phone. Rose guessed the elephant to be nine months old, although it looked malnourished. It would have been dependent on its now dead mother for milk... and protection. A broken arrow shaft protruded from its belly.

Rose cupped her hands and shouted down to the head ranger. "Don't shoot a tranquilliser dart. A blanket thrown over its head should suffice. It's very weak. And I need it lying on its right side so I can remove that arrow and treat the wound."

The rangers formed a loose circle, about twenty metres in diameter, around the elephant. Those on the slope opposite Rose's vantage point moved forward, herding the tottering elephant towards flatter ground at the base of the elephant corridor.

When it stumbled down the slope into an area clear of thorn bushes, two rangers unceremoniously threw a blanket over its head and wrestled it to the ground. It barely moved, but another two rangers still secured its legs to prevent it escaping or injuring someone.

Thabiti ran down the slope to film close-up shots of the rescue. Rose collected her large green medical bag and followed him. She shouted to three rangers, now standing around watching the proceedings, to collect the buckets and containers of water.

Rose examined the calf's wound and the abscess forming beneath its thick skin. She didn't think any major organs had been damaged, which was a relief.

The head ranger spat, "Poison arrow, like the ones that killed its mother." Despite Mount Kenya National Park being protected, and designated a UNESCO World Heritage site in 1997, poachers still infiltrated it. They were a constant frustration to the Mount Kenya Trust Rangers.

"It's a young male." Rose cut an incision in the calf's skin beside the arrow and stood back as greyish pus and sand bust forth, dislodging the arrow in its lava flow.

Rose wiped her cheek with the top of her sleeve. "Thabiti, can someone else film? I need your help and some water pouring." A young ranger, in his teens, took the phone and warily continued filming. Thabiti tipped the contents of the jerrycan into a yellow plastic bucket.

"I'll hold the flap of skin open," said Rose, doing so with her latex-gloved hands. "Pour the water into the wound to flush out any more pus and debris." They repeated the procedure until Rose nodded in satisfaction.

Rose stood, arching her back to ease the stiffness. "Can you pour more water into the bucket?" she asked Thabiti. She searched her bag and extracted two bottles. "An antibiotic and antiseptic solution." She poured povidone-iodine and a dash of potassium permanganate into the bucket, which turned the water a light purple.

Returning to the prostrate elephant, she opened the damaged flap of skin with her gloved hand. "Pour in the liquid," she directed Thabiti. She swilled the mixture inside the wound and over the surrounding skin. They flushed it with more water until Rose was happy that the wound was clean.

From a white plastic tub, she gouged out handfuls of green clay, smearing it around and inside the wound. The rangers bent forward to view her work. "Why do you cover it in mud?" one asked.

"This clay is a natural remedy which fights infection and speeds up the healing process. It's also easy to apply and keep in place."

The ranger poked the contents of the tub with his finger, but quickly removed it as his colleagues laughed. It helped release the tension in the group. Rose sat back on her knees and patted the elephant.

"Ready." She looked at Thabiti. "Can you find the pickup driver?" Standing, she addressed the rangers. "Right, men, we need to move the elephant onto that large green tarpaulin so you can carry him to the vehicle."

The rangers set about their work excitedly, although not particularly gently. Thabiti assisted the pickup driver, signalling and manoeuvring him around the largest stones and bushes as he reversed towards the group.

They lowered the tailgate and, with cries and grunts, the rangers lifted the small but heavy baby elephant off the ground and deposited it in the back of the pickup. Two rangers volunteered to accompany the calf and climbed in beside it. Rose arranged a shuka blanket over its body as a forlorn elephant eye opened.

CHAPTER THREE

Rose arrived at Gaia Conservancy airstrip ahead of the pickup and baby elephant. She had not visited Gaia since it had been granted wildlife protected status. The conservancy was an amalgamation of three former cattle ranches.

Commercial cattle husbandry had given way to wildlife conservation and tourism, although Maasai tribes still kept cattle on surrounding land. Staff from the conservancy helped them prepare their animals for market and worked with them to prevent overgrazing.

The airstrip was a kilometre of mown grass with a white windsock on one side, drooping in the still air, and a hangar sheltering two small planes on the other.

Rose felt insignificant as she gazed across the conservancy's vast plains, spread out in all directions until they reached distant hills. It was April and the recent rains had tinted the landscape a shade of green. It looked barren and empty, but light aircraft pilots were not deceived.

They always flew low over the airstrip, searching for wild animals and hoping to frighten them away with the aircraft's noise, before they turned, re-approached, and landed. Rose spotted a warthog family cross the runway, stop, look at her, turn and trot away with erect tails. Within metres they repeated the sequence. Rose smiled.

It was approaching midday and the sun burnt like a lonely brazier in a clear sky. Rose felt her skin prickle. She opened her second bottle of water and drained half its contents. Thabiti did the same and burped. They both laughed.

Three people waited beside a grey and white fixed-wing plane. One, presumably the pilot, wore grey shorts, white shirt, dark sunglasses and a grey baseball cap.

An attractive and confident European lady in her late forties strode forward to meet Rose. Her outstretched hand recoiled as Rose stepped down from her battered red Land Rover Defender. Rose's appearance tended to be tidy and workman-like rather than fashionable, but today her sleeves were rolled up and her shirt partially untucked.

Her trousers were stained by contact with the red soil mixed with the solutions used to clean the elephant's wound. Sweating under the intense heat of the Kenyan sun added to her dishevelled appearance. Rose shuffled her feet but maintained her gaze. It was reflected in large gold-rimmed sunglasses.

The lady facing her looked immaculate in tailored trousers and a dazzling white shirt. "You must be Rose. Welcome to Gaia Conservancy. I'm Davina Dijan, Managing Director. What news of the elephant? Is it on its way?"

Yasir, the Nairobi-based vet who had called Rose earlier, hurried forward. He shook Rose's hand energetically. "Mama Rose, thank you for your help. What can you tell me about the elephant?"

"It's a male, about nine months, malnourished and weak," began Rose.

"When will it be here?" interrupted Davina.

"Soon, I hope," Rose responded. "The pickup couldn't carry him up the slope of the elephant corridor at the rescue point. I saw it driving slowly down the corridor floor in this direction. I parked my car up on the road so I didn't see anymore."

Davina tapped her foot and looked at her watch.

Rose and Yasir walked across to the plane. The Cessna Caravan could carry up to twelve passengers, but Rose saw someone had removed the rear seats to provide space for the orphaned elephant. A specially adapted double door lifted upwards, allowing easy access for the patient.

"I didn't have the equipment to provide an IV drip, but I think he'll need an electrolyte solution for the journey," Rose told Yasir.

They heard the strain of an engine and grating of gears, and they turned to watch the pickup lumber towards them and park beside of the aircraft. The rangers in the back looked grave. "Mama Rose, he not good." Rose and Yasir rushed over.

"He needs fluids now," said Yasir. He attached an IV line to the elephant's ear whilst Rose secured a bag of fluid to the other end of the clear PVC tubing. She passed it to one of the rangers to hold.

"As well as being malnourished," said Rose, "he has an injury on his left side. A poison arrow punctured the skin of his belly. We removed the arrow, and burst and cleaned the abscess. We've covered the wound in green clay."

"So that's what's lingering in your hair," laughed Yasir. Rose blushed as she picked hardened pieces of clay out of her curls. Yasir examined the drip. "The IV bag's empty. We'll move him into the aircraft, secure him, and attach the next bag of fluids."

Yasir called to some men from the conservancy, lazing under the shade of a small bead-bean tree. They lifted the elephant on its tarpaulin from the pickup into the plane. Yasir strapped it securely to the floor and covered it with another blanket. He attached a fresh fluid bag to the IV tubing and clipped it to the inside of the plane. The pilot secured the doors, jumped in, and the plane taxied up the runway.

Thabiti stood beside Rose as they waved the plane off. "I filmed some great footage of the rescue." He beamed proudly.

"Good, you can email it to me," stated Davina. "My property, so my rights to the film."

Thabiti shrank and hid behind Rose. He had anxiety issues which he forgot when distracted, as he had been during the excitement of filming the elephant rescue, but they resurfaced with Davina's challenge. Thabiti whispered to Rose's back. "The rights remain with the filmmaker. If she didn't want me filming, she should have told me at the time."

Rose smiled lopsidedly. "Sorry, Davina, the footage is for the Mount Kenya Trust. They need it to educate and prepare their rangers for future elephant attacks. It might also provide them with some marketing footage."

Davina stood with her hands on her hips, but Rose turned and walked casually to her vehicle. Thabiti followed like her shadow. "Jump in," she said to the two rangers standing forlornly by the airstrip. "I'll drop you in Timau." She started the engine, rolled down her window and shouted, "Nice to meet you."

She hit the accelerator, creating a cloud of dust which settled over Davina. Rose smiled, guiltily, but secretly satisfied.

CHAPTER FOUR

Rose returned home and kissed her husband, Craig, on the cheek. Home was a rented, one-bedroom, thatched cottage on the edge of Nanyuki town.

The house was small, but two guest cottages in the garden provided additional bedrooms. Rose and Craig chose the cottage when Craig retired as a farm manager, because it came with five acres of land.

There was space for a flower garden, vegetable and herb gardens, and Rose's menagerie of mainly rescued animals. These included a cow, horses, ducks, chickens, Potto her terrier, and Izzy her one-eyed black and white cat.

Craig was sitting out on the mabati tin-roofed patio. "Long morning," he commented. "Are you hungry?"

Rose slumped onto a large cedar sofa with striped kikoi-covered cushions. "No. We stopped at Chuckies Chips at Kisima Farm. Thabiti was complaining of hunger, as usual. The two Mount Kenya rangers with us were delighted with chips and cups of chai. The smell of chips enticed me, but I was defeated after half a bag. Thabiti finished them and I bought an apple from the fruit stall."

Craig placed his crossword on a wooden table next to his chair. "Did you find the elephant? Was it alive?"

"Yes, on both accounts." Rose rubbed at a mark on her sleeve. "Let me grab a bath before I tell you about it. I feel very grubby, especially after meeting the impeccably turned-out Davina Dijan."

The cottage did not have a shower. Instead, Rose ran lukewarm water into a chipped white enamel bath. The hot water heater was lit early in the morning and again in the evening.

Water was heated with a kuni tunnel boiler, kuni being Kiswahili for wood, which was the fuel burnt inside a metal tube to heat the water. It was highly efficient and more reliable and cost effective than electricity. That might be so, thought Rose, but she still had to boil a full kettle of water in the kitchen to make the temperature of the bath water bearable. She did not linger.

Rose returned to the patio, towelling her hair and wearing a fresh pair of jeans and blouse. She saw a large African man speaking to Craig, who she recognised as Sam Mwamba, an acquaintance from the Kenya Anti-Poaching Unit.

He stood to greet her, clasping her hands in one of his bearlike paws. Rose said, "News travels fast. Are you here to find out about the elephant poaching and rescue?"

Rose and Craig met Sam during Rose's first murder investigation, when an old school friend, Thabiti's mother, was murdered. Sam had appeared and disappeared throughout the case. Rose had considered him a suspect until he admitted to working with the victim and being part of the Kenya Anti-Poaching Unit. His job involved a lot of undercover work.

"Somewhat of a disaster finding a dead elephant, poached for its ivory tusks, on the doorstep of next week's inaugural Giant's Club Summit," remarked Craig.

"Yes and no," drawled Sam. Despite the pressures of his work, he always seemed relaxed with time to spare when he visited them. Maybe he was just being kind to two old mzungus, thought Rose.

Sam explained, "The Giant's Club Summit is to highlight the plight of our elephants and the increasing danger they face from poachers. Such a callous act, in a wildlife protected area, with an electric fence and regular foot and horse patrols, emphasises the cunning and greed of poaching organisations, and the need for a pan-African anti-poaching policy." Sam's nostrils flared like a horse detecting an unsavoury smell.

Rose sat up. She had not seen Sam so heated.

Sam continued, "Space for Giants has spent over a year planning this summit. Four heads of state are scheduled to be present and their countries represent over half the savannah elephant population, and three quarters of the remaining forest elephants. Our own President Kenyatta will be hosting, with President Bongo of Gabon, President Museveni of Uganda and President Khama of Botswana attending."

"What do they hope to achieve?" asked Rose.

Sam leant forward. "The political will, financial resources and technical capability to ensure a future for elephants and their habitats. Business leaders, conservation experts and key influencers are also attending."

"Key influencers? Who are they?" Craig asked.

Sam grinned and relaxed. "Celebrities. Rumours are Liz Hurley's coming."

Craig scratched his temple. "An English actress, I believe, though I can't recall what films she starred in."

"Never mind her films. She was Hugh Grant's girlfriend and wore a dress held together by safety pins." Rose grinned.

"She did what?" Craig's eyes widened. "Sounds like she needed a trip to mitumba."

Rose and Sam laughed. Mitumba was a large second-hand clothing market with unwanted garments sent from European countries. Rifling through the numerous stalls was one of Rose's favourite pastimes. She loved to pick up a bargain.

"Tell me about the elephant you rescued this morning," said Sam. "I heard some local women spotted it after we found its dead mother."

Rose was not entirely surprised that Sam had been a member of the group that found the dead elephant. He had a habit of appearing at poaching related incidents. "It was a nine-month-old male elephant, malnourished from the lack of its mother's milk, and with an abscess from a poisoned dart to the belly. The head ranger said poachers killed its mother with poison darts."

Sam grunted. "Unfortunately that's a common method, as arrows are cheaper and easier than guns to obtain and use."

Rose wiped her hands on the towel she held. "After treating the wound, it was driven to Gaia Conservancy. A plane and the old vet, Yasir, were waiting to transfer it to the Nairobi Elephant Orphanage. I hope it survived the journey. It needed plenty of fluids."

Sam shook his head. "We believe the elephants were part of a small herd, the matriarchal leader being the dead elephant's mother. The rangers think they passed back into the Samburu Reserve along the elephant corridor. They'll follow the rains north."

Craig sighed. "The young elephant would have been totally reliant on its mother."

"For food, protection and love," Rose mused. And she thought of her own son Chris, who she had barely spoken to in the past fourteen years.

Squeezing her eyes shut, she closed that door in her mind and turned to Sam. "Are you going to the summit?"

"I'll be round and about," he answered. "What about you?"

"I've received an invitation to the pre-event hosted by The Laikipia Conservation Society on Friday," Craig said, puffing out his chest.

Rose knew he was delighted to be invited. He had years of experience in conservation, farm and private conservancy management. His knowledge would be invaluable at the conference.

Also Craig was stranded at home now he no longer drove.

A childhood bout of polio damaged his left leg. He had learnt to live a full life despite it, but a few years ago a secondary illness invaded his body. He was often in pain and beginning to lose the use of the entire left side of his body.

"Davina Dijan is the main speaker at the conference, and she's also addressing the summit," Sam said. She runs the Gaia Conservancy where I presume the plane landed today."

"Yes. I met her." Rose's voice was flat.

"Doesn't sound as if she impressed you." Sam raised his eyebrows.

Rose lifted her arms. "The work I do is necessary, but I do have to get my hands dirty…"

"And other parts by the look of you earlier," interrupted Craig.

"Exactly." Rose dropped her hands. "Davina appeared put out having to wait for the baby elephant as if she had somewhere better to be. And she wasn't exactly dressed to help. Still, we'd have struggled without the use of her landing strip." Rose pursed her lips.

"It isn't actually hers. She's just the Managing Director of the Conservancy. Assisting orphaned elephants should be high on her agenda," Sam said. "Will you go to the conference?"

"I've no plans to," responded Rose. "I will be visiting the Mount Kenya Resort and Spa tomorrow, though. I've got my monthly clinic checking the resort's animals, particularly the horses the guests ride around the grounds. That reminds me. I need to prepare some of my herbal mixtures. Some of the horses were looking thin last month and might need to continue eating my digestive mix."

With that, Rose left the two men to discuss the plight of elephants.

CHAPTER FIVE

Cool mountain air permeated the open window of Rose's Defender as she drove up through the scattered forest and grassland of the lower slopes of Mount Kenya on Wednesday morning. She loved the smell of earth, trees and vegetation after rain, so fresh with the promise of new life.

She approached the entrance gates of the Mount Kenya Resort and Spa with caution. Three yellow oil drums stood on their ends, placed so she had to weave slowly between them. Usually the guard at the gate, who knew her from previous visits, waved her straight through. This time he signalled with his hand for her to stop.

"Habari, Mama Rose. Identification please." The guard wore a blue uniform with an elephant-head motif embroidered on his shirt pocket.

Rose sighed and reached across to the glove compartment. She extracted her folded red Kenyan driving licence and passed it to the guard. He gave it a cursory glance, returning it to her with a clipboard. She filled out her details, the car's registration number and the reason for her visit. She signed the last column.

"Preparing for the summit?" she asked.

"Yes. Security must be very good. And some guests arrive

early." The guard handed her a pass with the resort's name, a number and "Visitor" written on it. She placed it on her dashboard and drove through the now open gates.

The resort's horses were stabled on the left, just past the entrance. The head groom, known as a syce, appeared and greeted Rose coolly with a sharp nod of the head.

"Habari," she responded.

For the next hour she moved between the horses and ponies. Most of the time they plodded around the grounds carrying delighted guests, but once or twice a week the younger, fitter horses embarked on lengthy rides through the Mount Kenya forest.

Rose knew the syces were lazy and sometimes other staff helped who did not know the horses or the correct equipment. Too often they used ill-fitting tack which rubbed the horses, causing sores, particularly under their bellies where girths pinched soft skin, and in their mouths.

Rose had her own treatment for wounds, smearing on a mixture of iodine and honey, which she'd prepared in advance. Three elderly horses still looked thin so she handed the syce three bags of her digestive herb mix to add to their feeds. She had no idea if he'd give it to the three horses, all the horses, or none of them.

In the last stable she was checking a mare's foot when the light dimmed. Someone stood at the stable door. She placed the hoof on the floor and looked up at the strained face of Jabori Bundi, the resort manager.

"Mama Rose. Might I invite you to lunch when you've finished? I have a delicate matter to discuss." Rose's stomach clenched. She relied on the money she earned from the hotel's monthly clinic, even if they were not very prompt at paying her.

"I've nearly finished here. I've just the patrol dogs left to check," Rose responded.

"Good, good," the manager said, absent-mindedly. "I'll be in my office," he said, walking away.

CHAPTER SIX

R ose sipped a glass of chilled Sauvignon Blanc wine as
she leaned back in her chair to admire the view. The
Mount Kenya Resort and Spa was located within fifty acres of
landscaped gardens, and thirty acres of forestry, in the
foothills of Mount Kenya.

All eighty bedrooms in the two-storey white-washed hotel
commanded views of the majestic mountain. As did the
twenty-five single-storey villas scattered around the grounds.

Rose sat at a table on the shaded veranda adjoining the
main restaurant. Manager Bundi had been summoned to
placate a disgruntled diner. Warm sunlight illuminated the
snow which had fallen overnight on Batian Peak.

Manager Bundi returned, mopping his brow with a brown
and yellow kanga cloth. Once seated, he removed his round
wire-rimmed glasses and began their ritual cleaning.

Rose launched in. "I treated a number of mouth sores
today caused by wrong or ill-fitting bridles and bits."

"Ugh!" Manager Bundi screwed up his eyes.

"I think it would be beneficial to hold a clinic to show all
staff who deal with the horses how to find and fit the right
tack for the right horses."

"Perhaps, perhaps. Speak to me after the summit. I have more important matters to discuss than horses' mouths."

Rose tensed.

Manager Bundi slipped on his glasses and leaned closer to Rose as if examining her. Rose fought the temptation to lean back.

In a small voice, he said, "Someone has been stealing at the hotel." He looked around to make sure nobody had overheard him. He had purposely chosen a table in the far right-hand corner, away from the restaurant, to give them privacy.

There was only one group of early diners on the veranda. Most preferred to take lunch after one o'clock and rest during the hottest part of the afternoon.

"Oh," responded Rose. She sipped her wine to relieve her dry throat. She wondered why Manager Bundi was telling her this. Surely it was a matter for the police.

"I don't want to involve the police, not yet," he whispered. "They'll crash around the hotel, visibly upsetting and interrogating guests. This hotel has a reputation to uphold, one that could easily be ruined with a whiff of stealing or police involvement." He sat up, removed his glasses, and began cleaning them again. "I understand you know the commissioner. That you assisted him. No, let me rephrase that. I believe you solved a case recently for the commissioner."

"Well yes, I suppose I did, but I was helping a friend."

Manager Bundi reached over and placed his hand over Rose's. "Am I not an old friend?" Rose's insides squirmed. Summoning her self-control, she forced first her hand, then her face, and finally her chest to relax.

"I hadn't really considered it. Business associates, yes." Rose saw his shoulders slump. "But why not? Yes, we can be friends." She smiled. She needed the money from the clinic.

"Then, as a friend, can you help me? I presume you're

attending the Laikipia Conservation Society Conference on Friday?"

"Actually no, but my husband Craig is."

Manager Bundi sat up. "I'll get you an invite and you can stay the night. In fact, why don't you and your husband stay at the hotel until the matter is resolved?"

Rose shook her head. "I'm afraid your prices are out of our league."

"No, no." The stocky manager waved his hand dismissively. "Stay and eat at the hotel's expense. I'm sure you'll have solved my little problem by Monday." He looked down. "I hope so. I can't afford any problems over the summit. It's not only the reputation of the hotel to consider. There's my job."

Beads of perspiration appeared on his forehead. He used the same cloth as he used to clean his glasses, to mop them and jumped up. "Let's get food from the buffet. Give you time to consider my proposal."

An expansive three-course buffet lunch had been laid out in the restaurant. A central table was piled with fruits and tiers of desserts. The left-hand table, covered with a white cloth, exhibited two soup kettles, platters of cold meats and cheese, and baskets of assorted bread rolls.

Rose chose a small bowl of clear beef consommé, on which she guiltily scattered a spoonful of croutons. Manager Bundi ladled thick vegetable soup into his bowl and grabbed a white bread roll.

Back at their table, Manager Bundi asked, "Will you do it?" He slurped loudly.

"What exactly do you expect me to do? What's been stolen?" asked Rose.

"Here's the thing. The list is long and varied. The majority of the items have little value." He patted the pocket of his rumpled grey suit jacket. "I've lost the list. I'll get a copy whilst you choose your main course."

Rose had found the soup surprisingly filling. She

considered the vast array of food on the buffet tables, but she could not ignore a free lunch. Craig's voice sounded in her head: "No such thing as a free lunch."

She smiled ruefully and walked past a selection of curries, rice and chapatis provided principally for Asian guests. She chose a chicken breast poached in mushroom sauce and a variety of salads. She sneaked few chips onto the side. She returned to her table aware that her plate of food was twice the intended size.

Manager Bundi hurried over with a plate piled with African fair: ugali, a dry white porridge made of maize flour, sukuma wiki, which was braised kale, and meat stew.

He handed Rose a folded piece of paper, stained brown at one corner. She flattened it and read as she ate her lunch. Manager Bundi was right. Most of the items had little or no value: partially used toiletries from the bedrooms, sachets of butter, honey and Nutella, batteries from the TV remote controls, bottles of water, pens, loose change, and toilet paper.

But there were items of greater worth: medicines, alcohol from the minibar, towels and bathrobes, clothes and small items of jewellery.

"An eclectic mix," commented Rose. "When did this start?"

"It's hard to tell. Especially the smaller items. Many of the staff feel it's acceptable to take left-over fruit from the complimentary fruit bowls, or pick items out of guest's dustbins. An increase in the number of missing items came to my attention about six months ago. That's also when more valuable objects began to disappear."

He coughed as an Asian family stepped onto the veranda. They were a large family group. Amidst the noise of waiters moving tables to accommodate them all, Manager Bundi pleaded, "Please help me."

Rose sat back. She pushed her lunch plate to one side, feeling her stomach brimming over. Oh well, she wouldn't need any supper. She weighed her options. Craig was attending the conference anyway, and she was intrigued to hear Davina Dijan's presentation after their encounter at Gaia Conservancy.

It would be a treat to have free food and accommodation at this lovely hotel. She smiled, remembering that fires were lit in all the bedrooms at night, which created a cosy feeling.

"OK. I'll come to the conference and ask around about the stealing. It would be lovely to stay here on Friday night, but I am afraid Craig struggles with stairs and a lot of walking."

Rubbing his hands together, the tubby manager beamed. "We have a cottage on the second row reserved for agents and representatives from our parent company, the Belmont Hotel Group. I'll reserve it for you for the whole weekend. When your husband needs to come over to the main hotel, he can call reception and they will send a golf cart to collect him. The cottage is very peaceful, away from the main hotel, and has splendid views of the grounds and mountains."

As they left the hotel, Rose couldn't stop herself from picking a piece of nut brittle from the dessert table.

CHAPTER SEVEN

R ose arrived at Dr Emma's pharmacy, in the centre of Nanyuki town, as a tall African man carried a matted-looking dog into the shop. He was a typical Maasai, with a red-checked shuka wrapped over his clothes, several brightly coloured bead necklaces, and both his ear lobes were elongated, creating large loops below his ears.

Dr Emma was a qualified vet and technically Rose's boss. She preferred her patients to come to her premises, leaving Rose to conduct home visits in Nanyuki and the surrounding area. They performed basic operations together, although Dr Emma's pharmacy did not provide the sterile environment expected in modern operating rooms.

A space had been cleared in the centre of the shop for a table which was covered with clean but frayed towels. The Maasai laid the dog gently on top of them. Dr Emma was a diminutive figure, which contrasted with her huge round yellow glasses and unfashionably large afro hairstyle. Her bright manner dimmed as she clipped a lamp to the side of the table and inspected her patient.

"It doesn't look good," she told Rose, who was rolling up the sleeves of the white coat she wore for operations. "The leg's rather a mess. There's an open cavity with pieces of dirt and hair driven into the tissues, which only adds to the complication of infection."

Dr Emma used her gloved hands to examine the wound further. "The bullet has broken the radius and ulna in three places and some of the muscles are ripped and torn." Rose looked into the wound as Dr Emma continued. "His owner doesn't want the leg amputated. We either save it or put the dog out of its misery."

Rose caught her breath. "What happened?"

"Ask him." Dr Emma indicated towards the Maasai with her still bowed head.

Rose repeated her question to the man in Kiswahili. He answered in kind. "Men with guns broke through the fence into the conservancy. The dog chased them so they shot him."

Rose pursed her lips and returned to the dog. He didn't appear particularly distressed by his injury, but he would be if they didn't anaesthetise him before beginning their work. Rose pressed her thumb onto the top of the dog's leg to raise the cephalic vein, and Dr Emma emptied the anaesthetic contents of her syringe into it. The dog slipped into unconsciousness.

"Nairobi vets have external fixators, but I don't." Dr Emma frowned. "Alternatively, they would hold the bones together with a plate and several screws, but I don't have the experience to do that."

"Neither do I," said Rose. "I think that only adds to the chances of infection within the bone." Rose felt the bones. "If we remove this small middle section of radius we could use a single pin to hold the top and bottom sections together. Not much we can do for the smaller ulna but it should heal if the radius does."

"Can you insert the pin? I'd rather not." The petite Dr Emma was unusually reticent and quiet.

Squinting, Rose asked, "Are you OK?"

Dr Emma shook her head. "I forgot how much I hate gunshot wounds. Initially, I was concerned about treating and helping the poor dog. Now I'm angry that someone deliberately caused him such pain and injury."

Rose clapped her hands together. "Come on. Let's see if we can help him."

With Dr Emma's assistance, Rose inserted an intramedullary pin into the centre of the top piece of bone, pushing it into the marrow cavity. Then she worked it into the lower shaft.

"It feels stable, although there is a section with no bone, just the metal pin."

"Shall we clean and flush the wound?" suggested Dr Emma.

Rose hesitated. "No. I'm concerned we'd cause more damage or infection. Can you stitch it closed? It won't be easy. I'll give him a long-lasting antibiotic injection." She thought further. "I think we should bandage it with a splint. The bandage will keep the wound clean and the splint should stabilise it." Dr Emma got to work.

CHAPTER EIGHT

Rose returned home to find Craig and Thabiti absorbed in a crossword puzzle. As she sat on the sofa, Pixel, Thabiti's fluffy white dog, dashed over and yelped a greeting at her. Izzy, Rose's cat, seemed to take exception to the noise. She grew to her full height, arched her back, and hissed at Pixel. The dog ignored her. Rose patted Pixel on the head and Izzy stalked away without a backward glance.

Thabiti read, "Seven across, nine letters. Colour blindness especially confusion of red and green." He looked up. "I've no idea. Are there different types of colour blindness?"

Rose answered. "There's a range. I think red-green confusion is most common. It's a genetic condition carried on the X chromosome. Sons have a fifty-fifty chance of inheriting it if their mothers carry it. Girls are usually only carriers, unless their fathers pass the gene to them."

"So what do colour-blind people see?" asked Thabiti.

"I believe their whole colour vision is diminished. When you and I look at a fruit stall we see red apples, green limes, yellow lemons and a whole medley of coloured fruit. The world of a colour-blind person is devoid of colour as they'd see only a dull green wash."

"Wow, I had no idea someone could miss out on the amazing colours in Kenya. What's the answer?"

"Daltonism," said Craig. "After the scientist who first took an interest in the condition, as he had it."

Rose crossed to the outdoor dining table. She poured hot water from a thermos and made herself a cup of Kericho Gold tea. "Talking of conditions, how is Pearl?" she asked. Thabiti's sister, Pearl, had stopped eating after the stress of her mother's death. Although there were no signs of physical illness, she had been admitted to Nanyuki Cottage Hospital.

"Much better. I'm expecting her home next week." Thabiti smiled in an open, schoolboy manner. "Though, like me, she needs to find something meaningful to do."

Rose sipped her tea. "I thought she wanted to be a fashion designer?"

Thabiti shrugged. "I'm not sure how serious she is."

"One step at a time," suggested Craig. "You've just lost your mother. The whole experience was very distressing."

Thabiti tilted his head to one side. "You only realise how much you miss something when it's gone. I feel like that about Ma. I wasn't the son she wanted. Not strong, clever or ambitious." He bit his bottom lip. A schoolboy again, but lost and vulnerable.

"I'm sure she loved you as you are. There's a special bond between mothers and sons," said Rose.

"Perhaps." Thabiti tilted his head again. "Thank you for your help and support." Craig blinked and Thabiti grinned. "I know these morning visits to keep you company are just an excuse to make sure I'm OK, but I've appreciated our daily crossword battles."

"It sounds like they're coming to an end." Craig's mouth drooped.

"I've found a job at the Laikipia Conservation Conference on Friday, and if I don't mess up I'll work during the Giant's Club Summit as well." Thabiti's eyes pleaded for praise and mirrored Pixel's as she returned with an old green tennis ball clasped in her mouth.

"That's excellent news," exclaimed Rose. "What are you doing?"

"Working for the conference production company." Thabiti's eyes shone brightly. Rose had no idea what that meant. Thabiti continued, "It's the sound, lighting and technical side of the conference."

"Oh," said Rose. "The guys who sit at the back wearing headphones and twiddling nobs."

Thabiti's smile evaporated. "Rose, I think it's rather more technical than that," Craig chided her. Thabiti nodded. "Well done," said Craig. He lifted his chin. "I'm a delegate, so I'll see you there. I'm really looking forward to catching up with old friends."

Rose said, "I'm going, too."

CHAPTER NINE

Rose slid her Defender into a free parking space in front of Dormans Coffee Shop. Assisting Dr Emma with that morning's operation had thrown her. She'd completely forgotten her arrangement to meet Chloe for coffee and was fifteen minutes late.

Dormans was located in the town centre, fronting a small road which ran parallel with the main thoroughfare. It occupied the left third of a single-storey white building; other building occupants included a health food shop, up-market gift shop, travel agents and internet provider. Most customers sat at the wooden tables in the front courtyard. Shade was provided by a canopy that extended from the building, or large umbrellas above individual tables.

A metre-high wall enclosed the area with a picket fence on top. Various green-leafed plants eked out an existence on top of the wall, providing a buffer between customers and the dust thrown up by passing vehicles. They also screened those within from the insistent street hawkers selling anything from pirate DVDs to beaded jewellery and plastic Tupperware.

The coffee shop had opened as Dormans with Nanyuki's first commercial coffee machine. Rose couldn't call it by its rebranded name, "I love Nanyuki" Coffee shop, although she approved of the "I Love NY" logo.

Chloe sat at their usual corner table, tapping away on her phone. Rose believed her to be in her late thirties. She was slim, attractive, and wore her long blonde hair loose. Rose frowned.

Chloe wasn't the vision of couture elegance she had been on her arrival in Nanyuki two months earlier. Maybe she was just relaxing into the simple Kenyan way of life.

"Chloe. So sorry to keep you waiting," said Rose. "I had an emergency operation with Dr Emma this morning."

"It's OK. I've nothing else to do." Chloe's voice was flat.

Rose looked directly at her companion, but her face was concealed by very large sunglasses. She ordered a Kericho Gold tea, having failed to finish her earlier cup.

Chloe lifted her sunglasses and lodged them in her hair. She rubbed her bloodshot eyes.

"Not sleeping?" asked Rose.

"Something like that. I'm lonely when Dan's away with work, which is most of the time. But when he's back he hits the bottle. He's becoming increasingly withdrawn, volatile and hard to live with." Chloe pressed her lips together.

"I'm sorry to hear that." Rose's voice was gentle. She had seen similar situations before. Ex-Army men dragged their wives away from the comfort and familiarity of the UK, promising them sunshine and a safari lifestyle.

Most worked in the security sector and were away in dangerous places, leaving their wives on their own. More than one marriage had failed recently in such circumstances.

"You need to find something to do. To keep you occupied." Rose was businesslike. "Sister Lucy, who runs our church orphanage, is always seeking volunteers."

Chloe's face reddened as she avoided Rose's gaze. "Rose, I know you are just being helpful. Children... well, it's rather a sore point at the moment." Huge tears slid down Chloe's cheeks.

Rose realised she'd made a serious blunder. All she could do was place her hand over the one Chloe rested on the table.

"I've lost another baby." Chloe reached for a napkin and wiped tears and snot from her face. "And it's all my fault."

"Why do you believe that?" Rose asked.

"I've seen doctors and specialists in the UK, too many to mention. They've prodded, investigated and tested, but can't provide an answer as to why I can't hold onto a baby. One specialist thought it might be my own immune cells attacking the placenta. There's no scientific proof, so he suggested we try again. Seems my own body killed my baby."

"That's just one suggestion. As you say, nothing scientific, no proof it is you. I am very sorry, though."

Chloe sniffed. "So you see, I don't really want to be around children or babies." She wiped her eyes and face again.

She wrapped both hands around her tall latte glass. "Animals are OK. Before you arrived I overheard two ladies discussing a baby elephant rescue. I gather you were involved."

Rose was relieved to be discussing a safer topic. "Thabiti and I helped. Poor thing had been wandering around with a poison arrow stuck in it. Hadn't eaten for days, either, as its mother was killed by poachers."

"Poaching is terrible, and so is the decline in elephant numbers. One reason I agreed to help at the Laikipia Wildlife Society Conference and the Giant's Club Summit. It'll also keep my mind off... other things." Chloe placed her sunglasses over her eyes and appeared to retreat behind them.

"Good for you. I met one of the main speakers recently, Davina Dijan."

"She's really important in conservation circles. I think Dan does some work on her conservancy. She's due to launch a book at the summit about the plight of elephants. I've pre-ordered a signed copy."

"You should find the conference and summit interesting. And The Mount Kenya Resort and Spa is a lovely venue."

"I know." Chloe burst into tears again.

CHAPTER TEN

On Friday morning Rose dressed in a pair of light blue trousers and a flowery blouse. Both were purchased from mitumba and, as usual, the trousers were a little too short, stopping above her bony ankles.

She also wore a pair of green court shoes instead of her usual boots or trainers. She and Craig had finished breakfast and were preparing to leave for the Laikipia Conservation Society conference.

Craig opened the door of the small wardrobe in their bedroom and moved aside jackets and the few dresses Rose owned. He called, "Have you seen my brown tweed jacket? Today is the perfect opportunity to wear it."

"You haven't worn it in ages. I've no idea where it is."

"Well I'd like to wear it today." He turned and leant on his walking stick.

"Can't you wear something else? You hate being late and I've no idea how long it will take to find it." Rose fought to suppress her irritation.

"No, it has to be the tweed jacket." Craig's tone was cool and final.

Rose's shoulders slumped. "I'll see if Kipto knows." She

and Kipto searched for Craig's jacket in cupboards and on hooks throughout the house. Eventually Kipto discovered it hanging amongst some old suits in one of the guest cottage wardrobes. Rose had to admit Craig looked very smart in the jacket, which he wore with beige cord trousers and a brown paisley tie.

Rose braked hard, pulled the steering wheel, and swerved around an impala—a medium-sized antelope—skipping across the road.

"Rose. Slow Down!" Craig gripped the passenger grab handle.

"Sorry," Rose said as she accelerated away.

Only two cars were ahead of them at the Mount Kenya Resort and Spa entrance gate, but it took a full five minutes to clear the security checks and enter the hotel complex. Rose recognised Boris, one of the security dogs, masquerading as a sniffer dog. She pointed him out to Craig. "The only thing he'll be sniffing out is meat to fill his belly." She grinned.

They were directed to the right-hand side of the hotel and the main porticoed entrance. Rose felt rather self-conscious parking amongst an array of Range Rovers, Porsche Cayennes and Toyota Land Cruisers. A uniformed African man consulted a clipboard and announced, "Cottage 25." His younger colleague assisted Craig down from the vehicle and snatched the keys out of Rose's hand.

"One minute. My bag." Rose opened the rear passenger door to remove a green canvas Sandstorm tote bag. She had been given the bag in lieu of payment by a client who, she suspected because of a small black stain inside, had already used it. Still, it provided ample room for all her clobber, including notebook, iPad, phone, water and glasses.

Rose offered her arm to Craig, who leaned on it whilst using his wooden walking stick, with a horn handle, in his right hand. They followed a group of farmers Craig knew from the west of Laikipia County.

At the entrance to the conference area, Rose was relieved to see the immaculately turned out version of Chloe, standing behind a gold-clothed table. She confidently chatted to conference attendees, efficiently handing out name badges. She was assisted by a pretty Asian girl in her early to mid-twenties.

"Rose, these are for you and Craig." Chloe handed Rose two name badges with clear plastic covers and safety pin backs. "Marina, two more delegate bags please."

Rose was handed two cloth bags with KenyaSimu printed on them. She moved back to the group of farmers Craig was speaking with. They excused themselves and headed for Chloe's table. Rose pinned on her own and then Craig's badge.

"Would you like some coffee?" A table with various hot and cold drinks, as well as cakes and biscuits, was located to one side.

"Think I'll wait until the break. I don't want to disturb anyone by having to get up for a pee in the middle of a talk." Craig smiled ruefully.

"Let's go inside," said Rose. "The room's filling up."

Rose and Craig entered a large room with a stage at one end and rows of gold-cushioned chairs facing it. More than two thirds of the seats were occupied or had been reserved with folded jackets or conference bags.

Rose wanted an end seat so she could leave without disturbing anyone. It would also provide an easy escape route for Craig should he need one. She moved a bag and a jacket further down a row and pulled the end chair out of line. Craig sat and stretched out his sore leg.

"I wonder who's speaking this morning," said Craig.

Rose handed him one of the bags Chloe had given her. "Have a look in there and see if you can find an agenda."

Craig held up the bag. "KenyaSimu. They must be

sponsoring the event." He withdrew a pile of coloured leaflets from inside the bag. "Doesn't Davina Dijan's husband run KenyaSimu?"

"Second husband. Yes," Rose responded. She bent down to collect the leaflets discarded by Craig as he searched for the conference agenda.

"Here we are. The conference information pack. There's so much other rubbish."

"Craig, you know it's expensive to run these events," said Rose. "They need money from sponsorship and advertising."

Craig grunted and opened his delegate pack. "Opening address. First talk to be given by the head of the Kenyan Wildlife Service. Davina Dijan's address is after the coffee break. Then I guess she'll take part in the panel discussion. We have a buffet lunch and more panels and discussions in the afternoon."

Rose lifted her hands, then let them fall. "Do you mind if I skip the first part? I need to look into this theft business for Manager Bundi, but I want to be back to hear Davina speak."

"I'm OK here. In fact, once you leave I think some of my old muckers might come over to see me. Shame I can't mingle."

Rose wrinkled her nose. "Well, if you're sure you're OK, I'll see you later. If you need any help, ask Chloe."

Rose made her way against the tide of incoming delegates. To one side, near the back of the room, she spotted Thabiti sitting at a table surrounded by computers and electrical devices. She thought he was wearing a baseball cap back to front.

A black-shirted European man in his late twenties was explaining a piece of equipment to him. The man wore a pair of headphones around his neck and frequently listened through one ear-pad before twirling dials in front of him.

Rose waved tentatively, not wanting to disturb them. Thabiti beamed back before returning to his companion. In the entrance, Chloe, without the assistance of Marina, was shepherding the remaining guests into the conference room.

"Rose, we're just about to start," she said briskly.

"I know. I have some hotel business to attend to first."

CHAPTER ELEVEN

Manager Bundi hovered outside the conference area entrance. He hurried over to Rose. "Is everything OK? Has everyone arrived?" He bounced on his feet, agitated and trying to peer over Rose's shoulder. She stepped to one side but he mirrored her. "Don't want to be seen. Mustn't interfere."

"I believe it's about to begin. The final attendees were being ushered to their seats." Rose took Manager Bundi's arm and walked him out of the conference area. "I'm about to begin my task. I need to work out how, and from where, the missing items were taken. Can a staff member explain the hotel's routine and perhaps show me some of the rooms?" she asked.

Manager Bundi removed his glasses and began rubbing them with a cloth. Green and orange today. "Kenneth will be best. He's been with us about a year and is a former member of the British Army, so he's hard-working, reliable and disciplined, except when he's had a little too much brandy. He lives in one of the staff houses with his young son."

Manager Bundi looked along the corridor towards the hotel entrance. He hurried away towards a steward descending the main staircase, carrying a silver tray and the remains of breakfast. Rose was summoned with an upturned hand gesture.

"Kenneth," said the agitated manager. "This is Mama Rose. She's looking into… efficiency and waste in the hotel. Yes, that's right. Rose, this is Kenneth, who is responsible for the rooms on the first floor of the East Wing. Please answer her questions, Kenneth, and show her around."

Manager Bundi scuttled away to the hotel reception. Rose shifted her feet uncomfortably. She hated being dishonest.

"Mama, I would shake your hand, but I might drop something from this tray. Would you like to follow me to the kitchen? It's time for my break and perhaps you could ask your questions over a welcome cup of chai."

Kenneth was a moderately sized man, but he had a rocky hardness about him. As Rose ran to keep up, she imagined him carrying two trunks of wood under his arms rather than balancing the silver tray.

In the cramped staff room, Rose accepted a chipped mug of chai: water, milk and tea boiled together in a pan. She preferred European tea, but did not want to offend her host. "Kenneth, I'll come clean. I'm no good at subterfuge and you'll soon pick up that I know absolutely nothing about hotel waste or efficiency."

"Are you looking into the thefts?" Kenneth asked in a matter-of-fact tone. "I'm fed up of fingers being pointed in my direction. I do my work, do it well, and I ain't stealing from no one."

Rose leaned back. "Well, that makes life easier. Yes, Manager Bundi wants me to investigate possible thefts. He's not keen to call in the police."

"Well, I don't blame him. I know some of the guests have been stealing, usually those with the most money. I've had slippers, towels, bathrobes and pillows disappear from my bedrooms. Usually from the suite." He whispered, "Some of those guests were senior officials, even police officers and their so-called wives."

Rose, not wanting to become involved in a discussion about adultery, said innocently, "I think that happens in most hotels. They accept those losses as part of the room costs." Kenneth frowned.

Rose continued. "I have the list Manager Bundi gave me." She removed the stained piece of paper from her tote bag, together with her reading glasses and notebook. "I've grouped the items in my notebook. So you're saying that these items, towels, bathrobes and pillows were most likely taken by guests."

"Yes, that's what I believe," nodded Kenneth.

"What about corkscrews, cutlery, bowls and plates from room service?" asked Rose.

Kenneth scratched his head. Then he laughed.

"I caught a senior business leader's wife trying to hide a silver fruit bowl in her oversized handbag. Not real silver, but it was large. And she tipped the unwanted fruit on the table, so oranges and apples rolled onto the floor. She looked straight at me, turned with a flick of her head and kicked an apple for good measure as she walked out. Some people are so brazen. So the answer is yes, guests do help themselves to those items."

Rose looked down at her notebook. "Then there is a whole bunch of things with little or no value: left over fruit, magazines, tea, coffee and sugar sachets, partly used hotel toiletries, loose change, toilet paper, and sachets of Nutella, jam and butter." Kenneth nodded again.

Rose continued reading. "I've got a random section which includes pens, bottles of water and batteries from the remote controls. The most valuable items appear to be cosmetics, clothes, jewellery, watches, a picture frame and prescription medicines."

Kenneth sipped his chai, whilst Rose ignored hers. "Is there a pattern? A particular time or specific day they vanish?" She looked over the frame of her glasses.

"Time is hard. Guests tend to realise something is missing

only as they finish packing on the morning they depart. Half the time I think they've already packed it and have just forgotten."

Rose twiddled the pencil in her mouth.

Kenneth said, "When I think about it, guests make the most fuss at the weekends. Especially the American ones. A tour company specialising in African holidays for more mature American clients uses the Belmont chain of hotels. One of their group always complains something is missing."

Rose realised that her task was far from straightforward. "Do hotel guests follow any kind of routine?" she asked.

"They generally use the hotel facilities in the morning. After lunch they rest before more activities and supper. Apart from resting and changing for the evening, most guests hardly use their rooms during the day."

"So there would be plenty of opportunity for someone to enter and search the rooms," stated Rose.

CHAPTER TWELVE

R ose and Kenneth walked along the first floor corridor.
"I can't show you the suite as Robert Dijan and his secretary are working there. This room is free, though." Kenneth produced a plastic keycard, which he inserted in a hole above the chrome door handle. The light turned green and they entered.

The room was light and airy. It was elegantly furnished and decorated in coffee shades. Rose ran her hand along the fake fur blanket folded over the end of the king size bed.

"Can you explain how that works? Can a card open the door of another bedroom?" asked Rose.

"No. Each keycard has a magnetic strip." Kenneth turned his over. "Reception codes a new card for each guest, which allows them access only to their room for the duration of their stay."

"But your card opens all the doors?" Rose's eyes narrowed.

"On this corridor. Sometimes I cover downstairs and have to sign for a separate card from Manager Bundi."

Rose repositioned the tote bag on her shoulder. The system sounded secure and logical, except... "Have you ever lost your card?"

"No. That's a sackable offence. One of the cleaning ladies lost her job towards the end of last year. Swore someone had taken her keycard, but didn't know who." Rose looked around the immaculate room. The cleaning staff appeared to do their job well.

"Where did she work?"

"This wing, actually."

Rose walked over to the window, moved the voile shade curtain aside and stared out. "And most of the valuable items were taken from this wing?"

Kenneth frowned. "Remind me what those are?"

Rose put her glasses on and consulted her notebook. "Clothes, not sure what exactly."

"I know," said Kenneth. "There was a pair of ladies, nearly new, Louis Vuitton shoes, Armani jeans, and a pair of men's Air Max trainers. Oh, and two sets of Agent Provocateur lingerie. They still had their labels. The embarrassed American lady who reported them stolen must have been in her sixties."

Rose had no idea what Agent Provocateur was, but doubted her own underwear would emulate it. She coughed.

"Taken from rooms in this wing?" she asked.

Kenneth rocked his head seemingly working through her question. "Yes, you're right. The trainers from this floor and the others from the floor below. Not all were the American clients'. The owner of the shoes reported them missing on Tuesday, but she checked in on Sunday."

Rose and Kenneth discovered a similar pattern with the theft of jewellery, cosmetics and medicine.

Kenneth asked, "Does your list include a bottle of whisky?"

Rose checked her notebook. "No!"

Kenneth grinned. "Manager Bundi was furious. An American gentleman was very vocal one Saturday evening about his missing $300 bottle of whisky. Highland Park, it was from a distillery on Orkney, Scotland. Of course, he shouldn't have had it in the hotel and Manager Bundi was not sympathetic. The guest even accused him of confiscating it. Manager Bundi puffed himself up like a peacock and the tour group leader swept the guest away to buy him a drink 'on the house.'"

CHAPTER THIRTEEN

A hotel waitress handed Rose a cup of tea. She popped a shortbread biscuit on the saucer and carried them through to the conference room. Craig was standing, leaning on the back of his chair, in earnest discussion with an important-looking African man in combat fatigues. Chloe walked onto the stage and clapped her hands.

"Ladies and gentlemen, please take your seats." There was a bustle in the room as attendees found their chairs. The uniformed gentleman patted Craig on the shoulder, positioned a green beret on his head, and left the room.

Rose helped Craig onto his seat and sat down next to him. "Interesting morning so far?" she whispered.

"Very. That was the director general of the Kenyan Wildlife Service. Presented a detailed account of his organisation's challenges, successes and future strategy."

A hush fell over the room. A man and woman climbed onto the stage. The man addressed the room. "Ladies and gentlemen, please welcome our next speaker. She is a prominent wildlife conservationist and managing director of Gaia Conservancy, the most recent area of Kenya to be granted wildlife protected status. Her new book about the plight of elephants in Africa will be released next week. If you would like to pre-order a copy, see the ladies at the conference entrance. Please welcome Davina Dijan."

Davina Dijan was dark-haired with a dark, tanned complexion. She towered over the audience who clapped politely. She wore a navy trouser suit with a single-breasted jacket and red high-heeled shoes. "The title of my talk today is 'Importance of Conservation'…" She looked round at the large screen behind her and stopped. The words on the screen read "Gaia Conservancy, Strategic Plan, Funding Wildlife Conservation."

"No. No. That's the wrong one. It's the one about enhancing wildlife and supporting local communities." She directed her comments to someone behind Rose. "I gave you the flash drive. Where is it?" she snapped.

Rose looked round. The man she had seen with Thabiti was on his feet, waving a small item in his hand. He shrugged his shoulders. Rose spun back round to the stage as Davina stormed down the steps and strode to the back of the room.

"You idiot." Her mike was still turned on. "That's the wrong presentation. Where's the other flash drive?" Rose did not hear the response. The young man's face was flushed. Marina rushed over to the table. "Go get my bag," Davina demanded.

Marina rushed off and returned a minute later with a red and gold handbag. Davina rummaged around in it before handing a second flash drive to the young man. "Get this one right." She stormed back to the stage. At a small table, she poured herself a glass of water.

The audience waited in excited silence as the correct title appeared on the screen. Davina looked at it, rolled her shoulders and turned to her audience, smiling.

"Conservation can be defined as the protection of plants, animals and natural areas, particularly from the damaging effects of human activity."

Davina discussed the need to separate wildlife from human activity, the history of cattle ranching in Laikipia, and the recent move towards the co-existence of farming alongside wildlife conservation. Rose agreed that local communities needed to engage in the process, though was not sure how, and was delighted to hear that the wildlife biomass in Laikipia had risen by 7.5%.

However, her mind kept drifting back to the incident with the wrong presentation. She turned and looked towards the table at the rear of the room. Thabiti appeared relaxed and was chatting to Marina.

Rose smiled. She had not seen him so comfortable with a girl before. Usually he shrank into his shell, tongue-tied or stammering. The technician beside him looked up from his screen towards Davina, his eyes hidden behind a pair of red-tinted glasses.

CHAPTER FOURTEEN

After the conference, Rose and Craig rested and changed for supper in their cottage in the hotel grounds. They returned to the main hotel and were directed to a lawned area in front of the hotel and its main bar, The Bongo Bar. They claimed two of a set of four canvas safari chairs that were positioned around a burning metal fire pit.

The damp grass sloped gently down to an oval-shaped outdoor swimming pool, and the air was moist in the aftermath of a heavy rainstorm. Rain rarely fell gently in Kenya. Heavy water-laden clouds gather and tip their contents in a deluge on the land below. As soon as they're empty, the rain ceases and the sun appears, evaporating wispy plumes of moisture.

It was half past six and the sun slid out of sight behind the hotel. The warmth of the day faded with it. Kenneth appeared with red and green checked shuka blankets. He unfolded one and laid it over Rose's bare legs.

Rose thought dining in the hotel restaurant was one of the rare occasions she should dress up, and she wore an attractive peacock coloured skirt. Craig remained in his cords, but had removed his tie and exchanged his jacket for a green woollen jumper.

Kenneth returned with several drinks on a tray. He handed Rose and Craig a glass each. "Dawas, courtesy of Manager Bundi."

Rose took a tentative sip, grimaced, and shook her head. "That's strong. Could you transfer it to a larger glass and add some soda water?" Kenneth grinned. "Yes, of course. Let me hand out the other drinks first."

Chloe and Marina arrived, followed closely by Thabiti and the young man he'd been working with at the conference.

"I hope we haven't kept you waiting. We've had lots of tidying up to do." Chloe flopped into a spare chair, whilst Marina hovered behind her.

"Take the other seat." Thabiti said to Marina. "Hugo, let's fetch those spare chairs." Thabiti and Hugo completed the circle around the fire pit. Marina held her hands over the fire, warming them.

Kenneth returned to pick up Rose's dawa. "Can I get anyone a drink?" he asked.

"What's that?" asked Chloe, pointing at Rose's glass.

"A dawa. Our speciality. The base is cubed limes, brown sugar, crushed ice and a twist of honey. Vodka is poured over it."

"Wow, I should try one," Chloe exclaimed. "I need a stiff drink. It was harder work than I expected today."

Craig passed his drink to Chloe. "Have mine. I haven't touched it and would prefer a Tusker. Tusker for you, Thabiti? And your friend?" Both men nodded their acceptance.

Craig turned towards Marina, his hand raised in her direction. "A fresh passion juice, please," she said.

"Are you sure that's all you want? Nothing stronger?" Craig asked.

"No thanks. I need something refreshing, and I don't drink alcohol."

Kenneth departed in the direction of the bar. Thabiti leaned over and took a shuka from the back of Marina's chair.

"Thanks," she said, wrapping it around her like a Maasai warrior.

Rose watched Craig. He was glowing and not purely from the heat of the fire. Craig had always been an active and influential member of the community. He was often frustrated when his leg prevented him getting out to events and meetings. She knew he had enjoyed the conference: the people, the discussions and the feeling of being included. He appeared to relish hosting the small group relaxing around the fire.

"Chloe, I believe you know our daughter Heather back in the UK," said Craig.

"That's right." Chloe crossed her legs. "Heather helped me organise our move out here. My husband Dan got a job in a security company."

"Ex-Army officer, is he?" Craig asked.

"Yes. He left after a difficult Afghan tour." Chloe looked down at her drink.

Craig addressed Marina. "Marina, I don't know you."

"No, Sir. My family are based in Nairobi. I'm currently working as a tour and lodge relief manager. I take over when the existing managers are on holiday or sick. I agreed to help today, as I'm leaving early tomorrow to take a tour group to Samburu National Reserve."

"And the young man at the end. Is it Hugo?" Craig asked.

"It is, and you're…?"

"So sorry, I'm Craig and this is my wife, Rose. We live in Nanyuki and are friends of young Thabiti."

Hugo asked, "Is Nanyuki the town we passed through to reach the hotel?"

Craig nodded. "Yes, it's a market town serving much of the county of Laikipia."

"I'm rather new to Kenya. Haven't travelled much out of Nairobi yet."

"Do you have family here?" Rose asked.

"I'm looking…" The return of Kenneth interrupted

Hugo's answer. With one hand Kenneth deftly positioned two tables between the group on which he placed crisps, nuts and various drinks.

"If that's all?" Kenneth asked. "I have to return to my steward duties. The lift has stopped working, so I need to chase the engineers."

Rose said. "Thank you, Kenneth. And for your help this morning."

Craig turned back to Hugo, but Chloe announced: "This drink is great. I feel so much better. Do you know, I think I'll see if they have a free room tonight. Do you mind if I join you for supper? Dan is still away, and I don't want to return to an empty house."

"That's a great idea, Chloe," exclaimed Rose. Chloe jumped up, taking her nearly empty glass with her into the hotel.

There was a silence. "What are you all doing tonight?" Rose asked.

"Hugo and I are staying in small rooms at the back of the hotel until the end of the summit," answered Thabiti. "I think they're usually kept for drivers or tour guides. We're free for supper though, aren't we?" Hugo shrugged his shoulders. Unusually, Thabiti was taking the lead. It was great to see him gaining in confidence.

"I'm going to grab a plate of food and take it my room," said Marina. "I still have itineraries to work on ahead of tomorrow's departure."

Chloe returned, eyes bright and glass full. "As I helped today, they've given me a great deal. A small room at the back of the hotel. No mountain views, but who cares. And tomorrow I can lounge by the pool before I return home."

"What will you wear?" Rose asked.

Chloe laughed. "I always pack a bag of essentials: makeup, clean underwear and change of clothes. Never know what might happen. I threw a bikini in thinking I might have time to sunbathe today. No chance. Too much to do, especially with the demands of Davina Dijan."

Chloe sipped her drink. "And she's at it again. I witnessed her berating a boy, well he's probably in his early twenties. She shouted at him, 'It's my book. You work for me so the matter's closed.' Her husband dragged her away to The Bongo Bar, but I saw him turn back and mouth 'sorry' to the boy."

"It must be humiliating, like walking a dog which constantly strains its leash to attack other dogs," said Rose.

"You can choose your friends, but you can't choose your family," quoted Craig.

"Mrs Dijan's not a very nice person," stated Marina.

"Only interested in herself. No thought of how her actions affect other people," muttered Hugo.

Thabiti jumped up. "Don't let Davina Dijan spoil our evening. Who's hungry?"

CHAPTER FIFTEEN

Davina Dijan and a distinguished looking African gentleman waited to be seated as Rose's group arrived at the hotel restaurant. Rose guessed the man to be in his late fifties, but he had aged well and appeared to keep himself in shape. There were no signs of double chins and his belly fitted neatly into his belted grey trousers.

"Mr and Mrs Dijan. Good evening. Table for two? Please follow me," said an elderly African waiter with tightly curled white hair.

"Three, please, I'm expecting my secretary to join us," responded Mr. Dijan.

"Really, Robert. Why can't he have room service?" quipped Davina.

"Because," Robert said through gritted teeth, "He has been stuck in our suite all day helping me prepare contract documents. He needs a break, and frankly," he looked across at his wife, "He's better company than you when you're in this mood."

"What mood?" Rose heard Davina ask petulantly as she followed the elderly waiter to a table. Davina shook her head, looked around, and pointed towards a table in the back right hand corner. It was set for five people. The waiter shook his head.

A waitress appeared in front of Craig. "Table for five?"

"Yes, please." The waitress led them to the corner table favoured by Davina. Rose took her seat and looked up. Davina was glaring at her. Temporarily defeated, Davina stood with hands on hips surveying the restaurant.

She stormed across to a table set for four, not far from Rose, and sat down heavily. Picking up a menu, she refused to acknowledge the gesticulating waiter. Rose watched Robert Dijan place a conciliatory hand on the waiter's shoulder and offered him something with his other hand. Money, Rose presumed.

"Never a dull moment," beamed Chloe.

"Will you excuse me," Hugo said, his face pale. "I need some peace and quiet. Conferences are so full on. They take it out of me." He gave a weak smile and left.

"So, Thabiti. How did you get the job assisting Hugo?" Rose asked.

"The guy who was to help him fell off his Boda Boda motorbike," said Thabiti. "He's stuck in hospital. Hugo called me after the Mount Kenya Trust sent him my elephant orphan rescue footage to edit. When he found out I lived in Nanyuki, he asked if I wanted to help and I agreed. It was really interesting discovering how the different monitors and controls work."

"Marina seems a nice girl," Rose said softly.

Thabiti smiled at her. "Do you think so? She's so kind, but also very organised. She helped me this morning when I didn't know where to find things."

Craig coughed. "There's a large group of Americans entering the restaurant. I think we should order our food to avoid delays."

Rose searched for a menu amongst the crockery, cutlery and array of glasses in front of her. She found it hidden under the foliage of the table decoration. There was a choice of four items, including a vegetarian option, for each course.

The waitress appeared to take their orders. "Butternut squash risotto followed by salmon and spinach fettuccine, please," said Rose. Thabiti and Craig ordered fillet steak for their main course.

"Steak for me, too. Medium, please," requested Chloe brightly. Good, thought Rose, it might help build up her strength.

The waitress returned with the bread basket as Davina kicked off again. "These sizzling garlic prawns are too spicy. I asked for mild."

"Here, swap with me. These chicken wings aren't hot," suggested Robert.

"No, I want the prawns. Bring me some less spicy ones," Davina demanded, holding her plate aloft until the waiter took it. She lifted a champagne flute and swirled the contents around.

A young man with fair skin, glasses and short wavy red hair tentatively approached Davina's table. Robert stood up. Rose overheard him say, "Ah Ethan. I ordered you the same as me. Buffalo chicken wings for starter. I hope that's OK?"

"Of course it's OK," screeched Davina. "He's only a secretary. He'll eat what he's given and do as he's told. Won't you, Ethan? Just a small step out of line…" Rose missed the rest as their waitress arrived with their starters. The smell of garlic tingled in the air. Rose's risotto was rich, creamy and filling.

Suddenly there was a crash at Davina's table. Ethan jumped up, grabbing his napkin, and tried to mop up orange juice as it spread across the white tablecloth.

"Oops, clumsy me," Davina slurred.

"Davina, you've had too much to drink," declared Robert.

"Don't fuss, there's nothing wrong with me," responded Davina.

Rose's main course arrived, and as Davina's ranting

appeared to have subsided, it was easier to talk about other subjects. Rose, Craig, Chloe and Thabiti chatted happily.

When their main courses had been cleared, Rose heard Davina say, "I feel rather sleepy."

"Then let me take you to our room." Robert helped Davina stand and escorted her from the restaurant.

There was an outbreak of excited chatter and laughter amongst the diners. Ethan poured himself a glass of champagne. He removed a sheath of papers, a small bottle, and a silver pen from his jacket pocket and settled down to read.

Craig patted his lips with a white damask napkin to remove any lingering chocolate fondant. Robert returned and sat opposite Ethan. He leaned in, talking quietly, so Rose was unable to eavesdrop. Then they both stood and left the restaurant.

"Anyone fancy a nightcap?" asked Thabiti.

"Good idea," said Chloe. "Shall we move through to the Bongo Bar?"

Rose looked at Craig, who removed his glasses to rub his eyes. She said, "I think we'll turn in. It's been a busy day."

Rose and Craig found a golf cart and driver outside reception, which drove them slowly the hundred metres to their cosy one-bedroom cottage. Fires had been lit in the sitting room and bedroom. Rose sighed with contentment.

CHAPTER SIXTEEN

R ose loved the comfort of their hotel cottage with the crackling log fire in the sitting room. She placed the book she'd been reading on the coffee table. The Laikipia Conservation Society had collated an amazing collection of wildlife photographs within the hardback book. She switched on the kettle and walked into the bedroom.

Rose had already helped Craig change into his pyjamas. He was propped up with pillows on the bed, reading a report he'd downloaded on Rose's iPad.

"I've put the kettle on. Would you like a drink?" she asked.

"A glass of water for the night would be just the ticket," he replied.

Someone knocked urgently on the cottage door. "Mama Rose, come quickly."

Surprised, Craig looked at Rose. "Expecting anyone?"

The knocking continued until Rose flung open the door. "What's so urgent? Can't it wait? Oh, Manager Bundi!"

The manager was pale and his skin clammy, with beads of perspiration on his forehead. He pushed past her into the little cottage. "No. It can't wait. Definitely not," he said.

"Is it a horse or dog? I'll need my medical bag from the car," said Rose.

"Horse? Why are you always talking about horses? It's Davina Dijan. She's dead." The hotel manager was shaking. He removed his glasses, revealing dilated pupils.

"What? She was larger than life in the restaurant earlier this evening. She had been drinking and was rather unsteady on her feet. Did she fall? As long as it's not murder... too many suspects!" Rose gave a shocked bark of laughter. It cleared her head and reality returned. "Sorry. I can't believe she's dead. I only saw her two hours ago."

The glasses quivered in the portly man's hand. "Quite, quite. It is terrible. The effect on the hotel, next week's conference." Manager Bundi was also in shock.

"Sit down," said Rose. "We both need a sweet cup of tea."

"Tea!" Manager Bundi squawked.

"Yes, now calm down," Rose instructed.

"Is that Manager Bundi? What's happened?" Craig called from the bedroom.

His deep steady voice and matter of fact tone calmed the anxious manager.

"Yes, just a minute, Craig."

Rose poured two cups of tea. She added three teaspoons of sugar to Manager Bundi's cup, and, as an afterthought, half a spoonful to her own.

Carrying her tea and a bottle of water, she walked into the bedroom. Manager Bundi followed. He was deferential now. "So sorry to disturb you at this late hour."

"Sit down," said Craig. "Explain the situation." He placed Rose's iPad on the bedside table.

Manager Bundi perched on the end of the bed. "It's Davina Dijan. She's dead. Someone stabbed her."

"That's no accident," sighed Rose. "Who found her?"

"Her husband, Robert, in their suite. He was working in the living room and checked on Mrs Dijan at ten o'clock. He found her lying on their bed with blood covering her neck and side."

Still shaking, the rotund manager gulped his tea. "Mr Dijan said he tried to wake his wife. When there was no response he sent his secretary to find me. She certainly looked dead. Pale skinned against red-stained cream sheets." Manager Bundi shivered. "I locked both doors to the room and came in search of you."

"Me!" exclaimed Rose.

"Yes, with your veterinary training I thought you could confirm she's dead. Tell us when and how she died."

"She's not a doctor. You can't expect Rose to provide the time of death," said Craig.

"But I might be able to establish how she died. Have you called the police?"

"Well, no." Manager Bundi looked at the floor. "That's the other reasons for seeing you. I don't want an army of policeman tramping around the hotel, creating noise and disturbing guests. I wondered... can you call Commissioner Akida? I understand you have a... working relationship."

Rose pinched her mouth. "Very well." She found her phone in the living room. "Commissioner Akida, it's Mama Rose," she said when her call was answered.

"It's who?" he shouted back. There was a tumult of background noise.

"Mama Rose," she responded in kind.

"Just a minute." Rose presumed the commissioner was finding somewhere quieter as the sound of voices faded.

"Sorry about that. Couldn't hear an elephant sneeze in there. Did you say Mama Rose? Why are you calling so late?"

Rose explained, "I'm at the Mount Kenya Resort and Spa. One of the guests has died. The manager thinks she was stabbed, but he's rather anxious. Because of next week's summit, he wants the matter dealt with... delicately."

Manager Bundi stood in the doorway between the living room and bedroom, nodding appreciatively.

"I'm in Nairobi, at the Suffolk Hotel," said the commissioner. "I've security meetings all weekend about the summit. I am not sure how a murder will affect next week's plans. Sergeant Sebunya's on duty at the moment."

The line went quiet. "That's no good. He's the least delicate man I know." Rose waited. "Best if I call Constable Wachira. She knows how to be discrete. Intelligent, too. Of course you have met her. Can you check the body while you wait for the constable to arrive? I'm afraid we shall have to leave it in situ until morning, but we need to make sure nobody has access to it."

Rose was about to finish the call, but the commissioner continued giving instructions. "Work with Constable Wachira. Record the names and contact details of all witnesses, potential witnesses and interested parties. Try to establish what happened, but save the main questioning for tomorrow. I suggest Constable Wachira stays at the hotel tonight."

If Commissioner Akida had been in the room, Rose would probably have saluted him. She wasn't one of his subordinates. Through clenched teeth, she said, "Commissioner, the dead woman is Davina Dijan."

"It gets worse. She's a leading figure and speaker at the summit. I'll return as soon as I can." The commissioner hung up.

"Thank you, Mama Rose." Colour had returned to Manager Bundi's face. "Come, you must examine the body."

"Rose," Craig called from the bedroom.

She walked through. "You're not getting involved in another murder enquiry are you?" His expression was serious and worried.

"All I'm doing is establishing how Davina Dijan died and the main facts of the case. Commissioner Akida is stuck in Nairobi, but he's sending that nice Constable Wachira. The pretty one who's friends with Sam."

Craig grunted. "At least she's sensible. I suspect if she's involved, Sam won't be far away, which is reassuring. Be careful."

Rose kissed Craig on the forehead and left the cosy cottage.

CHAPTER SEVENTEEN

Davina Dijan was sitting up on the king sized bed, covered in a lilac silk dressing gown tied loosely around her waist. A matching camisole and lace edged shorts were visible beneath it.

As Rose looked at the body, she noted the left-hand side of her neck and dressing gown were red. Blood had seeped onto the pillows beneath the body and into the bedding. There was even a small splatter pattern across the mocha shade of the bedside lamp.

Davina's left arm was across her body, whilst her right hand hung by her side, palm up and covered in sticky red blood. Rose followed the direction of the open palm. She knelt on the floor by the bed and found a silver-coloured knife. How strange. There was an engraving of a cartoon elephant on it.

Rose tried to avoid Davina's dead eyes. They were spooky, only partially closed so the bottom whites were visible.

Rose realised it would be difficult to examine the wound thoroughly without getting covered in blood or disturbing the crime scene. She should have brought a pair of surgical gloves from her medical bag.

Carefully, using only her thumb and index finger, she

examined the area on the neck where the blood flow appeared to start. There was a smooth-edged hole, similar in width to the knife blade on the floor.

Rose turned as the attractive Constable Wachira walked into the room, wearing jeans and a sweatshirt instead of her police uniform.

"Mama Rose, what have you found?" asked the constable.

"The stab wound. I think you'll find the weapon, a small knife, under the bed. It entered here, at the side of her neck." Rose prised open the wound for the constable to see. "I cannot tell if it penetrated the jugular vein, found under the skin, or the deeper carotid artery."

"There's a lot of blood," commented the constable.

"Yes, I believe she bled to death. Unfortunately, she accelerated her own demise by removing the knife." Rose stared at the blood on her hand.

"How do you know?" The constable wrinkled her nose.

"It's the natural reaction." Rose pursed her lip. "Remove the knife and get rid of the pain. The knife could have been sealing the hole in the blood vessel and removing it allowed the blood to escape."

"Poor soul." Constable Wachira's eyes were large and sad.

"Taking a person's life is a crime, a tragedy. But I suspect few people will be sympathetic if her behaviour today is typical. She treated others appallingly. I fear we may have a long list of potential suspects. People she upset, injured or mistreated." Rose finished examining the body and backed away from the bed. "I'm just going to wash my hands."

Rose entered the spacious bathroom adjoining the bedroom. A large mirror hung above double sinks inlaid in a marble top. The rear wall was also marble, with a large shower unit set into it with a glass door. Very smart, thought Rose. She washed Davina's blood from her hands and patted them dry on the hanging towel.

In the bedroom, Constable Wachira placed the knife in a plastic bag. She had remembered her gloves. Rose looked about the room. It was similar in decor to the one Kenneth had shown her, but more opulently furnished. Fire embers glowed in the grate and the floor-to-ceiling windows created a small alcove for two comfortable chairs and a table. An open laptop and some papers were scattered about the table.

One suitcase of men's clothes rested on a stand, partially unpacked. Rose slid open the wardrobe door in the passage opposite the bathroom. There was an array of ladies clothes: jackets, blouses, skirts, trousers, and even a couple of evening dresses. Shoes were scattered over the floor. Rose slid opened a drawer. It was full of expensive-looking underwear.

A vase of lilies shared the top of a wooden dressing table with various cosmetics and a silver box overflowing with bracelets and necklaces.

"I don't think it was a robbery gone wrong," said Constable Wachira, examining a pearl necklace.

"There's nothing more I can do here tonight," said Rose.

Constable Wachira secured the external bedroom door, leading into the hotel corridor, with the loop and ball door latch. They walked into the living room.

"I'll sleep on this sofa," said Constable Wachira. "Make sure nobody enters and disturbs the crime scene." She checked that the windows onto the small balcony were secure, then opened a door in the side wall and stepped through. Returning, she asked, "Who's sleeping in there?"

Rose shrugged her shoulders. "I've no idea."

"Never mind, it will be easy enough to find out." The constable closed and secured the interconnecting door. She moved across to a large desk and began sifting through papers. Rose opened a door in the corridor, leading to the suite entrance, and found a small bathroom.

Constable Wachira looked up from the desk. "Business papers about an internet company. Does Robert Dijan run KenyaSima, the telecoms company?"

"I believe so. I overhead him say he'd been working on

contract documents today with his secretary. Kenneth, the steward for this floor, said they were working in this suite."

"Maybe the interconnecting door is to the secretary's room. Mrs Dijan might not have been happy with her sleeping next door."

"The secretary is male. Young red-haired man called Ethan," Rose said.

"Sorry, mustn't jump to conclusions. Shame, as it rules out a crime of passion and jealously." Constable Wachira removed her gloves. "I think we should gather witness statements before they all fall asleep."

CHAPTER EIGHTEEN

Constable Wachira locked the door to the suite. Kenneth the steward hovered in the corridor. As he approached Rose and the constable, an American voice shouted, "Can we go now? We've been waiting over an hour and I want my bed."

A group of four Americans, three women and a gentleman, all in their late sixties or early seventies, were seated on brown sofas in an alcove at the end of the corridor. Their drink glasses were empty. So was their patience, as they tapped their feet and crossed their arms.

"Just a minute," Constable Wachira called back.

"Constable Wachira," said Rose. "This is Kenneth, the steward who looks after the rooms on this floor."

Kenneth said, "Constable, the two lift engineers at the other end of the corridor have to return to Nairobi. Can you speak with them first?"

The young constable hesitated. "Of course," responded Rose. "Kenneth, ask the Americans if they would like another drink, on the house." He nodded.

"Why were the men working on the lift?" asked the constable.

"The doors failed this afternoon," replied Kenneth. "They

wouldn't fully open or close. Although we called the repair company immediately, their men didn't arrive and start work until nine."

Rose and the constable turned to their left, and then made a right turn down the corridor towards the lift. Rose stopped. "It's rather dark here." She looked around. "Those wall lights aren't working." She pointed at the two closest to them.

Constable Wachira peered around a light fitting. "The bulbs are missing. We must ask Kenneth about this later."

Had someone started stealing lightbulbs? Rose wondered.

Two yellow-overalled men slouched sullenly against the wall by the lift. A large battered metal toolbox and coil of flex lay at their feet. "Can you make this quick? We need to go," said the younger engineer.

"As long as you answer my questions clearly and truthfully, you'll soon be on your way," said Constable Wachira. Rose realised that although the pretty constable was young, and female, she was not intimidated by her job or the people she dealt with.

Standing with a straight back and holding their gaze, the constable began her questions. "Where and when were you contacted about the faulty lift?"

The older engineer answered, scowling. "I was on my way home when I was called back to the office."

"I hadn't left," the younger engineer said, chewing gum. "The call came through at five. As I was still around, I was sent here."

"When did you arrive?" asked the constable.

"Eight forty-five. I wrote the time in the sign-in sheet at the gate if you want to check." The older engineer stood. "Why does it matter?"

Constable Wachira's gaze did not waver. "That's not your concern." The older engineer continued to glower, but the younger one hid a smile behind his hand. He said, "We waited at reception for the steward. I would say it was around nine when he collected us and brought us up here."

Now for the key questions, thought Rose, just managing to restrain herself and allow the constable to continue interviewing the two men.

"Who did you see in the corridor?" asked Constable Wachira.

"Only the steward." The younger engineer picked up the coil of flex. "Once we began work, he left us and started checking the rooms. We last saw him leaving the room up at the top of the corridor, where it's darker."

The older engineer grunted. "Apparently someone stole the bulbs out of the lights up there. The steward said he'd have to fetch new ones, but I guess he hasn't had a chance yet."

Constable Wachira relaxed her stance. "And you saw nobody else in the corridor or enter or leave any of the rooms?"

The two engineers shook their heads. "Can we leave now?" the younger one asked.

The older engineer lifted the toolbox and they strode away. Constable Wachira sighed. "Time for the American guests."

They found the Americans enjoying their free drinks and chatting animatedly. "Is it true there's a dead body in one of the rooms?" the gentleman asked.

"Is it Divina Dijan? One of the charities I give money to back home, the Supporting Africa Foundation, donates to her conservancy," said a lady with a short grey-haired pixie cut.

Constable Wachira held up her hands. "Please, we can't give out any details at present. I just have a few questions to ask before you go to bed. Firstly, I need to take your names for my report."

The lady with the pixie haircut was called Joan, and she was sitting next to Linda, who had a pink tint to her hair. Opposite them were Ronald and a lady with long grey hair called Nancy.

"What time did you come upstairs?" continued the constable.

Linda said, "We left the restaurant just after this lady's party." She pointed towards Rose. "Around nine?"

Rose considered the question. She and Craig arrived at their cottage at ten past nine, but they had chatted to Pearl and Thabiti outside the Bongo Bar. "That sounds about right," she replied.

Constable Wachira nodded. "And who have you seen whilst you've been sitting here?"

"To start with, just the steward. He asked if he could turn our beds down and light our fires," responded Nancy, with the long grey hair. Her hand shot to her mouth. "Oh, my fire's probably gone out by now."

"I'm sure Kenneth can relight it for you," Rose said.

"Good. Later on a young man with bright red hair dashed out of a room at the far end, down this corridor and through the door to the stairs." The stair door was on the right as Rose looked down the corridor.

"He looked a bit peaky," said Joan.

Ronald interrupted. "I guess he went to fetch help. The manager and steward returned with him to the far room. After a few minutes the manager came out, leading the young man who was supporting an older African gentleman. They ignored our questions and headed down the stairs. The steward stayed in the corridor, although we couldn't see him when he was around the corner. Then you arrived," he said to Constable Wachira. "But I didn't see you until you came out with her," he accused Rose.

"I entered the suite by the bedroom door with Manager Bundi," Rose said. The American gentleman's eyebrows knitted together.

Constable Wachira turned to Rose. "Do I need to ask about anything else?" It was the first time her confidence had wavered. Rose needed some air and space to think. She shook her head.

"Thank you for your patience," said the constable. "We may have more questions for you tomorrow." The Americans bade each other goodnight and retired to their rooms.

Constable Wachira balanced on the edge of the sofa and read through her notes. She tapped her pen. "Interesting that the Americans didn't see you enter the suite, but the lift engineers didn't tell us they had."

"Maybe they didn't feel they needed to because I was with Manager Bundi," suggested Rose.

The young constable kneaded her chin. "I'm not convinced their statement is entirely accurate. Access to the room might be the crucial point in this case."

Rose surveyed the corridor. "You mean because the suite is on a corner and it's impossible to see both doors from either part of the corridor?"

"Precisely." Constable Wachira jumped up. "There is also the adjoining room." She marched back along the passageway.

"But it still opens onto the corridor, so anyone entering or leaving would have been seen by the Americans." Rose trudged after the athletic constable.

"Unless someone hid in here… is still hiding." Constable Wachira produced a keycard, opened the door, and turned on the lights. They began to search the room. It was untidy, with bedclothes strewn across the bed and clothes hanging out of a navy suitcase, but no one was concealed in the room or its ensuite bathroom.

"What about the windows?" asked Rose.

"The ones in the suite were bolted." The constable pulled aside the curtains. "So are these."

"The Americans said Robert Dijan and his secretary left with Manager Bundi. Does that mean they were in the suite when Davina was killed?" said Rose.

"Looks like it. Our prime suspects."

CHAPTER NINETEEN

On Saturday morning Craig and Rose decided to eat breakfast on the restaurant terrace. It was cool and small wispy clouds hovered over the grounds. Mount Kenya was not yet visible.

"Are you sure you're OK out here?" Rose asked Craig.

"Bracing air. It's good for me," Craig replied. Rose was not certain he was right, but decided not to argue. She felt the first rays of sun warm her face.

"May I join you?" Constable Wachira sat down, wearing the same clothes as the previous evening. She shivered. "I was in such a rush to get here yesterday that I forgot to pack spare clothes. Still, the cool air should clear my head. I didn't sleep very well."

"Neither would I with a corpse next door and a killer on the loose," said Rose.

Craig cleared his throat. "I presume Commissioner Akida will take over the investigation today, or send a senior officer." Rose noticed the young constable lock her hands into fists and compress her mouth. Craig must have noticed as well. "I'm not doubting your ability, Constable, but there has been a rather gruesome murder of an influential woman."

"I spoke with the commissioner," the constable said

through clenched teeth. "He is not sure when he will be released today, if at all. The news of the murder is likely to raise more security concerns rather than diminish them. He is expecting a grilling and wants me to keep him updated regularly."

"Who is he sending to help you?" Craig asked.

Constable Wachira shifted uncomfortably in her chair. "Well… he hoped Mama Rose would." Steam was not actually rising from Craig's nostrils, but they flared violently. The constable continued quickly. "Only Sergeant Sebunya is available, and the commissioner mentioned something about not finding something from his elbow." Constable Wachira was so straight-faced with her delivery that Craig laughed.

He composed himself. "Rose is not an extension of the police force. From what I understand the lethal blow was delivered with some force. Our killer is dangerous and likely to still be in the hotel," argued Craig.

"Even so, I can't see why they'd want to harm me," said Rose. "I still need to help solve the hotel thefts for Manager Bundi, so I might as well help the constable at the same time." Rose winked at the constable, who grinned.

"What was that?" asked Craig. His eyes narrowed.

Rose leant forward and put her hand over Craig's. "Whilst we're here and assisting Manager Bundi, we both get free board and lodging. Kenneth told me a number of people are due to arrive today ahead of next week's summit. I think you'll enjoy their company. And what better surroundings than these."

Rose opened her arms as the last clouds lifted from Batian Peak and the sun shone majestically on Mount Kenya.

CHAPTER TWENTY

R ose left Craig on the terrace drinking his second cup of coffee and finishing the report he'd downloaded on her iPad. She needed to find Thabiti and ask if he would help with her theft enquiries. Constable Wachira had gone to wait for the ambulance from the Community Hospital which was taking away Davina's body.

They had agreed to meet at eleven o'clock to interview Robert Dijan and his secretary. Rose realised they also needed to interview Kenneth. She would try to find him this morning.

As Rose reached the central area of the hotel, by the entrance to the Bongo Bar and within sight of the main staircase and hotel reception, she saw Chloe greet a European man. Rose froze.

"Chris. This is unexpected. What are you doing here?" exclaimed Chloe.

"Ma'am," the man responded politely but warmly. "Could say the same about you. Is the major here?"

"Dan's away. Up country, I think, on a security job." Chloe secured her sunglasses in her long hair.

The man clasped his hands in front of him. "Me, too.

Security that is. I've been sent over from the UK to help with this big summit event they're holding here next week."

"Didn't you grow up in Africa?" Chloe tilted her head.

The man nodded. "I did, not too far from here, actually."

"Are your parents still living here? Will you visit them?" asked Chloe.

"I'm not sure. Expect I'll be busy with work and we don't really talk." The man spoke to his polished brown shoes. "They didn't approve of me joining the regiment. Well, not as a soldier, anyway."

"Oh. I'm sure they'd be delighted to see you," Chloe said brightly.

The man lifted his head and looked over Chloe's shoulder. "I might call… Mum?"

Rose's feet were glued to the floor. If they hadn't been she would have turned around the moment she saw her son. She could have prepared herself for their awkward reunion. And what would Craig say when he knew Chris was staying in the same hotel?

Chloe swung round, her eyes wide. She saw Rose and stammered, "Morning, Rose. Can I introduce you to…"

"My son, Chris." Rose was still firmly rooted to the ground. Chloe walked across to her with an uncertain wrinkle across her brow.

"Did you say your son?"

"Yes. And he's right, we're haven't spoken for a long time. Too long." Rose began to feel herself crumble. That was no good. She had a job to do. A killer to find. And she needed space and time to think. This was her chance to get her son back. Possibly her only chance, and she mustn't mess it up. She summoned her strength and resolve. She lifted one foot and then another.

To Chloe, she said brightly, "Did you sleep well? Craig is on the terrace finishing breakfast if you want to join him."

Rose did not let Chloe answer and ignored her jaw-drop expression. She walked across to her son uncertain whether to hug him. Her arms remained limply by her side. "Chris. I'm delighted to see you, but it's rather a shock. For you, too, I expect. You need to settle in and I have a job to do this morning. Why don't we meet tonight for sundowners?"

Chris swallowed. "Dad's here as well?"

"Yes."

"I'm not sure I can cope with a joint reunion. Better if just the two of us meet." He held Rose's gaze. "You're right, I have to get sorted with work. But I'll find you later."

Chris stepped back, half bowed to Chloe, and returned to the reception area. Rose felt her legs wobble. Chloe rushed over, placing a supporting arm around her. "Rose, you're very pale. Come and sit down."

Chloe escorted Rose to the Bongo Bar and plumped up several cushions on a covered bench against one wall. She went to the bar.

Rose replayed the scene in her mind, uncertain how she felt. She had longed for a chance to explain to Chris why his father had been so angry, but did it really matter anymore? Her son was a mature man, possibly with a family of his own. No, her daughter Heather would have told her if he had married or had children.

She knew Heather kept in contact with her brother, and she occasionally told Rose snippets to reassure her Chris was still alive and well, despite being sent to some dangerous places with the British Army.

"I've ordered you some tea with honey. I think you're in shock." Chloe sat beside Rose.

Thabiti walked in as Rose's tea arrived. He was excited and dressed head to toe in black, with a loose fitting black shirt and baggy low-slung cotton rapper trousers.

"Who or what are you supposed to be?" demanded Chloe.

"Now I'm working as a DJ, I need to look the part." He flicked his fingers.

"Thabiti, you're working as a sound and technical engineer at a serious event," Chloe admonished him.

"Chill sister," Thabiti replied. Chloe sat back and folded her arms.

"Mama, why you so quiet? Spill the tea?" Thabiti chimed.

"Leave my tea alone." Rose wrapped her hands protectively around her cup. She ignored whatever gesture Chloe made to Thabiti and sipped her tea in silence. Slowly the warm sweet liquid penetrated her body and mind. She shook her head and focused on Thabiti.

It was time to get back to the business at hand. "I can probably put up with you dressed like a rapper, but there's no need to talk like one. Sit down." Thabiti slumped onto a chair. "I'll tell you what's happened, but in confidence. I might need your help." Rose explained, to her rapt audience, the events of the previous evening and how she came to be involved.

"As well as a killer to identify, I also told Manager Bundi I would help him find a thief or thieves. The hotel has been suffering from a series of robberies over the past six months. That investigation is how Craig and I can afford to stay here. Payment for my 'detecting' services."

Thabiti laughed. "No need for that," Rose chided, but she smiled and felt herself relax.

"It's just that with each case you take on, I think you'll gain a characteristic until you morph into Miss Marple," Thabiti said.

"Don't be ridiculous. I need your help, Thabiti. I know you are here to rest, Chloe, and have your own problems, so there's no need for you to get involved." Rose spoke in a business-like tone.

"Au contraire. This is far too exciting to miss," declared Chloe.

"It's not a game." Rose frowned. "Craig's right. There is a dangerous killer in this hotel."

Chloe clasped her hands in her lap. "Sorry. You're right. Davina might have been a disagreeable woman, but her death is still awful. What do you want us to do?"

Rose placed her teacup on the table. "I need you to pursue

these thefts. I think we have two perpetrators. One who takes valuable items, pieces they can probably sell easily. The other is someone who only takes stuff they think has been discarded, or won't be missed."

Rose fished the notebook out of her bag and wrote a list of the higher value items and another of the least valuable. She agreed with Kenneth, up to a point, about the guest thefts.

"There." She tore the page from her notebook. "Go on a treasure hunt and explore the hotel. Especially the staff and private areas. If anyone asks what you're doing, say it's hotel business, which they should take up with Manager Bundi or me."

"What are you going to do?" Thabiti asked.

"Find Kenneth and ask him about last night."

Chloe leant across to Rose, placing a hand on her leg. "Are you sure you're OK?"

"Better for the tea. Thank you. Better for having something to do." Rose knew she used her work, or whatever activity she could find, as an excuse, a barrier against dealing with emotional problems.

Chloe and Thabiti left. Thabiti looked back at Rose and started questioning Chloe, but she just shook her head.

Rose drained the contents of her teacup. She should be joyous. Her son had returned and they were staying at one of the most beautifully located hotels in the world. She picked up her bag and left in search of Kenneth.

CHAPTER TWENTY-ONE

R ose had sent Chloe and Thabiti on a treasure hunt, but found herself scavenging for Kenneth. He was not on the first floor, where a group of white clad men stood in the doorway to Davina's bedroom. Neither was he at reception or the Bongo Bar.

In the staffroom she found the remnants of chai in a chipped cup, and half a glass of orange squash. She couldn't spend all day looking for him. Reception would have his mobile number and could call him.

Rose left the staff room and passed an old wooden-framed window with a cracked pane. She stopped abruptly, returned to the window, and used her shirt sleeve to wipe away enough grime to see through.

In the rear delivery yard, Kenneth was playing football with a young boy of about nine. The boy wore a shiny blue shirt and skilfully dribbled the ball around Kenneth. He scored a goal by kicking the ball against a wall crudely marked with the outline of a goal post.

Rose tapped on the window. The boy picked up the ball whilst Kenneth walked across and peered at Rose.

"We need to talk," Rose shouted through the cracked pane. Kenneth consulted a chrome watch.

He held up five fingers and shouted back, "Five minutes."

The door at the far end of the corridor opened and Thabiti stuck his head round. "Mama Rose. I thought I heard you shouting." He beckoned to her with his hand. "Come and see who we've found."

Rose joined Thabiti who led her into the large hotel kitchen. There was a sweet smell of caramelising onions. Rose had peeked inside a number of restaurant kitchens in Kenya. Most were small and shabby with tiled or wooden surfaces and domestic standalone gas cookers. Some kitchens were more outdoors than indoors, with vegetable peeling, washing up and open fire cooking undertaken outside, behind the restaurant.

This hotel kitchen did have some white-tiled splashbacks, but the large industrial ovens were impressive and the stainless-steel counters shone. Rose stared at the unusual sight of a dishwasher, from which a waiter removed plates before carrying them into another room. In most establishments, washing up was done by hand.

Thabiti said, "Look. Our quest has uncovered Joel, former chef at Avocado Catering." A young bald-headed man stopped slicing chicken pieces and smiled amicably.

"I had enough of Avocado once I found out Vincent used it as a front to steal from the houses in which we cooked. I'm only a junior chef here, but I'll receive training in many different areas: meat, fish and even pastry. Maybe one day I can open my own restaurant." His smile became a grin.

"Good for you," said Rose. "But I have to meet Kenneth." She turned back to the door.

"Just a minute," said Chloe, who was leaning against a stainless-steel counter. "Joel might have some information on the thefts." Rose faced the chef.

Joel looked around sharply and said in a low voice. "Not here. I've got lunch to prepare, but I will be finished by two. Meet me outside the exit to the maze down in the grounds. There's a bench where I often sit and watch the mountain."

CHAPTER TWENTY-TWO

Rose returned to the staff room. The young boy drained his glass of orange squash, high-fived Kenneth, and ran off. Rose waited.

"My son, Darren. He's a good boy and looks after himself, but I try and spend my breaks with him at weekends."

"Where's his mother?" Kenneth's ears reddened. Rose felt the back of her neck tingle. She'd miscalculated. The boy's mother was probably dead.

"Back in the UK," Kenneth said with finality.

Rose quickly changed the subject. "As you know, I helped Constable Wachira last night after Davina Dijan's body was found. Commissioner Akida is still in Nairobi, so I'm continuing to assist the investigation."

Rose removed her notebook and glasses from her tote bag. "We interviewed the lift engineers who confirmed you met them at reception at nine o'clock. What were your movements from the time your left us around the fire pit until nine?"

Kenneth leaned back in his chair and crossed his arms. "I suppose someone has to ask these questions. Better you than some boorish policeman. But you could send that attractive constable." He grinned.

"You look strong, but you should see her boyfriend. At

least I think that's what he is. He's a man mountain. Anyway, you're stuck with me." Rose formed her hands into a steeple on the tabletop and looked expectantly at Kenneth.

"I made my way around the first floor rooms, closing curtains. All except the one next to the suite. There's a red-haired young man staying there who works with Mr Dijan."

"Yes, his secretary, Ethan."

"He said he was getting changed and had already drawn his curtains."

"Were Mr and Mrs Dijan in their suite?" asked Rose.

"No, it looked as if they had already changed for supper. I returned a couple of damp towels to the bathroom, which had been thrown on the floor."

"Were all the lights working in the corridor?" Rose leaned back and crossed her ankles.

"You mean because two wall lights weren't later? Yes, when I first went up, all the lights worked."

"So what did you do after drawing the curtains?"

Kenneth tapped his fingers on his leg. "I returned to the kitchen. I delivered four room service orders. Two to the first floor and two to rooms on the ground floor. The ground floor steward was working in the restaurant during peak service. That's when I noticed the lights weren't working, but I didn't get a chance to replace the bulbs."

"Who did you see in the first floor corridor?" Rose asked.

"When I first went up, I met two of the American guests with their tour guide. I presumed they were heading down for supper. The red-haired young man passed me as I was taking the second room service order. Later, I followed Mr Dijan down the stairs when I collected the room service trays. About ten minutes later, I met the lift engineers."

"So you saw Robert Dijan on the stairs around ten to nine."

"I guess so." Kenneth watched Rose. He appeared relaxed and unconcerned. Maybe too unconcerned.

"The lift engineers told me you left them to check the rooms. Did you go into the suite?"

"Yes, Mrs Dijan had changed into her night clothes and was sitting on the bed reading a book. She kept yawning and asked me to make her a cup of coffee, which I did."

Rose sucked her pencil. "Apart from the killer, you might be the last person to see Davina alive." Rose noticed Kenneth suddenly stiffen.

He stammered. "That can't be right. Her husband?"

"Did you see him?"

"He wasn't in the living room when I entered the suite, but he was pouring himself a drink as I left. He asked me if Davina was asleep and sighed heavily when I told her I had made her a cup of coffee."

"Did you notice anything else?" Rose leaned towards Kenneth, who hesitated.

"Mr Dijan looked rather ruffled, and his hands shook as he lifted his glass. I noticed the door to the adjoining room was ajar. Now, I really need to get back to work."

"Yes, of course, but Kenneth, I think you've realised you're currently a prime suspect, and potentially the last person to see Davina alive."

His voice shook. "Mama, I didn't do it. I don't want any trouble with the police." Kenneth's eyes were pleading.

As they walked into the main hotel, Rose put a hand on the trembling man's shoulder. "I'm sure the police will get to the bottom of this."

"But you believe me, don't you? Will you stand up for me?"

Gently, Rose said, "As long as you're telling me the whole truth." Kenneth gulped.

An American voice said, "Ma'am, you gotta minute?"

Kenneth fled as Rose turned to Joan, with the pixie hairstyle. Her friend Linda, with the pink shade of hair, hid behind her. Rose checked her watch. Ten forty-five. She had fifteen minutes until the interview with Robert Dijan, which she didn't want to miss.

The three ladies seated themselves by a full-length window in the Bongo Bar. The hotel swimming pool was visible below them, beyond the grass terrace where they had enjoyed pre-dinner drinks the evening before.

Chloe strode past the window wearing a vest top and kikoi sarong over her swimming costume. The three ladies gazed at her. As if aware of the scrutiny, Chloe turned towards them and waved. Rose waved back.

"She a friend of yours?" asked Joan. Rose nodded. "How well d'you know that steward?"

"Kenneth?" asked Rose. "Not particularly. Seems a decent chap. Why?"

Linda whispered. "I think he may've stolen my phone." Joan patted her friend's leg. "I began charging it before supper. On the small table by the window in my room. When I woke this morning it wasn't there."

"Did you check last night before going to sleep?"

"No. 'Twas late and I was tired."

Rose checked her watch again. "I'm sorry, ladies. I have to meet the police constable. Why don't you search your room again? Double check your phone hasn't fallen down the back of a chair or that you haven't left it in a bag. Then speak to reception. Someone might have handed it in. If it's still missing, find me this afternoon and I'll see what I can do."

The ladies nodded in appreciation. "Thank you, ma'am."

CHAPTER TWENTY-THREE

Constable Wachira had converted the living room area of the Dijan's suite into her incident room. Manager Bundi reluctantly agreed after she pointed out that the suite could not be used by guests.

Rose dashed into the room. "Sorry I'm late. I was waylaid." Rose presumed Robert Dijan had been given another room. She wondered whether his secretary had also moved from the adjacent bedroom as the latch was still secure across the door leading to it.

Papers had been cleared from the large desk and under it she spotted a rolled up sleeping bag and pillow. One of the windows had been opened onto the balcony. The gauze shade curtain moved slowly back and forth as fresh air filtered into the room and stale air escaped.

"Who's she?" Robert Dijan asked Constable Wachira. He raised his arm in Rose's direction. "I saw her in the restaurant last night, so I presume she's staying at the hotel."

Rose felt another pair of eyes examine her. "She doesn't look like a police officer," said the red-haired young man standing to her right. It was Ethan, Robert Dijan's secretary. He scowled at her.

"You don't look like a secretary," Rose said. "Don't judge a lion by its mane." Rose raised her chin and squared her shoulders.

"Why not? All male lions have manes," Ethan sneered.

"Actually, they don't," responded Rose. "I've watched maneless male lions in Meru National Park."

Constable Wachira coughed. "Mama Rose has been asked to assist me by Commissioner Akida as he has to attend security meetings in Nairobi. Last month Mama Rose investigated two murders and prevented a third. She was called in yesterday evening as she has some medical knowledge."

"Oh, you're a doctor," said the younger man.

"No, a vet, actually." She did not add "community" as she guessed her answer would be treated with derision. She was right.

The young man snorted. "So the murder of my employer's wife, an important woman, is being investigated by two women. A police constable and an elderly amateur with dubious medical qualifications." He had a point... she had no medical qualifications.

The young female constable was not standing for such talk. She walked forward and confronted the young man. He was smaller than Rose realised, as Constable Wachira eye-balled him.

The secretary stepped back a pace, but further retreat was blocked by the dividing wall with the suite bedroom. "The first forty-eight hours are critical in an investigation. You should be assisting us rather than insulting my colleague. If there are no leads or suspects in a case within that time, the chances of solving the case are halved. Luckily, we have a number of suspects." She glared at her prey.

The pale face of the young man contrasted with the bright spots on his cheeks and his shock of red hair.

Robert Dijan moved across and offered a hand to his secretary, guiding him to safety. "Please excuse Ethan." Robert's deep voice broke the tension. "It has been a tough night for us. Until the commissioner or someone senior arrives, we will help you as best we can. Perhaps we should all sit down."

Constable Wachira tightened the kanga scrunchy at the base of her neck, around her long braided hair. She gracefully seated herself in an empty chair. Ethan perched on the arm of the sofa looking out through the fluttering curtain.

Robert undertook the role of host with ease and efficiency. Perhaps his way of coping, thought Rose. "Would anyone like a drink?" He opened the minibar, hidden in a cupboard located against the bathroom wall.

Rose took a water, Constable Wachira a Diet Coke, and Ethan a Sprite. Robert tipped a can of tomato juice into a glass and added the contents of a small clear bottle. Vodka, Rose guessed. Maybe he was not as calm and composed as he liked to portray.

Constable Wachira directed her opening question at Mr Dijan. "Can we start with your movements yesterday? Did you attend your wife's presentation at the conference, sir?" Clever girl, thought Rose. He was more likely to open up to someone who respected him. As the managing director of the nationally important company, KenyaSimu, he was used to being treated with reverence.

Whether it was the constable's words, her manner, or the effects of the vodka, Robert Dijan appeared to relax. He leaned back in the sofa and crossed his black-clothed legs. "No. I have an important acquisition completing next week. Ethan and I spent all day in here working on the legal documents. We even had a cold buffet lunch provided by the hotel. Davina joined us."

"How did she seem?" The constable's pen was poised above her notebook.

"As always, elated after speaking and consuming a glass of champagne. Then she started her comedown. She complained about some poor technician who put up the wrong presentation. Her research assistant pointed out that she'd handed over the wrong flash drive and she lunged at him. Ethan and I had to restrain her. Gabe grabbed some sandwiches and left."

"Gabe?' asked Rose.

"Gabriel Baker, her research student. The conservancy has an arrangement with a UK university. It will involve money, to the conservancy's advantage, I'm sure. A student gets a year's placement on the conservancy and Gabriel is the second such student."

Rose remembered Chloe's comment the previous evening. "Was he the young man your wife shouted at early yesterday evening? I believe you removed her to the Bongo Bar."

Robert Dijan uncrossed and re-crossed his legs. "Yes. I'm not sure what that was about," he said to the room behind Rose. His left eye twitched. He's lying, Rose thought.

"Did your wife return to the conference after lunch?" asked the constable.

"Yes. Ethan and I had a video call with my lawyers in Nairobi. Davina reappeared at five o'clock, but she ignored us, poured a glass of champagne, and retired to the bedroom."

"Slamming the door," added Ethan. His mouth tightened.

"She did seem a little upset," murmured Robert.

"A little!" Ethan's eyes blazed. "The whole wall shook. And it wasn't just one glass. She carried the rest of the champagne bottle with her."

Robert sighed. "My wife was a passionate woman."

CHAPTER TWENTY-FOUR

R ose had seen the Dijans during supper and witnessed Davina's behaviour, but she still needed to establish a timeline. She asked Robert, "What time did you go downstairs yesterday evening, and did you and Davina go together?"

"Yes, we changed and headed down. The clock in reception said seven o'clock. Davina and I had a drink in the Bongo Bar before moving through to the restaurant, which is where I saw you." Robert drained his glass.

Rose felt herself blush. "I think your wife wanted our table. She was very vocal and... demanding."

Robert stood and crossed to the minibar where he removed a can of Tusker beer. "You need to understand, my wife worked hard and she was ambitious. Her desire to be recognised as a major player in conservation, in Kenya, seemed to increase with age. Ours was not a standard marriage and we spent much of our time apart: Davina at the conservancy, whilst I remained in Nairobi. We both travelled extensively, but usually separately, with our work." Robert returned to his seat.

"You were her second husband?" Rose asked. She was not

sure how much background knowledge Constable Wachira knew or had discovered.

"Davina's English. She married a surgeon and lived in London until he died of a brain tumour. She developed a passion for Kenya after working here as a young twenty-something on an elephant conservation project. She became a journalist, specialising in wildlife conservation and Africa. After her first husband's death, she moved to Kenya and worked on a conservation project up north. Later, she moved to Gaia and sort of took over." Robert leaned back to stare at the ceiling.

"How did you meet?" Constable Wachira asked.

"In Nairobi, at a fundraising dinner. She could charm the spots off a leopard when she put her mind to it. Certainly pursued and captured me." Robert smiled and his eyes became distant.

"Do you think she loved you, or just wanted your money and influence?" The constable spoke in a flat tone.

Ethan jumped up. "I'm sorry, but what kind of question is that?" Robert patted Ethan's thigh.

"A valid one. I was gullible to think a young, attractive and glamorous woman would fall in love me with me. I've come to accept that she needed my contacts to propel her onto the next rung of her career ladder. Don't get me wrong, it hasn't done my reputation or business any harm. A handsome woman on my arm, one with an acclaimed environmental voice, had huge business advantages, especially with our overseas partners."

"You didn't have children?" Constable Wachira continued.

The light dimmed in Robert's eyes. "No. Davina didn't want any. She saw them as a hindrance to her career progression."

"And with her first husband?" the constable probed.

Robert shrugged half-heartedly. "No, not that I'm aware of."

Constable Wachira cleared her throat. "Sorry to ask this, Mr Dijan. Do you know if she was having an affair?"

There was a pause. Robert picked at the cuff of his shirt. Ethan gave him a nervous glance. "I expect so. It wouldn't be the first time. Some young man she wanted to impress or influence. Once she'd exploited what she needed, she'd discard him and search for new prey." He flicked imaginary dirt from his sleeve.

"Did this bother you?" Constable Wachira was working hard.

"No. I have my own… friends." Robert continued to look at his hands. Rose noticed his left eye twitch again. Ethan repositioned himself on the arm of the sofa.

Rose jumped in. Time to change direction. "Was Davina drunk last night?"

Robert looked up. "She could handle her drink, but after champagne in the suite, a drink at the bar and more fizz at the table, I'd say so. You witnessed her knock over her glass." Rose nodded. Robert continued, "She refused to let me take her upstairs. Later, she complained she was sleepy, so I did help her to our room."

"What time was that?" asked the constable.

"I'm not sure. Ask the steward. He followed me back downstairs."

Rose turned to Ethan. "You joined the Dijans for supper. Is that usual? Davina didn't seem very happy with the arrangement."

Ethan bit at his nail. "She had worked herself into a state."

Rose peered at him. "Do you think she resented you?"

His head shot up. He glanced at Rose and quickly looked away. "Resented? Why should she?"

"Because you spent so much time with her husband," Rose stated.

Ethan shook his head. "We had a lot of work to do. This acquisition next week is a big deal for the company."

Robert added. "It'll greatly improve internet access outside Nairobi."

Rose looked at Constable Wachira, who shrugged. She said, "So... the two of you left the restaurant before us. Around nine. Did you go straight to your rooms or stop at the bar?"

"My room," muttered Ethan.

"Me, too," echoed Robert.

Rose asked, "Did you check on your wife?"

"No. I needed to finish some paperwork. The steward told me she was still awake and had even told him to make her a coffee."

"No doubt trying to sober up," Ethan added.

"I finished reading and went through to the bedroom. That's when I found her... body." Robert swallowed hard.

"Did you see or hear anyone else apart from the steward?" asked Rose.

"No one." He slowly shook his head.

Rose busied herself with her bag, preparing to leave. "One last question. Where were you when the steward entered the room?"

Robert looked confused. "Sorry, what do you mean?"

"The steward told me the living room was empty when he passed through to the bedroom. He only saw you when he came back."

Robert picked at his cuff again. Rose waited. "I must have been in the bathroom," Robert said.

"And you?" Constable Wachira asked Ethan.

"In my room. All evening."

"Is there anyone you can think of who wanted your wife dead?" asked Constable Wachira.

"She upset a lot of people. But I don't know of anyone who would kill her." Finally, tears ran down Robert's cheeks.

CHAPTER TWENTY-FIVE

Rose stood at the entrance to the Bongo Bar, which was busy. Many hotel guests were taking advantage of the light lunch served in the bar. The room was bright and airy with large floor-to-ceiling windows on the far wall and glass doors opening onto a patio. The sweeping lawns, distant forest and stately mountain provided an impressive backdrop.

The four American guests Rose had met the night before were seated on stylish wooden chairs on the patio under the shade of a canvas umbrella. Their heads were bowed in confidential conversation with a middle-aged European woman in khaki lightweight trousers and a tan polo shirt.

Kenneth was on duty behind the bar in the centre of the room. He popped the metal caps off two bottles of Tusker beer and placed them on the bar. He turned to speak to an African teenager washing glasses in a sink to one side of the bar. The youth's uniform shirt hung loosely over his skinny frame.

A waiter carried the bottles of Tusker, with clean pint glasses, to two European men seated at a small round table between Rose and the patio. The younger one, with long sandy hair tidied up in a ponytail, was talking earnestly to a slightly older man with a chiselled face and dark spiky hair.

Rose spotted Craig, Thabiti and Hugo sitting at a window table. She joined them as they discussed the current crossword clue.

"The first two words, 'edgy pair,' are an anagram. The clue is in the rest of the sentence 'out where everyone comes out,'" said Craig.

"It sounds like a party to me," said Thabiti.

Hugo was scribbling on the bottom of the crossword puzzle paper. "Got it. It is a party of sorts. Gay pride," he said.

"What sort of party is that?" Thabiti asked.

"Usually a parade with rainbow-coloured banners and flags to raise awareness of, and equality for, LGBT."

Thabiti scratched his head and asked, "LGBT?"

Craig coughed. "Thabiti, ask Hugo about it later. It relates to homosexuality, which of course is illegal in Kenya."

Hugo's eyes widened. "Really?"

Rose knew Craig was in his element, imparting information to his rapt audience. She collected menus from the bar and lowered herself into an empty chair.

Craig continued, "Under Kenya's Penal Code, sexual acts between men are a criminal offence. The maximum penalty is fourteen years in prison." Something clicked in Rose's brain. "Hugo, read out one more clue before we stop for lunch," Craig instructed.

Hugo read, "Eight down. Love child of unmarried parents." He shifted in his chair.

"How many letters?" asked Thabiti.

"Twelve." Hugo's voice was shaky. The waiter placed a small bowl of crisps on a table next to the crossword. Rose watched in amusement as Thabiti's right arm pumped backwards and forwards between the bowl and his mouth. Hugo reached over, but the bowl was empty. He looked accusingly at Thabiti.

"What? I'm hungry," Thabiti spluttered. Rose handed him a menu. "The answer's illegitimate," he said before his attention moved to the food on offer.

Chloe flopped into another chair. She had exchanged her sarong for navy shorts and wore a wide-brimmed straw hat.

"I need a drink." Chloe removed her hat and fanned her face. "Lovely out there, but I'm roasting." She smiled to the group. "Have you had a good morning, everyone?"

Craig tried to straighten up in his chair. "Yes, thank you. Very relaxed. And you?"

Chloe whispered, "Thabiti and I did a bit of sleuthing for Rose. Then I baked myself by the pool. The water is freezing, but soon cools you down."

Thabiti lifted his head from his menu. "Hugo and I have been editing material from yesterday's conference."

Rose frowned. "Have you seen anything unusual on the tapes?"

Thabiti laughed. "It's digital. Do you mean anything which might relate to Davina's murder?"

"Yes, just a thought. Keep your eyes open," Rose said.

Thabiti passed his menu to Chloe. "Has to be the Bongo Burger for me. What about you Hugo?"

Hugo's expression was unfocused. He jolted as if Thabiti had nudged him with an electric cattle prod. "Oh...Yes. That sounds good."

"How do you like it cooked? Rare with blood in the middle?"

Hugo shivered. "Well done."

Craig signalled to Kenneth, who sent the teenager across to collect their orders. His face fell as everyone started shouting at once.

"Slow down," Rose said, and motioned the boy to her side. "Two Bongo Burgers." He wrote "2 berga." Club sandwich became "cub sadwig" and Greek salad "geec sad." "Well done," she told the boy. His hands shook as he gave her a slow, haunted smile.

CHAPTER TWENTY-SIX

R ose looked up as Joan approached her. "Ma'am, may we speak with you again?"

Rose followed the lady onto the patio. It was hot outside, so Rose shifted the empty seat into the shade before sitting down. The rest of the group stopped talking.

"Nicki, this lady works for the police. She might be able to help us," said Joan to the European woman Rose didn't know. Did a flash of fear appear in the woman's eyes?

"I don't really work for the police." Rose paused. Actually, at the moment she was working in official capacities for both the police and the hotel. "I suppose you could say I've been seconded. Did you find your phone?" Rose looked towards Linda.

"No. We've looked everywhere." Linda threw her arms in the air. "Someone's gotta have taken it."

Rose turned to the lady who'd been introduced as Nicki, but she avoided Rose's gaze. "Are you the group's tour guide?"

"For the first part of the tour." Nicki straightened her polo shirt. "I meet the guests when they arrive at the airport. We stay in Nairobi the first night and then here for two nights. I escort them to Lake Elementaita, in the Rift Valley, where we spend the fourth night. Another guide takes them on to the Mara."

Rose asked. "Have other tour members lost anything?"

Ronald said, "I think I lost some money the first night. Hard to say. I exchanged five hundred dollars and received a stack of those one thousand shilling notes. It appears that's the highest value bank note. Still, I'm pretty sure the pile in my bedside drawer shrank."

Nancy turned to Linda. "Eloise and her husband, Matt, were on this tour over Christmas. She said someone took her gold bracelet."

Nicki jumped in. "I went over that with her. She admitted it had a loose clasp and it's likely she dropped it. Now, I have itineraries to prepare. Enjoy your lunch." As Nicki stood, Nancy whispered, "Eloise swore she didn't drop it." Nicki pulled at her shirt collar and left the group.

Rose asked Nancy, "Do you know where your friend was when she lost her bracelet?"

"Yes, the hotel by the lake. She couldn't find it to wear for supper. Nicki said she must've worn it during the game drive and lost it when the vehicle bumped over rough ground." Rose clasped her hands together, watching Nicki's retreating back.

Joan leaned over and touched Rose's arm. She whispered, "You still involved with that murder?"

"Yes, I'm helping the police until their commissioner arrives."

"Well, you know I said I donate to the Supporting Africa Foundation. I emailed the charity's director about Davina's death. His reply said the strangest thing: that he'll never know where the money went. Watta ya think he meant by that?" Joan raised her hand to her mouth.

"I've no idea." Rose saw the African teenager carrying plates to Craig's group. "Will you excuse me? My lunch has arrived."

She stood, but leaned on the back of her chair. "Can you

ask other members of your group about missing items? Their own or people they know from previous tours. Write down what went missing and where they were staying at the time. I can't promise to get your phone back, but if someone is stealing, we need to put a stop to it."

Rose turned and saw Craig lift the crossword from the table to make space for the lunch. His pen rolled onto the floor unnoticed.

The African teenager bent down to pick it up. With his head tilted to one side, he looked around furtively. Hugo noticed him. The boy's body went limp as he placed the pen in Hugo's outstretched hand. Hugo thanked the boy distractedly.

Rose was waylaid by a sweating Manager Bundi who diverted her to the corner of the bar counter. "Any progress?" he asked.

"With what?" Rose was lightheaded and her mouth watered at the smell of Thabiti and Hugo's burgers.

"The thefts. What else?"

"I'm currently helping the police with their investigation as well," said Rose.

Manager Bundi's shoulders slumped. "It's all too much. And with the summit next week."

"I really must eat some lunch." Rose sat down and stared at her club sandwich. The edges of the toast had curled. She popped a fry into her mouth and stared out the window.

It was no good. She had ingested too much information to think straight and her mind returned to Chris. She wondered what he was doing and if he was also eating lunch. She hadn't spotted him in the Bongo Bar.

She continued to pick at her food, whilst Chloe and Hugo enthusiastically explained the rules of croquet to a bemused Thabiti.

CHAPTER TWENTY-SEVEN

R ose felt trapped. Both in the sense of having been indoors all day, and in her head. She wrapped half her sandwich in a napkin and pushed her plate across to Thabiti.

"Not hungry?" asked Thabiti with raised eyebrows. Clearly the concept of not finishing lunch was to Thabiti like a lion refusing to hunt a zebra.

"I just need some air," Rose told him, and time by myself to think, she told herself.

As Rose walked past Craig, he leant back and placed an arm on her thigh. "Are you all right? You look tired."

Rose rubbed her eyes. "I am. It's been a hectic morning. Can you manage without me?"

"Of course. Are you going back to the cottage to rest?" Craig asked.

"No, I'd prefer to sit outside. I'll find a seat in the garden." This idea had come from Joel, and she remembered their two o'clock meeting.

"Chloe, Thabiti. Don't forget we're meeting Joel by the maze exit at two." She was not sure they had heard as they were too busy laughing.

Rose walked out of the Bongo Bar via the patio. Below, on the grass terrace, chairs and fire pits were being arranged for the evening sundowner drinks. Beyond the terrace, the oval-shaped swimming pool was surrounded by sun loungers with blue and white striped covers. Rose's path led her through borders of coloured flowers until she saw a wooden sign proclaiming, "Maze Entrance."

She followed the path around to the left and stopped by a wooden bench under the shade of a large black sweetberry tree. Clumps of small green berries wrapped themselves around branches at the nodes of dark green leaves.

Bursts of colour were provided by flower-laden bushes of bougainvillea on either side of the bench: one red, the other magenta. She felt shielded by the bushes.

Sandwich forgotten, Rose leaned back and closed her eyes. Immediately images of Chris appeared: as a baby, a young schoolboy, and the angry youth who had slammed closed the door on their relationship eighteen years ago.

The temperature was pleasant and the filtered sunlight refreshed her face. It penetrated through her skin and into her brain. The angry images of her son evaporated as she began to float with the calming hum of numerous insects.

Opening her eyes, Rose watched sunlight dance through the leaf canopy and thought of the investigation into the death of Davina Dijan. The shards of information she'd gleaned today were like the light fragments. They twisted around inside her mind.

Davina Dijan had been an ambitious woman who had been respected but not well liked. Last night she had been alone in her bedroom. The suite could be accessed from the corridor through two doors: one directly into her bedroom and one via the living room.

The suite was located on the corner of the hotel, which meant nobody in the corridor could see both doors. Witnesses at either end only saw Kenneth entering and leaving the suite.

Robert assisted Davina to her room at quarter to nine. Kenneth confirmed Davina was alive when he checked on her, sometime after ten past nine. So Kenneth was the last person to see Davina alive, and was clearly a prime suspect. Although he had the best opportunity, Rose hadn't discovered a motive, or indeed any connection between Davina and Kenneth.

Robert Dijan and his secretary, Ethan, both claimed they had not left their rooms after they returned from supper at nine. Rose paused. Davina's death would not have been silent. She must have cried out with pain when she was stabbed, and again when she removed the knife, if that's what happened.

The lift engineers might not have heard if they were using equipment such as drills. The Americans might not have heard or realised the significance of the noise if they were chatting loudly. But surely Robert or Ethan must have heard something. Especially Robert, who said he was completing paperwork in the adjoining room.

Rose felt something was not quite right. At the moment, the most likely perpetrators were Davina's husband Robert, his secretary Ethan, or the hotel steward Kenneth.

As Rose played these men though her mind, she heard male voices from beyond the red flowered bougainvillea.

"Will you return to the UK now that Davina's dead?" The voice was strong and deep.

"Why should I? The university has an agreement with the conservancy, not Davina. I shall stay on as planned until the end of July. At least now I can continue my research without further interference." The second voice was taut with suppressed anger.

"And what of the summit?"

"The organisers have asked me for Davina's notes, her presentation, but they weren't hers. I was putting together the presentation and I did the research, so I should speak in her place." The second voice now sounded petulant.

"But you're not an attractive, glamorous, esteemed conservation manager. I'm not sure the attendees would be impressed by a scruffy, ponytailed student." Ponytail. There had been a young man in the Bongo Bar earlier who fitted that description. Rose wondered if his companion was the chiselled-faced man he'd been with.

"That's what she said about the book. That nobody would buy from an unknown author, but with her name it would sell like suntan lotion on Diani Beach. But she left my name off altogether, without even a research acknowledgement." Now the second voiced sounded strangled.

"So what will you do?" the deep voice asked.

"Not sure. Maybe I'll speak to her husband, or you could write an article about it. I've plenty of information to tarnish Davina's reputation."

"I'm not sure it would be popular, condemning a murdered woman." The first voice had acquired a rough edge.

"Is this because you were sleeping with her? Suddenly developed a conscience? I thought she dumped you? Last week you were preparing to uncloak her."

"Well, I'm not now," the first voice hissed.

"You mean she threatened to tell Gill about your dalliance."

"Enough. I just think it best to let sleeping lions be. I suggest you do the same. Go back to your elephants." The icy voice made Rose shiver.

The sound of the men diminished. Rose presumed they were walking away. So, two new contenders for the crime. Rose was certain they were the men from the bar. The tight voice had belonged to the young ponytailed research student. Robert had called him Gabe.

She thought the other had been the attractive, dark-haired man. A journalist by the sounds of it. He'd been having an affair with Davina until she broke it off. Although he sounded unconcerned, men like that had their pride. A crime of passion?

CHAPTER TWENTY-EIGHT

J oel the chef joined Rose on the bench. "Who were those men? Were you talking to them?"

"No, but I did overhear their conversation. Increases the complexity of the murder case." Rose shook her head. "So how are you? You're looking well."

Joel leaned back, hooking an arm over the back of the bench. "I am. Taking a position at the hotel has been a great move." He looked around. "I love to sit here. Its peaceful, hidden away, and just what I need after a busy shift." Joel yawned.

"I'm staying at the hotel at the request of Manager Bundi," said Rose. "He's concerned about the number of possible thefts over the past six months. I'm struggling, though, because of the range of missing items. Some are valuable, such as jewellery or designer clothes, but many are low cost, practically worthless."

"I told you I had some information about that, the low value things." Joel sat forward, elbows resting on his knee. "Since Vincent plucked feathers away from my eyes I've been more vigilant and observant. I think Wanje is taking them. I spotted him removing some bread rolls from a basket he cleared from a table last night. The rolls couldn't be served again and would have been thrown away, but that's not the point, is it?"

"No," agreed Rose.

Joel flexed his fingers. "I also heard Kenneth tell Wanje off for looking through guests' waste bins. The trouble is I now think he's becoming bolder or more desperate. I saw him hide some sachets of butter and Nutella in his pocket. These had been returned from breakfast, but they would have been displayed again and not thrown away."

He sighed. "I need to persuade him to stop before he gets into trouble. He needs this job."

"Who is Wanje?" asked Rose.

"An African boy, a teenager."

Rose thought of the lunchtime incident with the pen. "Was he working in the Bongo Bar over lunch?" she asked.

"Yes, bringing the orders and delivering the food." Joel shook his head. "Poor boy, I know he didn't finish school, but I struggle to understand the orders he takes."

Rose smiled. "I know. I saw his spelling when he wrote down our orders. Do you know his story?"

Joel leaned back again. "I asked Kenneth. Wanje came on a community apprentice scheme about a year ago. He lives in a village on the mountain and his father was a Mount Kenya trust ranger."

Joel crossed his arms. "About eight months ago his father got caught up in a snare. He was freed, but his foot turned septic and he died. Wanje was left as the sole provider for his family. There's a grandfather, his mother, and at least three younger siblings."

"That must be hard for him." Rose thought about all the children in Kenya who didn't finish their education. Their families needed them to work on their shambas, growing crops, tending to cows, sheep or goats, or looking for paid work. Some parents even sent their children to towns and cities to beg.

This happened in Nanyuki where American and

European tourists often stopped on their way north. Paid work helped the family through their immediate problems, but the kids couldn't improve their position in life and would, most likely, repeat the pattern.

"Wanje's a good boy. He works hard and often volunteers for extra hours. He has a room in the staff quarters which his mother sometimes visits. She makes quite a scene, shouting, crying and pleading with him for money and food. If you've seen the boy you'll know he's like a scrawny chicken. He only eats what he can scrounge from the hotel and I suspect he sends all his wages home."

"You make him sound like the model employee and son. Why do you think he's stealing?" Rose asked.

Joel stared up at the tree branches. Only a little sunlight filtered through as the day darkened. "I think his mother's pushing him to steal. I saw her whispering in his ear and then wave her arm in the direction of the hotel. It's hard for her when she sees the guests, their cars and all the wealth and opulence. She probably feels she's entitled to a small piece of it. "

Rose thought of her dead friend Aisha, Thabiti's mother. She had strived for a vision of Kenya with security and economic prosperity for all. But that was far from the current reality. "If Wanje loses his job for stealing, he won't get a reference or another job like this. Then how would he support his family?"

"Exactly," said Joel. He shivered as the temperature dropped and darkening skies foretold rain. "And he's not the only one. I've walked on paths up the mountain where there are numerous shacks and small villages scattered about, and all of them in poverty. What must this bright white beacon of a hotel look like to them?"

Rose and Joel were silent. They could not solve the issues of poverty, hunger and inequality between them.

Joel leant forward again. His eyes shone. "I've been putting together an idea. One you could discuss for me with

Manager Bundi. I'd like to set up a community food bank scheme and find a way to fairly distribute food, which would only be thrown away, amongst the local people."

Rose smiled. "That's a great idea and generous of you. I'll be happy to speak to Manager Bundi, but after the summit's finished. He's too agitated to listen to any suggestions at the moment."

"He's like a strutting guinea fowl with puffed up feathers." Joel grinned.

Rose pursed her lips. "The best way forward is to stop the thefts. Then he'll view the scheme more favourably. Especially if you're willing to monitor and prevent items going missing in the future. But we need to persuade Wanje to stop, and I'm not sure how to do that." Rose frowned.

Joel said, "Why don't I speak to him, and to Kenneth? I can put aside some food for him that is to be thrown away. Maybe Kenneth can do something similar, such as oversee Wanje sorting through the dustbins, separating out the items to be recycled from general rubbish. There will be some things he can allow Wanje to keep."

Rose stood. "That sounds like a plan. I'll leave it with you. Let me know when you've spoken to Wanje. I have to decide what to tell Manager Bundi. Now I think we should head back to the hotel before it rains."

CHAPTER TWENTY-NINE

R ose shivered as she stepped into the Bongo Bar from the patio. A chilly breath of moisture enveloped her as the storm broke. She turned to watch Mother Nature in action.

Rose remembered an article she'd read about Gaia Conservancy. "Gaia" was the personification of Earth as a loving mother. A mother who cares and protects. Who sends rain to hydrate the land, preventing drought and famine. But people cut down trees and cover the earth with solid surfaces so rain floods the land, causing death and destruction.

Mothers should protect their sons. Had she failed Chris? Rose shivered once more.

"Rose, come inside. You'll get wet standing in the doorway and I can't afford for you to catch a chill." Constable Wachira touched Rose gently on the shoulder and led her into the bar area.

"Sorry, I was miles away," admitted Rose.

"I've been speaking with the commissioner. He has to attend more meetings in Nairobi tomorrow and asked if we can continue. Are you free now to review our progress?"

Rose and Constable Wachira walked to the first floor suite.

"The hotel has replenished the drinks. What would you like?" the constable asked as she opened the mini bar.

"I'm dying for a cup of tea." Rose examined the sachets in a brown leather display box. "Great, my favourite, Kericho Gold." She turned to the constable. "Thinking about drinks, did you find the empty champagne bottle in Davina's bedroom?"

Constable Wachira consulted her notes. "No bottle in her bedroom. There was an open bottle in the mini bar. About two-thirds full."

"I wondered about that. Davina didn't strike me as a heavy drinker. Sure, she'd probably have a glass to celebrate a successful presentation, but I don't think she'd want to lose control. Far from it. I believe she'd prefer to stay sober and watch others drink so she could take the opportunity to obtain information from them or funding for her conservancy."

Rose shrugged. "It's just a guess, a feeling I have from watching her yesterday and listening to others talk about her."

Constable Wachira poured herself a diet Coke. "Interesting you think that, and about the drinking. I was speaking to the barman in the Bongo Bar before you arrived. He was on duty last night. He said Davina drank a fresh lime and soda in the bar, and took an orange juice through to the restaurant."

They sat down by the window which was now closed.

Constable Wachira drew back the voile curtain and they surveyed the rain falling like a volley of arrows on the ground below. "Why would Mr Dijan and his secretary want us to believe Mrs Dijan had been drinking all evening, and was so drunk she had to be escorted back to her room?"

Rose thought about the events of the previous evening. "I saw Davina with a glass of champagne in her hand, but I didn't actually see her drink it. She knocked over a glass of orange juice. When we arrived in the restaurant, she was loud and tiresome, but during our main course we were able to talk normally as Davina had calmed down. I did not hear her again until she complained of being tired, which was when Robert escorted her out of the restaurant."

Constable Wachira swallowed some diet Coke and said, "But she was awake when Kenneth entered her room. She asked him for coffee, so either she was trying to sober up, as we have been led to believe, or she felt drowsy and wanted to rouse herself."

The two women stared out of the window as the pounding of the rain drowned out all other sound. Noise, thought Rose. How does one person stop another from hearing something? How does someone not hear a loud noise made near them?

"Can I see the list you made of items found in the suite?" Rose asked, reaching into her bag for her glasses.

The young constable handed Rose her notebook and enquired, "Are you looking for anything in particular?"

Rose marked her progress with a finger and looked up. "Yes and no. I'm looking for something that doesn't fit."

She returned to her examination. "Here we are. After 'plastic container of Seven Seas Complete Multivitamins' you've written 'bottle of liquid melatonin, orange flavour.'"

The Constable leaned forward, reaching for her notebook, and looked at the offending item. "What is melatonin? Why is it significant?"

Rose leaned back and removed her glasses. "Melatonin is a natural hormone released into the blood by the body's pineal gland. It makes sleep more appealing. The synthetic version has not been scientifically proven, but people believe it helps induce sleep. As it occurs naturally in some foods, it is not regulated and can be bought over the counter."

Constable Wachira's eyes drew together. "Are you saying Mrs Dijan was drugged to make her sleepy and appear drunk? If so, why?"

Rose twisted her glasses. "I keep coming back to noise. Why didn't Robert and Ethan hear Davina when she was attacked?"

CHAPTER THIRTY

The rain stopped abruptly as if someone had blown the final match whistle and the cloud players retired from the pitch.

Constable Wachira said, "Robert Dijan is my primary suspect. He appears too calm, apart from drinking vodka at eleven o'clock this morning…"

Rose interrupted. "You spotted that as well?"

The constable nodded. "But it's the only sign I've seen that his wife's death has affected him."

Once more Rose thought back to the scene in the restaurant. "Last night at dinner he seemed both resigned to his wife's behaviour and… disgusted by it."

Constable Wachira shifted in her seat. "I don't have experience of marriage myself, but disapproving or disliking your spouse isn't generally a motive for murder. Not on its own."

Rose and Craig suspected the young attractive constable was seeing the elusive anti-poaching agent Sam, and Rose didn't want to dim her perception of marriage.

She said, "Davina's behaviour might have started to impact her husband's reputation or business. He admitted he works with foreign companies and her work was an asset to his business relationships. But what if that changed and she began to embarrass him?"

Outside the sky had cleared, the sun shone and the earth steamed dry. Constable Wachira said, "I read a paper about homicides in America in non-violent relationships. Half the killings were classified as intimate partner violence, with women being killed by their partners because of jealousy and concern they would leave them. Mr Dijan admitted his wife had affairs and, whilst he appeared relaxed about it, he could be acting. What if he thought his wife would leave him this time?"

Constable Wachira was a bright girl.

Rose spoke her next thoughts out loud. "It depends on whether she'd gained a new love interest recently. It sounded as if she got rid of her last one a few weeks ago..."

Constable Wachira sat up quickly and a few drops of Diet Coke splashed her trousers. "How do you know that?"

"I overheard a conversation in the hotel grounds, but I didn't see who was speaking. A man admitted he'd had an affair with Davina and I'm pretty certain he was the ruggedly handsome European man I'd seen earlier in the Bongo Bar. A journalist," said Rose.

The younger woman's eyes gleamed. "This is an interesting development. One I'll follow up in the morning. A journalist, you say, and a handsome one. That American article also stated that if the motive is jealousy, most men stabbed or beat their partners to death." Constable Wachira sat back.

Rose hesitated. "I'm not so sure that rings true in this case. The attack was violent, but it wasn't frenzied."

Constable Wachira picked up her pad and pen, business-like again. "Back to our list of suspects. I shall speak to the journalist. I'll also look for a motive for Mr Dijan. Opportunity is clear, as he admitted to being in the room next door. His secretary also had the opportunity to kill Mrs Dijan, but no motive that I know of."

Rose said, "But it's unlikely he would have killed Davina without Robert knowing, as he would have to pass through the living room where Robert was working."

The Constable scribbled in her notebook. "Good point. Mr Dijan could be covering for him."

Rose tapped her fingers together. "Very possible. There's more to that relationship," she muttered to herself.

Constable Wachira looked up. "What was that?"

Rose's fingers stilled. "You're right."

Constable Wachira's forehead wrinkled, but she moved on, consulting her notebook. "That leaves our final suspect, Kenneth." Her hand flew to her mouth. "I haven't shared what I found on Davina's laptop. Well, what Thabiti found when he cracked her password."

Rose grinned. "Glad the boy's been of use."

Constable Wachira unfolded an A4 sheet. "Thabiti printed this off."

Rose donned her glasses and recognised the name of an English newspaper. The title of the article read "Son kidnapped by war hero father."

She read about a soldier who returned from a tour of Afghanistan to find his girlfriend living with another man. She'd taken their son with her. Her new partner had threatened the soldier, preventing him from seeing his son or former girlfriend.

The soldier had finally been allowed to visit his son, but failed to return him after a day out. Rose read out loud, "Former parachute regiment solider, Kenneth Magori, is believed to have kidnapped his son and returned with him to his former home in Kenya. Police are continuing their enquiries."

Rose held the printout in one hand and grabbed Constable Wachira's arm with the other. "Is this our Kenneth?"

"I think so." The Constable took the paper and pointed to a small, black and white head shot of a soldier in uniform wearing a beret. "The photo's not very clear and shows a young man, but there's definitely a resemblance with steward Kenneth."

"And I saw him playing football with a boy yesterday who he said was his son," added Rose.

Constable Wachira sat up. "I've no idea how Mrs Dijan found this article, but it provides us with another suspect who had both the opportunity, and strong motive, to kill her."

CHAPTER THIRTY-ONE

A screaming woman woke Rose early on Sunday morning. The voice was in her head. She was becoming used to the reoccurring cry, which had started during her first case, but she was no closer to understanding why it plagued her. Investigating the murder of her childhood friend had re-opened wounds Rose had tried hard to conceal.

The aroma of fresh baking and cinnamon hung in the air of the hotel restaurant. Rose couldn't resist a cinnamon roll with her tea as she sat alone, admiring the snow-topped mountain.

She hadn't seen Chris the previous evening. He said he would look for her but it had been hard to resist the urge to seek him out. She understood he did not want to see Craig, at least not at first, but she was hurt he hadn't found her. Patience, she reminded herself. After so long she had to control her own feelings and give him time to reach out to her.

She finished her tea and strode towards the hotel entrance, hoping to reach her car without being spotted. A glowing neon-clad Chloe stretched a leg on a low wall in the courtyard, opposite the entrance to the Bongo Bar. She called, "Great morning, Rose."

Chloe removed her leg and glided over, sipping from a pink water bottle. Small white headphones dangled around her neck and connected with her phone, strapped to her arm in a transparent pouch. "Are you attending a patient?"

"Church, actually," Rose replied.

Chloe bent double, her palms pressing against the floor. Out of politeness rather than curiosity, Rose asked, "Have you been for a run?"

"Yes, I managed 5 ks around the grounds. Not bad since my app says we're at seven thousand feet above sea level." Chloe grinned. "You told me training at this altitude helps Kenyan athletes to be the best distance runners."

Rose began walking backwards, "You've acclimatised well. I must go. Can't keep our Lord waiting."

"Bye." Chloe jogged around the back of the hotel.

In the reception area Rose met Constable Wachira hovering around a desk, attempting to catch the receptionist's attention. She still wore the same clothes she had on Friday evening.

"Everything OK?" Rose asked.

"I need to call the station. Get a car sent up to take me to the morgue."

"I'll give you a lift. I'm driving into Nanyuki for church and I can drop you at the Community Hospital."

Constable Wachira brightened. "Thanks." She picked up a white plastic bag. When she noticed Rose peek at it, she flushed and said. "I also need some fresh clothes."

Rose stepped out of the front door and was grabbed by the constable as two helmeted Lycra-clad cyclists screeched to a halt. She watched Thabiti and Hugo dismount. Thabiti's legs buckled and he leant against hotel wall for support.

Hugo grinned. "You did an amazing job keeping up. With some training, you could do well. Kenya has interesting road and mountain bike races." Hugo offered a hand to Thabiti who'd collapsed on the floor. "Stand up, you need to keep moving."

Rose decided she could only describe Hugo as nondescript. His skin was still pale, despite his move to Kenya. His short brown hair was neatly cut and he was of medium height and build. Actually that wasn't quite true. As his arm tensed to help Thabiti to his feet, Rose realised how prominent his muscles were. So, a fit and strong, nondescript young man.

"Morning, Rose. Constable," said Thabiti, hobbling towards them. "On your way to church?"

Rose nodded. "Thabiti, can you look into something for me? Do some digging on the internet?"

Thabiti slumped against the door frame. He dropped a green plastic tube he'd been sucking from. Rose blinked. The tube appeared to extend from his back. "Sure," said Thabiti. "What would you like to know?"

Rose stepped towards him and lowered her voice. "How Gaia Conservancy is financed. Which organisations give donations? And are there any hints of misappropriation of funds or accounting irregularities?"

Thabiti whistled. Rose continued, "I could be sending you to search for a cuckoo's nest. There again, you might discover something that cracks the case open. Everyone involved with this case appears to have something to hide."

A vigilant valet had collected Rose's car and parked it outside the entrance. Rose climbed in. She felt this Sunday was not going to be a day of rest.

CHAPTER THIRTY-TWO

R ose and Constable Wachira drove down from the hotel towards Nanyuki. At first the road passed through grassland with a few trees and small herds of impala.

They passed through the roofed gateway that marked the boundary of the Mount Kenya National Park and into an area of scrubby wasteland. Children played and watched over their families' herds of grazing sheep and goats, whilst their parents attended church.

Constable Wachira extracted two paperback books from the white plastic bag propped between her legs. "I found these in Mrs Dijan's bedroom. One open on the bedside table, and the other open on the floor, as if someone had thrown it."

Rose swerved around a stray sheep, with dirty matted wool, before glancing across. She had expected wildlife-related books, but these had pictures of young women on them. Victorian-looking servant girls. "What are they about?"

"They're not to my taste. One is about a baby girl abandoned with a piece of yellow ribbon tied around her wrist. Years later, when the woman who cared for her dies, she seeks her real mother. The second is the reverse. It's about a mother who seeks the baby she was forced to give up."

Rose concentrated on the road as they entered Nanyuki. "Which book did you find on the floor?"

"The second one," replied the constable.

"They're not the sort of book I would expect Davina to read." Rose paused. "I see her reading psychological thrillers." She braked as they reached a junction, and turned towards the Community Hospital. "But then I've learnt to my folly not to judge a book by its cover."

Constable Wachira grinned as she climbed down from the Land Rover Defender. "Don't wait for me. I've no idea how long this will take."

"I'll call when I'm finished," Rose shouted after her.

CHAPTER THIRTY-THREE

R ose lifted herself onto the pew from her kneeling position on the hassock. She felt an inner peace which spread through her mind and body, grounding and strengthening her.

Rose endeavoured to attend mass each Sunday at Christ the King Catholic Church in Nanyuki. The stone church was located towards the northern edge of the town, opposite the police station. It was cool inside, and the stained glass windows refracted light into rainbow coloured patterns.

Rose leant against the pew in front, staring towards the altar. Her focus blurred as figures ran though her mind like snippets of cine film. Children. A boy sitting at a window waiting for his father. The same child playing football. Another boy trying to hold back the tears that insisted on flowing as Rose left him at the entrance to an imposing school building.

Rose blinked away her own tears. The images continued. A baby crying for its mother. A young boy looking down at the dead body of his father dressed in a green ranger uniform. The same young boy waving a sad farewell to his family. A mother crying over the loss of her husband and the departure of her son.

The service began. Father Matthew also had children and families on his mind as he began his sermon with the fourth commandment. "Honour your father and your mother, that your days may be long in the land which the Lord your God gives you."

But it was another Bible verse which resonated with Rose when Father Matthew spoke it. "Isaiah 49, verse 15. Can a mother forget her nursing child? Can she feel no love for the child she has borne?"

Organ music rang out as the congregation shuffled to their feet. Rose was singing the final hymn when she felt, rather than saw, a covert figure enter her pew. She closed her hymn book and knelt, bowing her head for the final blessing.

"Mum?" The quiet male voice permeated the air around her. She did not open her eyes. Instead, she breathed in deeply through her nose and exhaled slowly, allowing a ribbon of breath to leave her mouth. "Mum, it's Chris."

Composing herself, Rose sat on the pew, turned to face her son, and smiled. She was relieved when Chris responded with his own warm smile. Without speaking, they moved across and hugged each other.

Rose and Chris squinted in the light as they left the sanctuary of the church.

"Sorry I didn't look for you yesterday," Chris blurted. "Ever since I accepted this job I've wondered how best to contact you, but I hadn't expected to see you the moment I arrived. Sorry." His hands trembled. Chris was not much taller than Rose, probably just shy of six foot she thought.

He had Craig's round face and, despite being lean and fit, retained his boyhood chubby cheeks. But it was his eyes which captivated anyone he spoke with. They were warm, intelligent and an illuminating blue. His smile was thin and appraising. Handsome, Rose thought proudly.

Unsure how to respond, Rose asked, "Coffee?"

Chris looked around. "Not in town. Let's find somewhere small and local. Are you happy to walk up Lunatic Lane?"

The road ran alongside the church from a junction with the main Nanyuki highway.

Rose nodded. "Have I told you how this road was named?" she asked.

"Probably, but tell me again," said Chris, grinning.

"It's hard to see with all the houses which have sprung up, but this road was originally built in the 1930s on a ridge linking the Nanyuki and Liki Rivers. Adjoining land was divided into plots of ten acres and small houses were built for retired Europeans or as weekend fishing lodges. An odd couple moved into one house. The wife made a habit of running down the road to the Nanyuki Sports Club, about half a mile behind us, shouting, 'Help, get that lunatic away from me.' Minutes later she was followed by her husband brandishing an axe or kitchen knife."

Chris laughed. "Crazy. No wonder the African termed white men of European descent mzungu. Isn't it from the brilliant sounding Kiswahili word for dizzy?"

Rose thought. "You mean kizunguzungu."

Chris clapped his hands. "Exactly, just saying it makes you feel the motion."

Rose grinned. "I'm not sure who was supposed to be dizzy. The Europeans for always rushing around, or the Africans watching them."

They sat down on wonky, rough wooden benches outside 'God's Favor Butchery' and Hotel. It was a narrow single-storey wood and tin building with an unrecognisable animal carcass hanging behind a sheet of glass in the front window. A corridor led to the rear sleeping quarters.

Chris laughed again. "These places always remind me of Sweeney Todd. I imagine guests entering the hotel alive, being murdered in their beds, and made into stew to be served to the next set of unsuspecting visitors."

"Please," said Rose smiling. A young girl carefully carried a tray to their table. Rose chose a Ketepa Pride Tea and Chris,

Nescafé coffee. The girl was surprised they both refused sugar, as no African would.

Rose placed her cup on the wooden table. It was time to address the elephant in the room. This was her chance to make things right between her son and herself. "I'm sorry, Chris. It's your life and we should have been more supportive."

Chris watched children running around in the street chasing a bicycle tyre. "It seems so long ago. I was so unhappy away from you, away from the farm. School wasn't the place for me. The other children knew it and teased me. The boy from the bush, the boy from Africa."

Rose heard the wail of a baby from inside the butchery. "Even at Pembroke? I thought it was full of country children?"

"It was, but most of their parents owned their own farms, or managed them for Europeans. You sent me to school at six without having taught me the basics of reading and writing. I could speak three tribal languages but none of them were English or Kiswahili."

Rose blushed and looked down at her hands. When Rose was arrested for shooting a poacher, forty years ago, Craig lost his job and with it their home. By the time Chris was born, Craig had found another position managing a small bush farm for a Kikuyu man living in Nairobi.

That's when Rose had begun her community vet work, payment for which was generally items of food which she gratefully received. They were able to save enough money from Craig's meagre salary to send Chris and Heather to an English-style boarding school near Lake Elementaita. Rose hadn't realised how much Chris hated it.

Chris touched her arm. "Don't look so dejected. The taunts didn't last long. Nobody could catch me, and if I caught them, I'd learnt a trick or two about fighting from my African friends on the farm. And I wasn't stupid, I just didn't want to be inside all day," said Chris.

"So what happened in England?" Craig had insisted the children receive their secondary education at boarding schools in the UK.

Chris's smile vanished. "The bullying was worse there. The boys ganged up on me. Do you remember the broken arm? It wasn't from playing rugby." Rose gasped. Chris moved his middle finger around the tabletop. "By sixth form I'd had enough. Did my GCSE retakes as Dad wanted, and left. Has he forgiven me for joining up as a soldier and not taking the officer route?"

Rose watched a young boy pull a plastic bottle along the ground attached to a piece of string. She said, "He has now, and he has followed your career with interest and pride. At the time, he thought you were throwing your education away. We had no idea what you went through, but did you ever consider how your father felt?"

"I knew he'd be disappointed I hadn't achieved the standards he expected," said Chris.

Rose's voice was weak as she said, "I'm sorry that's what you thought, but we sacrificed so much to send you to school. We ate only what we grew or I was paid as part of my veterinary work, and we only wore what we were given or could buy cheaply."

Chris winced. "I'm sorry too. I think I did know what you had given up to send us to school, but I resented it. It's one of the reasons I wanted to make my own way in the world. I chose the anonymity of a solider over the pomp and tradition of an officer, which was too much like school."

"I can see that now," said Rose. Her voice was still dull.

Chris finished his coffee. Rose had drunk most of her tea. Enough of the past. She could not change what had happened, but she could help shape the future. She asked Chris, "How did you get here?"

"I ran. It was downhill." Chris grinned. "Can you give me a lift back to the hotel?"

CHAPTER THIRTY-FOUR

Rose was alone as she parked outside the hotel reception. Chris had insisted on getting out at the entrance gates. Reluctantly, Rose promised him she'd not tell Craig they'd met.

Chris wanted to approach his father directly and talk with him. Rose hoped he'd act soon. Her son had returned and they were friends again. She couldn't keep it a secret for long. She smiled, humming a hymn as she handed her car keys to the valet.

She stopped humming as she thought of Craig. She had woken early, and as he wanted a lie in, she'd left him in the cottage, but she wasn't sure he'd manage to dress himself. She'd better go back to the cottage to help him, but first she wanted to check if Thabiti was around and had made any progress with his research.

As Rose suspected, Thabiti was in the Bongo Bar. His laptop was open on the table in front of him. She was relieved to spot Craig seated by the window with his customary crossword and a cup of coffee on the table beside him.

He turned and smiled weakly at her. Rose's throat ached. Craig looked old and in pain. He was slumped in his chair and the wrinkles on his forehead were more conspicuous. She moved swiftly to his side and pecked him on the cheek. She pulled up a stool and sat opposite him, grasping his hand. "Are you in pain?"

Craig tried to sit up. Rose stood and helped him. "That's better," Craig said. "I feel like an old baboon slumped in my chair. I'm afraid the last couple of days have taken their toll, old bean. I won't be much help to you today."

"I'm sorry I left you. I hadn't realised how exhausted you were."

Craig curled his hand around hers. "I called reception and asked them to send young Thabiti over." He lowered his voice. "Bit embarrassing for him helping an old codger like me get dressed. Much appreciated, though."

At the sound of his name, Thabiti joined them. "I was happy to help and it gave me a break from Rose's task. You didn't have much breakfast. Can I fetch you anything?" Thabiti asked Craig.

Craig raised his arm. Whether in homage or surrender, Rose wasn't sure. "Thank you for your help." Craig paused. In a brighter voice he said, "As for food, I'm saving myself for the famous Mount Kenya Resort Sunday BBQ." Rose's mouth watered at the thought and her stomach grumbled.

She watched Thabiti lean over Craig's crossword as they discussed a clue. Like so many Africans, he had amazing patience with the young, the old and the infirm. Perhaps it was the sense of family, of tribe, which had been lost in many Western cultures.

At the thought of family, Rose smiled.

"Good service?" Craig asked.

"Yes, and I resolved an issue that's bothered me for some time," Rose replied.

Hugo and the ponytailed youth entered the Bongo Bar, spotted Thabiti, and moved towards him.

"Rose, you might want to join us," said Thabiti before returning to his seat. Rose squeezed Craig's hand and placed it on his lap. She dragged her stool across to Thabiti's table.

He'd added a second table, onto which the ponytailed youth emptied his folder.

"I don't think you've met Gabe," said Thabiti. "He's a student from the UK on a placement at Gaia Conservancy." Gabe's straggly hair was tied back and stubble scattered his chin.

"Hello," Rose said politely.

Gabe answered with a flippant, "Hi." So Gabe was Gabriel, Davina's research assistant. He was also the man Chloe witnessed Davina shouting at on the evening of her murder. Was he also one of the men Rose overheard in the hotel grounds?

Rose greeted Hugo: "Morning, Hugo." Hugo remained seated with his face turned away, partially hidden by the hood of the top he wore. Despite his early morning bike ride, he looked pale.

"Hugo and I were discussing the task you set me this morning, looking into the conservancy's finances. Gabe and Freddie overheard us," said Thabiti.

"Freddie?" enquired Rose.

"He's a journalist," answered Thabiti. "He's covering the summit and its build-up."

Gabe swallowed and added. "He's also investigating rumours of embezzlement at Gaia Conservancy. That's where we met."

"Freddie's collecting his laptop and then he'll join us." Thabiti patted his knees.

"So what's all this?" Rose asked, pointing to the papers scattered on the table.

Gabe sat straighter. "They're what I've collected whilst at the conservancy: scribbled notes, printouts, records of conversations I've had."

"About what?" Rose asked. She moved the papers about with her hand. Gabe had certainly been busy.

"Let me tell you how it started." The youth appeared more confident. Probably discussing a subject he knew well.

"Soon after I arrived at the conservancy, I came across a list of employees. I copied their details, as I wanted to interview them about their own experiences with wildlife. All too often, researchers forget about the people on the ground carrying out the everyday jobs. But when I searched for the employees, I found they were all dead." Gabe pulled his ponytail.

"Could it have been a list of people whose families the conservancy was assisting financially?" Rose suggested, but she thought she knew where this was heading. It would not be the first organisation in Kenya to pay ghost wages.

"That's what I thought at first, so I checked again the next month. The same names were on the list and I noted down their job titles. I searched different areas of the conservancy and spoke with current employees. Most had never heard of anyone on the list, although some older men remembered a couple of the names. They were people employed on one of the ranches, before the ranches were amalgamated to form the conservancy."

A deep voice said, "That's when he met me."

CHAPTER THIRTY-FIVE

The strong voice behind Rose made her jump.

"Sorry to startle you." It was the handsome dark-haired man Rose had seen the previous day in the Bongo Bar. He extended a hand, closing it firmly around hers as he vigorously shook her arm. "Freddie Shaw. I hear you're the unofficial side of the law around here."

"I wouldn't go that far." Rose couldn't help blushing.

"I would," said Thabiti. "Rose found my Ma's killer and I bet she's a good idea who murdered Davina Dijan." Four pairs of eyes stared at Rose enquiringly.

"Not yet. I think there's still much to be uncovered in this case." Freddie, Hugo and Gabe all looked down at their feet. Even Thabiti shuffled in his chair.

Freddie recovered quickest. "I met Gabe at Gaia Conservancy. I'd been sent to write a piece on Davina ahead of the summit and the launch of her book." Gabe groaned. "More on the book later."

Freddie grinned, stretched his legs out, and clasped his hands. Rose thought he was enjoying performing to an audience. "I spend some time each year in the States and I was there last spring when Davina conducted one of her fundraising tours. I have to say, she was impressive and wowed her audience. From that tour alone, she secured half a million dollars from Supporting Africa Foundation, and at least the same again from Africa 2050, Renton Bright Wildlife Fund, and an individual donor, Blake Holiday."

Freddie looked around his rapt audience. "I sense a but here," said Rose.

"Exactly. When I returned to America in January, I discovered Blake Holiday had tried to get his money back. The general feeling is Davina allowed herself to be enticed into his bed so she could secure his donation."

"Takes one to know one," muttered Gabe.

Freddie gave him a sharp look, but continued. "Apparently, once Davina returned to Kenya, she wanted nothing more to do with him. He was furious, and when she refused to refund him, he sent an accountant to pore over her accounts. She'd been away and returned to find the accountant scaring her staff and complaining about missing money. She sent him packing, but the damage was done. Back in the States, Blake Holiday was gleefully stirring up rumours of embezzlement."

"Exciting, isn't it?" said Thabiti.

"Unforgivable if it's true." Hugo had chosen to join the conversation. "People trusted her. Gave her money to protect endangered wildlife and she was... stealing it."

Freddie threw his arms in the air. "Now hang on. This is pure speculation. The grudge of a jilted lover who felt cheated out of a substantial amount of money. I didn't get a chance to investigate if the allegations were true."

Rose faced Freddie. "Because as a disgruntled lover yourself, she threatened to tell your wife of your affair if you didn't drop it?"

Rose watched as the colour in Freddie's face drained like an egg timer. He stammered, "How could you possibly know that?"

"She's not the police's best amateur sleuth for nothing." Thabiti was enjoying himself.

"No, I'm not. But you need to beware of who is hiding in the corners of hotels or the far side of bougainvillea bushes in the grounds."

Freddie groaned. "You overheard Gabe and me talking yesterday."

"I did. Not that I can see how any of this helps me find Davina's killer. This Blake Holiday isn't masquerading as one of the American tourists is he?"

Freddie laughed. "No, you'd know if he was here. Loud is the best way to describe him. In voice, manner and dress. Undercover is not his style. Anyway, he'd send in men to do his work."

Rose looked out of the Bongo Bar glass door to the grass terrace beyond. Hotel staff were setting up blackened BBQs. "One point," Rose pulled her gaze and concentration back to her companions. "What is the issue with Davina's book, Gabe?"

"I think she overheard that as well," said Freddie.

Gabe sighed. "I suppose there's no harm you knowing. I've been studying for my Masters degree for two years back in the UK. Researching and writing a paper about African elephants, their habitats and migration routes. Bluntly, Davina stole that information and wrote it up in her book."

"In fairness, she told you what she was doing." Freddie was stirring the pot.

"Yes, but the book was to be co-authored. It was only when I saw the draft cover that I realised she'd cut me out. Now I know she'd not even given me an acknowledgement."

"That must have made you very angry?" suggested Rose.

"Furious. Two years' work. I might have to start again."

Rose murmured, "A strong motive for murder."

CHAPTER THIRTY-SIX

Constable Wachira tapped Rose lightly on the shoulder as Gabe blustered his innocence to the busy Bongo Bar. Guests, arriving for pre-lunch drinks, looked taken aback by the outburst. The constable's brow furrowed questioningly. "Tell you later," Rose whispered.

Hugo pulled Gabe into a corner. Gabe's face puffed up red and his eyes narrowed. He reminded Rose of a children's cartoon character where a bright red bird expanded with anger and blew up. Exactly, she thought, an angry bird. Hugo placed both his hands on Gabe's shoulders, calming him down.

"Can I speak to you upstairs?" Constable Wachira asked Rose.

Rose told Craig she wouldn't be long, and followed the constable. In the suite-cum-incident room, Rose poured herself a Sprite. She needed an injection of sugar.

"What was all that about in the bar?" asked the constable.

"Two men with possible motives to kill Davina, but no opportunity. I've learnt plenty about Gaia Conservancy's finances, but I've no idea if it's relevant to the case." She gulped her drink. "Sorry I didn't give you a lift back from Nanyuki."

"No problem. I told you I had things to do," said the constable. Self-consciously, she looked down at herself. "Fresh clothes and more for the coming days in case we don't get to the bottom of this case today."

The women carried their drinks to the chairs by the window. "What did you discover at the mortuary?" Rose asked.

"That the commissioner won't be happy." Constable Wachira crossed her legs. "Robert Dijan has refused to pay for the autopsy. Said it was obvious Davina was stabbed. Now the police have to pick up the bill and it's ten thousand shillings!" The constable shook her head.

"The stab wound was fatal, wasn't it?" Rose was worried she'd been wrong.

"Yes, you were spot on. The pathologist agreed Mrs Dijan may have been saved if she hadn't pulled the knife out. She bled to death, but it was relatively quick, probably three to four minutes."

Rose felt her own body squirm in protest as she touched her neck. "And was the weapon the knife we found?"

The constable held up the plastic bag, containing the small knife, between her finger and thumb. "He believed so, but said it was a strange little weapon. It reminded him of the knife in a christening set his niece was given last year." Of course, thought Rose. The cartoon image of the elephant on the knife's handle.

"The pathologist added that the attacker would be strong. The knife was used with considerable force," said the constable.

"Did he rule out a woman?" asked Rose.

"No, but said he'd rarely seen cases of women attacking other women with knives."

Rose pursed her lips. "I presume there were no traces of melatonin in her blood," said Rose.

"No, but it's difficult to test for, as the body produces it naturally. The pathologist received the body too late to check for the synthetic substance."

Rose looked out the window. The autopsy had told them precious little.

"I left the best till last." Rose turned towards the constable who grinned and said, "The pathologist told me Davina's had a baby. He thinks it was at least twenty years ago, as her perineal scar was only a pale white line."

"Now that is interesting." Rose's words were slow as she thought of the possible implications of the news.

"There's no record of a child with either of her husbands. I suppose it could have been between marriages, but unlikely, don't you think?" The constable's eyes sparkled.

Rose answered, "Yes, more likely before she was married. Possibly when she worked in Kenya."

CHAPTER THIRTY-SEVEN

R ose realised she needed to return to Craig. "Will you join us for lunch?" Rose asked the young constable. "The hotel is famous for its Sunday BBQ and carvery." Rose's tummy rumbled loudly. "Sorry. Must be the thought of food." Constable Wachira giggled.

As Rose and the constable reached the bottom of the stairs, they met the two lift engineers they'd spoken to on Friday evening. "Back already?" Rose asked.

"Trouble with the service lift," the older engineer responded.

"I wanted to speak to you again," Constable Wachira said. "In your statement you didn't mention seeing Rose and the hotel manager enter the room at the end of the corridor."

"No, well it seemed obvious since you're like the police." The younger engineer looked at Rose. His mouth moved continuously as he chewed gum.

"Problem is. I'm wondering what else you thought was obvious and didn't tell us." Constable Wachira appeared to grow as the two men shrank like scolded children.

The older one whimpered. "I didn't tell you 'cause I thought my eyes were playing tricks. The end of the corridor was real dark. But now I'm sure I'm right. It's about the man I saw leave the room at the end. He looked around before crossing the corridor to the staircase. When he pushed open the door, light fell across his arm. The man was a mzungu."

CHAPTER THIRTY-EIGHT

Rose and Constable Wachira found Craig, Chloe and Thabiti sitting on the patio outside the Bongo Bar. Chloe had commandeered a table under a large cantilevered umbrella. Thabiti located an extra chair for the constable and manoeuvred the arm of the umbrella until everyone was in the shade.

The day was bright and glorious but would be uncomfortable at the extra tables set for lunch on the grass terrace, which did not benefit from the shade of umbrellas.

Craig said, "This Sunday BBQ is popular. I hadn't expected so many diners."

"The pool was busy, too," said Chloe. "Became unbearable. Children playing and laughing is one thing but squaddies after a few Tuskers is quite another."

Thabiti looked puzzled. "What do you mean by squaddies?"

Chloe turned to him. "It's a slang term for British soldiers. Used particularly after they've consumed a few drinks."

Thabiti still frowned. "I get that, but how can you tell they're squaddies when you're sunbathing by the pool?"

Chloe laughed. "I've been an army wife. I don't want to stereotype, but they arrive in groups with camouflage rucksacks. Their arms and bodies are etched with tattoos and they think suntan lotion is for civvies. Look, there's a bunch of them over to the left."

They looked across to a group of young men standing and sitting around a table without an umbrella. As they watched, a man with red sunburnt arms pushed a man with a glowing red neck and tattooed arms to the ground. Most of the group doubled over laughing.

"OK. Point taken. Are they staying here?" asked Thabiti, pinching his nose.

Craig answered. "No, I asked a waiter. The hotel has a Sunday brunch deal for the British Army and local residents. They pay a set price for lunch and use of the hotel's facilities for the day. The hotel's created a problem for itself, though. The deal is either three thousand five hundred shillings for brunch, and you buy drinks, or six thousand shillings inclusive of drinks. Guess which the soldiers choose? And they ensure they get their money's worth."

The hotel was busy and Rose located most of the people she'd encountered since arriving on Friday. Robert Dijan, with a hand casually placed in his trouser pocket, guided his secretary Ethan around the serving tables offering Indian and traditional African food.

Rose watched a chef take out a ball of chapati dough, roll it flat and bake it like a pancake in a blackened frying pan on a tabletop stove. Robert lightly tapped Ethan on the arm and pointed out another interesting dish.

The American guests were seated at a large table on the grass terrace under the shade of two cantilevered umbrellas, Their tour leader, Nicki, walked past Rose's table speaking into a mobile phone. "He needs a cast? How much will that cost?" A pause. "Well, go ahead. I'll work out how to get the money."

Nicki stopped and slipped her phone into her trouser pocket. She turned away from her guests and wiped her eyes. With what looked to Rose like considerable effort, Nicki lifted her head, pinned her shoulders back and chiselled a smile on her face. She joined her tour party.

"Blow me away. That's Nicki O'Conner," cried Craig.

"The tour guide. Do you know her?" Rose asked.

Craig turned to Rose. "Don't you remember? She was married to that waster Dermot O'Conner. He was a drunk and I'm sure he laid a hand on her more than once. He emptied their bank accounts and fled to Mozambique, or so they say. Left her with two sons and a mountain of debts. I wondered what had become of her. Can't be easy, though. Her boys will be in their teens, so she'll have school fees to pay."

Chloe and Thabiti were talking with Freddie, Gabe and Hugo. Gabe and Hugo appeared to have become firm friends. The men left, moving in the direction of a large BBQ where slabs of meat were being cooked.

Chloe said to Thabiti, "You've been ditched for a ponytailed student."

Thabiti retorted. "Technically, I'm still a student. I think they're both homesick. They started discussing bars and clubs in Southampton and Bourn-something. To be honest, I'm relieved as Hugo's become really withdrawn and subdued."

"Do you know what brought him to Kenya?" Constable Wachira asked. Still in work mode, thought Rose. "Does he have friends or family?"

Thabiti frowned. "I don't think so. He changes the subject whenever I ask. I get the impression there is someone important to him in Kenya, but whether that's a family member, a friend or a girlfriend, I can't work out."

"Lunch anyone?" asked Craig.

Everyone nodded and pushed back their seats. "Shall I get yours?" Rose asked Craig.

Releasing a breath, Craig replaced his walking stick by his chair. "If you don't mind, old girl. I think I'll find carrying a plate over the uneven ground rather a challenge. You know what I like, mostly meat with some potatoes and a bit of veg. I can smell lamb on the BBQ. That would be lovely with some mint sauce."

Rose heaped a plate with pink beef fillet, a rib of lamb and a chicken and vegetable kebab. She added some boiled parsley potatoes and carrots. Craig drooled over the plate as she placed it in front of him. "Perfect. You've done me proud. Now don't hang around. You need to get your own lunch."

Rose chose a small chicken kebab and a portion of tilapia fish. She took small amounts of most of the interesting looking salads and garnished her plate with a freshly baked chapati. She returned to the table and was delighted to see the young constable relaxing with Thabiti and Chloe. I must ask her first name, thought Rose.

"Thabiti, have you chosen anything apart from nyama?" asked Constable Wachira.

Chloe looked up from a plateful of salad with a single chicken kebab. "Nyama?"

Thabiti picked up his knife and fork. "Meat. Technically, as this is BBQed meat, it is termed nyama choma."

Chloe's face relaxed. "Oh, I've seen signs with that written on around Nanyuki."

Constable Wachira swallowed. "You will have. It's our unofficial national dish. As you can see, Kenyan men pile it onto their plates." Thabiti forked a large piece of beef into his mouth. "And into their mouths."

Everyone at the table laughed, apart from Thabiti who nearly choked.

CHAPTER THIRTY-NINE

Rose wiped her mouth with satisfaction. Did she have room for a dessert? She spotted Joel, the chef, with a large basket refreshing the dessert table.

"Dessert" she announced, and strode over to Joel. She picked up two plates and whispered. "Have you had a chance to talk with Wanje?"

Joel continued to place individual tarts with a custard yellow filling onto a serving platter. "Yes." He looked up. "He's coming over now."

The scraggly young man Rose had previously seen working in the Bongo Bar carried a bowl in each hand. He gratefully dumped them on the table and shook his arms. "Careful," said Joel, as juice from the bowl of fruit salad sloshed onto the white tablecloth. "This is Mama Rose. She's the lady I told you about."

"Habari," the boy said. His voice was soft and quiet and could have been mistaken for that of a girl. Joel nudged Wanje. "Pole, Mama. I not mean to take anything worth money. I just need to help my family. My Pa is dead."

"I realise that," said Rose. "But it doesn't mean you can take things from the hotel." The boy's head hung forward. "Now I've discussed the matter with Joel, and he with

Kenneth." Rose looked up at Joel who nodded. "And they're going to help you out, but you must promise not to take anything else without asking one of them. Manager Bundi wouldn't be happy. Do you understand?" The boy, head still bowed, nodded.

"Good boy," said Joel. "Now, collect the chocolate roulade and apple tart from the fridge." The boy ran off. "Have you told Manager Bundi about Wanje?" Joel asked.

Rose picked up an individual cream tart with a strawberry on top. "Luckily I haven't seen him. I still don't know what to say."

Joel emptied his basket. "Kenneth's not working today. He's spending time with his son. We said we'd discuss exactly how to manage Wanje tomorrow."

Rose returned to her companions. She'd added a meringue with cream and a couple of pieces of nut brittle to her plate. For Craig, she'd chosen the chocolate roulade, lemon mousse and a meringue.

"So Judy, how long have you been going out with Sam?" Thabiti teased the constable. So her Christian name was Judy, noted Rose.

Constable Wachira's ears and cheeks flushed pink. "I'm not sure what you mean," she stammered.

"Come on, even Mama Rose knows you're a couple," said Thabiti.

The constable looked down and glanced over at Rose, "Really?"

Rose broke a piece of nut brittle. "Leave the poor girl alone." Then she asked, "When do you next expect to see him?"

Thabiti threw his head back laughing.

Constable Wachira sighed. "He's doing some prep work for the summit, but should be back by Tuesday or Wednesday."

Chloe, Thabiti and Judy—Rose wasn't sure she'd get used to calling her that—left to choose desserts as Manager Bundi bustled up and perched on the edge of a spare chair. "Mama Rose, I've been wanting to catch up with you. What news on... our business?"

"Hello, wonderful lunch you've laid on, and obviously very popular." Rose was stalling. "I think I've worked out how most of the items went missing."

"Yes?" The little manager held up his hands like a begging dog.

"I split the list up, as there was such a variety of items. Firstly, there were lots of little things which would have been thrown away or their absence ignored. I think they only became apparent when the overall volume of missing items increased."

Rose took a deep breath. "It appears that some staff took these not realising that technically they were stealing. I've spoken to those involved and I don't think you'll have any future problems."

"Staff? You better give me their names." The manager extracted a small notepad and pencil.

Rose shook her head. "That won't be necessary."

Manager Bundi spluttered, but Rose stared at him until he dropped his eyes. His shoulders slumped.

"In addition," Rose continued, "You have a guest theft problem. And it seems to be those staying in the most expensive rooms and suites."

"Oh no," said the dumpy manager. "How do I stop that?"

Rose pursed her lips. "You could charge an extra deposit, have an inventory of items for each room and deduct the cost of the items taken. But it would be difficult to cover everything. Alternatively, you increase the room price by the cost of a pillow or bathrobe to cover the thefts. I suggest you print a large sign listing the price of all the items in the room and reminding guests to purchase them from the hotel shop. It might nudge people in the right direction."

Manager Bundi jumped to his feet. "Excellent idea. Is that everything?"

"No. There's still the other items, the valuable ones like jewellery and designer clothes. I have a few thoughts, but won't have an answer today, especially with this murder case taking up much of my time. What about the cottage Craig and I are staying in?"

Manager Bundi waved a hand. "Keep it for as long as you need. Well, not that long. You will be finished by the summit, won't you?" The manager's eyes widened.

"The thefts or the murder?"

Manager Bundi shivered. "Both, I hope."

The others returned to the table. Chloe was joking with Thabiti whose bowl was piled with various desserts.

Rose's mobile rang. She looked at the screen and said to Craig, "Julius at the Animal Orphanage, probably calling about a sick animal."

CHAPTER FORTY

R ose collected her medical bag from her red Defender and walked through a hotel side gate into the Animal Orphanage. The orphanage was busy with families huddled together by low-fenced enclosures to watch porcupines, African lemurs abandoned as cubs, and a family of warthogs.

The orphanage cared for over a hundred and sixty animals. Its aim was to rehabilitate and return them to the wild, but it was not always possible. Patricia was a twenty-five-year-old ostrich who couldn't run because her foot bones had been injured and fused together. She wouldn't survive in the wild.

Rose navigated through the visitors to reach the central section of the orphanage, with a small administration block in the middle of a grass lawn. Concrete pens and wire enclosures had been constructed around the perimeter.

A girl Rose guessed to be ten or twelve grinned widely as she rode on the shell of Speedy Gonzalez, a giant tortoise estimated to be over a hundred years old. The girl slid to the ground and held out a cabbage leaf for Speedy, which he gratefully munched.

Julius, the chief warden of the orphanage, walked towards

Rose. His arms hung by his side as he shook his head. "Pole, Mama Rose, it's too late."

Rose and Julius trudged across to a high-sided monkey enclosure. Lying huddled at the back of the cage was the diminutive figure of a Patas monkey. His companions squawked but avoided him.

"I noticed his discomfort and called you," said Julius. "He was crouched in the corner, arms crossed over his chest with a sad expression on his face."

"Abdominal distension?" Rose asked.

"I think so. There are so many visitors here today it is hard to monitor them all."

"You think one of them fed the monkey something other than nuts the wardens hand out?"

Julius frowned and nodded. They left the enclosure as a warden removed the body of the dead monkey.

"Come and see the young bongo you helped deliver," suggested Julius. The previous month he had called Rose as a mountain bongo was struggling to deliver her calf. Rose, with the assistance of a youthful warden, had pulled the calf out after ensuring its legs were positioned correctly.

Bongos, one of the largest forest antelopes, were a critically endangered species. Rose leaned over the fence of the bongo paddock to watch the small bongo calf, with distinctive vertical white stripes over a chestnut coloured coat, skip around its patient mother. The adult was similarly coloured and adorned with slightly spiralled horns.

Rose noted Julius grinning like a proud father.

CHAPTER FORTY-ONE

A receptionist hailed Rose as she passed through the hotel lobby and handed her a note. It was from Constable Wachira, requesting her presence in the incident suite.

Rose arrived in the suite to find Constable Wachira adjusting the position of a large flip chart positioned on an easel. "Thanks for coming, Mama Rose. The investigation has ground to a halt, so I want to reconsider the suspects in light of our new evidence, that the man the engineers saw was a mzungu, a white man."

The constable dragged a chair in front of the board. Rose sat down gratefully with a cup of tea, while the constable stood beside the board gripping a black marker pen. "The engineers' news was unexpected, but I believe they were telling the truth. If we accept they saw a mzungu leave Davina's bedroom on Friday evening, it rules out Robert Dijan and Kenneth."

The constable wrote their names at the top right hand corner of the chart and crossed through them with a red pen.

"That leaves us with the secretary, Ethan." She wrote his name at the top left hand side of the chart.

"The problem is," Rose paused, "If it was Ethan the

engineers saw leave Davina's room, how did he get back to the suite unobserved so that Robert could send him out again to find Manager Bundi?"

Constable Wachira wrote "return?" next to Ethan's name. "But if Ethan didn't kill Mrs Dijan, who did?" She twirled her pen.

"Quite a puzzle," mused Rose. "The only person seen entering and leaving these rooms was Kenneth, and it was confirmed he used the living room door."

"Yes, the Americans saw him," said the constable.

Rose continued. "Nobody else was seen entering the rooms by either the Americans or the engineers."

"So our culprit must be Ethan, as he was already in his room?"

"So who did the engineers see leave? How did Ethan return to his room so he was present when Robert found his wife's body?"

Constable Wachira removed her scrunchy, fiddled with her hair braids and tied them up again. "We've come full circle."

"Exactly," said Rose. "Someone else must have entered one of the rooms before the engineers or the Americans took up their sentry positions."

The constable's eyes shone. "Oh, somebody was hiding?"

"I believe so, and I'd like to work out where they were concealed," said Rose.

Constable Wachira looked around. "I think it is unlikely our killer hid in the secretary's room unless he knew about the connecting door and was certain it would be unlocked. Mr Dijan was working here in the living room, so anyone hiding would have been spotted entering the bedroom."

Rose interrupted. "But our killer wouldn't know Robert planned to work. He could have hidden and sneaked out when Robert was in the bathroom, or wherever he went when Kenneth entered." Rose tapped her fingers.

"But then Kenneth would have seen the killer," said the constable.

Rose thought back to Kenneth's statement. "True, and Kenneth said Robert was in this room after he'd seen Davina alive. I think we can rule out the living room as a hiding place."

"So that leaves the bedroom." Constable Wachira wrote "bedroom" halfway down the right hand side of her flip chart and capped her pen.

Rose hadn't been in the bedroom, the scene of the murder, since Friday evening when she examined the body. Constable Wachira turned the lights on as the curtains remained drawn.

"The pathologist took the bedding." Rose was relieved, although there was still evidence of blood on the mattress, headboard, lampshade and floor. Constable Wachira handed Rose a pair of latex gloves before putting on her own pair.

The constable moved around the room, peering behind furniture. "There's no space under the bed as it's a divan. It would be possible to hide behind the curtains, but there's no room at the back of the dressing table."

Rose walked across to the wardrobe and opened the doors. "Someone could have hidden in here, but the floor is scattered with shoes, and none of them appear damaged or squashed."

She turned around and entered the spacious bathroom. It was bright and anyone hiding in or behind the bath, or under the double sinks, would have been spotted by Davina preparing for bed.

"Too bright in here to hide," said the constable walking in behind Rose.

"Do we know if Davina took a shower before bed?" Rose asked.

"I don't think so. Kenneth said he picked two wet towels off the floor when he drew the curtains, which was after Mrs Dijan changed and went downstairs for supper."

Rose looked at the shower door which was flush with the

rear wall. "And I don't remember any water on the floor, and the bathmat was hanging over the shower door as it is now." Rose opened the glass shower door and looked inside. She looked out and back in. Then she stepped into the shower, closing the door behind her.

"What are you doing?" asked the constable.

"Give me a minute," Rose called back. Constable Wachira waited. "Can you see me?" Rose shouted.

The constable walked across to the shower door and peered through. "Yes."

"No, not through the door like that. Go back to the bedroom and then enter the bathroom as if you're getting ready for bed, as Davina would have done." The constable did as Rose suggested, walking into the bathroom and sitting on the closed toilet lid. She looked across at the shower. "I can't see you from the toilet."

She crossed to the double sinks. "Or the sinks. Unless I'm near the shower door and actually looking for you I wouldn't see you." The constable opened the shower door and looked to her left. Rose was perched on a tiled shelf, flattening herself against the connecting wall. Rose held out a hand and Constable Wachira helped her down.

They returned to the living room. "So there are two possible hiding places: the shelf in the shower or behind the bedroom curtains." Constable Wachira wrote them both under the word "bedroom."

Rose considered the flip chart. "I remember when my kids played hide and seek at birthday parties," Rose said. "Someone hiding behind curtains was inevitably discovered as their feet stuck out, the curtain moved when they giggled or coughed, or it was just obvious the curtain wasn't hanging properly."

"But Davina wouldn't see any feet because of the chairs in the window," countered the constable.

"Except if she sat in one. Her laptop was open and there

were papers on the table. The killer would be taking quite a risk hiding so close to somewhere Davina might sit."

The constable sighed and added a question mark after curtains. "I agree, the shower is the most obvious hiding place. But how did the killer get into the room in the first place?"

CHAPTER FORTY-TWO

R ose and Constable Wachira stared at the flip chart. The constable clutched her arm and muttered, "This is a complex puzzle and we appear to be moving away from a solution."

Rose cleared her throat. "Let's work through the possibilities one by one. We've ruled out access via the windows?"

"Yes," confirmed the constable. On the right hand side of the flip chart she wrote "Access" and under it "windows." She scored through it with a red pen.

Rose continued. "The next option is using a keycard." The constable wrote this down. "The stewards and cleaners have universal key cards for each floor, but they are careful with them. Kenneth told me a cleaner was sacked a few months ago for losing one. I'll ask him tomorrow if he's misplaced his, as he is unlikely to volunteer the information."

Constable Wachira patted her thighs as she thought. "Do we know of anyone in the hotel, a mzungu, who could be a link between the cleaner's lost card and Friday night's murder?"

Rose lifted her teacup. It was empty. "We would have to check with the hotel. See if any guests were staying on both occasions." Rose kneaded her chin. "If there were American guests, Nicki the tour guide might have been."

Constable Wachira moved away from the flip chart and picked up her notebook from the chair by the window. "So we need to ask the hotel about the missing keycard, any other cards that have been mislaid, and current guests who were also staying at the hotel when any keycards vanished." She jotted something down in her book.

"I'll speak with Kenneth," said Rose.

"Kenneth," mused the Constable. "That's another issue, but I'll have to wait to take it up with the commissioner." Rose couldn't help feeling sorry for Kenneth, but she must remember the boy also had a mother who would be missing her son. At least Rose presumed she was. Back to the matter at hand.

Rose said, "Davina, Robert and Ethan would have their own keycards."

"I found some cards when checking the rooms." The constable leafed through her notebook. "Two cards still in their cardboard holders on the sideboard in the living room. Another card on the dressing table in the bedroom which was probably Davina's."

"I agree," said Rose.

"Robert handed me a card, and Ethan gave me two, before we closed off their rooms," added the constable.

"Are all they keycards accounted for?" Rose switched the kettle on.

"Yes. So where does that leave us?" The constable asked.

"With someone who was quick, entering one of the rooms as someone else left." Rose made her second cup of tea and returned to her chair.

"Robert said it was seven o'clock when he and Davina went downstairs, which I don't doubt. Kenneth went round the rooms closing curtains soon after he left us on the terrace, so between seven and seven-thirty." Rose sipped her tea appreciatively.

"He said Ethan was in his room, so he didn't go in." Constable Wachira perched on the arm of the chair with the window behind her.

"Yes. Ethan arrived in the dining room as the Dijans' starters arrived, just before mine appeared, so I guess around eight."

Constable Wachira returned to her flip chart. Towards the bottom she drew a line and wrote "7pm" on the left and "8pm" on the right of it. "So we need to find someone who had the opportunity to access the rooms between these times. Where were our potential suspects?"

"Robert and Davina were in the restaurant. At my table, Craig…"

Constable Wachira's eyes narrowed. "You couldn't possibly think he's our killer?"

"Of course not. I'm just working my way around the table." Rose used her fingers to count off the names. "There was Chloe, Thabiti and Hugo." Rose paused. "No. Hugo left. I think Davina's behaviour upset him, as he said he needed some peace and quiet."

"What time was that?" asked the constable.

"Quite soon after we sat down." Rose frowned, dragging the information from her memory. "Before Ethan arrived."

Constable Wachira crouched by her flip chart and wrote Hugo below the line.

"I can't think what motive Hugo would have. But two men with potential motives who weren't in the restaurant were Freddie, the dark-haired journalist, and Gabe, Davina's aggrieved research student."

Constable Wachira crouched and wrote their names above the line.

"Freddie told me about an irate American who felt Davina had swindled him out of a large amount of money. Freddie swears the man's not here, but said he could have sent someone to kill Davina in revenge."

Constable Wachira groaned. "The idea of an American

assassin would have been exciting yesterday, but now it's a complete pain. Another complication."

"A highly unlikely one when I think about it." Rose thought back to supper on Friday evening. "The party of Americans were in the restaurant." She paused. "But I can't remember if Nicki their tour guide was."

Constable Wachira wrote "Nicki?" and "American?" under the line.

"Craig told me a sad story about Nicki. Her husband ran off and left her penniless with two sons to support. I think I'll ask Thabiti to do a bit of digging." Rose finished her tea.

Constable Wachira turned the front page over to cover the flip chart. "I'm going to read through my notes. I don't think our suspects will be amenable to questioning this evening, but I might see if I can dig around in the hotel records."

Rose stood. "Any news from the commissioner?"

"He has a couple of meetings in the morning, but hopes to be with us by lunchtime, mid-afternoon at the latest."

"You'll be pleased to pass the case over?" Rose was fishing.

The bait worked. Constable Wachira bristled. "I think I, we, are doing an excellent job without him." Her shoulders slumped. "But far from solving the case."

CHAPTER FORTY-THREE

Rose returned to the Bongo Bar. It was quiet. The mountain was in shadow as the sun waned. Craig was slumped in a chair by the window and looked to be sleeping. Resting, Rose told herself.

Thabiti and Hugo were working on laptops in a corner. They wore large black headphones and despite the dimming light, Hugo wore red tinted glasses.

Rose joined them. Thabiti looked up and shouted, "Hi." Rose brought a finger to her lips and the men removed their headphones.

"Sorry," Rose said softly. "I don't want to disturb Craig just yet. What are you working on?"

"Final edits from Friday's conference. The summit organisers need it tomorrow to add to their material," said Thabiti.

"Did you find anything which might be relevant to Davina's death?" Rose asked.

"No. Just her storming off and on stage when we had to change presentations." Thabiti began to grin but it turned into a frown.

Hugo removed his glasses and blinked. "Are you OK?" asked Rose. "Isn't it a bit dark in here to wear sunglasses?"

"Oh, they're not sunglasses." Thabiti grabbed them out of Hugo's hand. "These are special. They're EnChroma glasses." Hugo snatched them back, blushing.

"It's OK, Hugo." Rose felt guilty for embarrassing the young man. "You don't need to explain."

Hugo looked down and mumbled. "I don't usually tell people. They'd find it strange given the work I do, and some might refuse to employ me. I'm colour-blind." Hugo looked up, a pained expression on his face.

"How do the glasses help?" Rose was curious.

"I'm red-green colour-blind." Hugo's voice was quiet. "Without the glasses my world is murky green with some black, white and blue. I don't think I can see colours as clearly as you or Thabiti with the glasses, but it's like moving from normal TV to HD."

"HD?" asked Rose.

"Sorry. High definition." Hugo's voice strengthened. "I believe the glasses increase the contrast between red and green. Red is way clearer now, as are associated colours such as purple."

Rose jumped as she heard Craig shout, "What? Who?" He covered his head with one hand. Leaning over him was Chris. Rose shifted round to the right, hoping Chris wouldn't spot her.

"Who's that with Craig?" whispered Thabiti.

"Shush," replied Rose. She wanted to listen.

"Dad, I didn't mean to startle you. I didn't realise you were sleeping."

Craig spluttered. "I wasn't sleeping, just resting." Rose kept her head down, but glanced across. Craig was trying to raise himself up in the chair. Chris tried to help, but Craig batted his hands away. Craig was clearly still befuddled.

"You remind me of my son. Who are you?" demanded Craig.

"Dad, I am your son. It's me, Chris." Chris squatted in front of his father's chair.

"You can't be. Chris is in the UK." But Craig reached out a hand to touch Chris's face. Rose felt her chest contract. Guilty about spying on them, she turned back to Thabiti.

Quietly she said. "When you've finished this, can you look into someone for me?"

"Who is it this time?" Thabiti asked. He sat back with his arms crossed.

Rose leant forward and whispered, "The American party's tour guide. A lady called Nicki O'Conner. According to Craig, her husband was a drunk and he ran off with their money and left her with two kids and huge debts."

Hugo muttered and shook his head.

"I think she's struggling, which is not surprising, and I doubt her job pays enough to support her family. I've a feeling all is not well, and wondered if you could dig anything up."

"Like a reason to murder Davina?" Thabiti bit his bottom lip.

"Yes," said Rose, although she didn't think Nicki would have one. Her struggles were different: surviving and providing for her sons. "Someone may have paid her to do it?" Rose said out loud.

"You're not serious?" Thabiti's eyes widened.

Rose realised she'd spoken her thoughts. "I know, it's far-fetched." Rose paused. "But a mother will go to extraordinary lengths to protect and provide for her children."

"Lucky them," muttered Hugo.

Thabiti raised his hands. "Ok, I'll look into our potential female assassin. See if she's advertised her services on Assassins for Hire."

"Thabiti! That's enough."

Thabiti scowled.

Rose heard raised voices bedside the window.

"No!" Chris stood up.

"But you must come home. Your mother needs you. If you

want to work in security, get a job here. There are plenty of them." Craig swept out his right arm.

"Not after the collapse in oil prices. Security firms are laying-off rather than recruiting in Kenya." Rose couldn't see Chris's face clearly, but he radiated self-control.

"What's keeping you in the UK? Have you a family you've hidden from us?" Oh dear, thought Rose. She could see Craig's face darkening.

"I've no family, Dad." Chris sighed. "But London is my home." Rose doubted this reasoning would satisfy Craig.

"Don't be ridiculous. You're a country boy. Brought up in the bush!"

"Dad, I'm thirty-six. My boyhood days are far behind me." Chris's arms were by his side, but he began flexing them.

"Well, I think you have a duty to us, to your mother." Bringing her into the discussion was bound to rattle Chris. Rose stood, but it was too late.

"I can't believe you're still trying to run my life, tell me what to do. I'll be returning to London after the summit."

Chris strode out of the room, his face burning and his fists clenched. Thabiti inhaled deeply.

"Don't say a word," Rose warned him. She was torn between calming Chris or consoling Craig. Craig wasn't going anywhere. She hurried after Chris.

"Chris," Rose shouted. No response. "Chris, wait."

Chris spun round. "I see you sneaked in to watch that little performance."

Rose bristled. "I was already in the room and I tried not to listen. A bit hard when you're shouting at your father."

"Well, he hasn't changed. He's just as controlling and demanding as he always was." Chris started to turn away.

Rose took a breath and said gently, "Chris, you surprised him. He's tired. It's been a busy couple of days for him. He can't get out much now. Not being able to drive frustrates him and I don't think he's being completely honest about the amount of pain he's in."

"Pain? What's wrong with him? Why can't he drive?" Chris's eyes were still cold.

"He has post-polio syndrome," Rose explained.

"But he had polio as a child. Isn't it a bit late for a secondary complication?"

"Apparently not. As with your father, it can appear years after recovering from the initial attack. It causes muscles and joint weakness, resulting in pain and fatigue." Rose held her hands out in a conciliatory gesture.

"It still doesn't excuse his behaviour," said Chris, his chin jutting.

"No, but it's rather a bombshell for him, for both of us, you turning up like this. Give it time. I'll speak to him."

"OK. But I'm not making any promises." Chris paused before hugging his mother.

CHAPTER FORTY-FOUR

Rose, Craig and Chloe ate breakfast in the hotel restaurant. It was quiet. A waiter told them many guests requested early breakfast on Mondays so they could return to Nairobi and their work. The American party were eating when Rose entered, but they had left.

"It's been an interesting weekend," said Chloe. "But I'm going home until the summit starts. Dan's back this afternoon for a couple of days. What about you?" Chloe delved into her fruit salad.

Rose cut a slice of omelette and replied, "We're heading home today as well. The last few days have been exhausting, haven't they?" Rose turned to Craig, but he only grimaced, concentrating on his full English breakfast.

Rose looked at Chloe who mouthed, "Is he OK?"

Rose shook her head but continued brightly, "It's been a lovely change, being here at the hotel, but it'll be nice to get home." She patted Craig on the arm.

He looked up, blinked and said, "Amazing spot this. Great food. But I'm looking forward to a few days peace and quiet." He returned to his breakfast.

"I'll probably have to come back," said Rose.

"Commissioner Akida is due today and Constable Wachira wants my help explaining our findings in Davina's case."

"Will you continue working on it?" Chloe asked. She drew back the foil lid of a pot of vanilla yoghurt.

Rose pursed her lips. "I'm not sure I'll be allowed, but I want to. The case is like a jigsaw, where only some of the pieces are turned over. Until I know the images on the others, I can't complete the puzzle." Rose sipped her tea.

"And your work in the hotel?" Chloe asked.

"One piece of that particular jigsaw is still missing."

Chloe stirred the froth on her cappuccino. "It all sounds a bit frustrating to me, like the maze Thabiti, Hugo and I explored in the grounds yesterday afternoon. Going around in circles with lots of dead ends."

After breakfast, Rose assisted Craig to the Bongo Bar so he could begin a crossword puzzle while she packed their belongings into the Defender.

The hotel lobby was full of chattering guests. She hugged Chloe farewell as Joan, the American lady with the grey pixie haircut barrelled over. "It's a disgrace. My iPad's missing and nobody's the least bit interested. Whatta you gonna do about it?" She planted herself in front of Rose.

"I'm very sorry to hear that." Rose was rather taken aback. "When did you realise it had gone?"

"This morning." Joan snorted. "I left it by my travel bag on the bed when I went to breakfast. The rest of my bags were brought down here, but my travel bag was still there, without my iPad." The lady shrugged a large cloth bag from her shoulder and opened it for Rose. It contained a book, glasses case, water bottle and countless other items—but no iPad.

"I am sorry, but there's not much I can do just now." Rose looked around at the melee. A friendly-looking African man and a uniformed hotel employee were lifting cases into the back of a matatu—a white Toyota minivan.

At the reception desk, an Asian man was checking out,

surrounded by numerous children, as two older ladies, in yellow and green saris, sat composed next to the desk.

"Do you have that list I asked you for?" Rose asked Joan, who was still standing in front of her. Joan opened her voluminous bag and extracted a paper.

"Here, but it won't help you find my iPad." She held the paper out until Rose tugged it from her hand.

"Thank you," said Rose. "You never know, it might."

Joan hoisted her bag onto her shoulder, pulled down her sleeve and prepared to leave.

"One minute," said Rose. "Have you heard of a man called Blake Holiday?"

"Sure, who hasn't? He wouldn't need to steal my iPad, 'cause he could buy this hotel." Joan looked around her, scrunching up her face.

"Did you know he donated to Davina Dijan's Conservancy?" asked Rose.

The words caught Joan's attention. "No, but it makes sense. The papers reported his relationship ending with an attractive and influential lady from Africa."

"Do you think he would be upset enough to kill her?" asked Rose.

"Hell no, even if she did take him for hundreds of thousands of dollars. Apparently, he landed a big deal last week. There's a photo of him on Facebook with an attractive brunette, half, no, two-thirds his age."

Nicki walked over carrying a clipboard. She nodded a greeting to Rose and escorted Joan to the matatu which the rest of her party had already boarded. As Rose watched it drive away, Manager Bundi materialised. "That's a relief," he said.

Rose jumped. "Manager Bundi."

"More trouble, I gather, with our American guests?" His forehead glistened.

"Yes," Rose paused, her brow furrowed. "The valuable

items that go missing, are they generally from the Americans?"

"Good question." The stout man rubbed his chin. "Yes, I'd say they are. Why? Do you know who's stea…" He lowered his voice to a whisper. "Who's involved?"

"I've an idea," said Rose. "I have to return to Nanyuki this morning to take Craig home. I'll be back later as Commissioner Akida's arriving. What about the cottage?"

"It's not booked until Thursday. Keep the key and use it if you need to. Just promise me everything will be sorted by Wednesday evening. We've the summit welcome drinks and supper."

Rose looked down at Manager Bundi as he rubbed his wrists. She said, "I only make promises I know I can keep."

CHAPTER FORTY-FIVE

C raig seemed relieved to be home. He cheerfully settled into his large cedar chair on the patio with the help of their house girl, Kipto, and smoothed out his unfinished crossword puzzle.

"Bomori, kahawa?" Kipto brought Craig his coffee and continued to fuss over him.

Potto, Rose's black and tan terrier, also wanted attention. He showed his delight at Rose's return by following her round the yard and field as she checked the well-being of her animals.

The cow and horses munched their way through the new growth of grass, whilst the chickens scratched about at grubs and insects on the ground, further proof of the life-sustaining power of rain and Mother Nature.

Only Izzy, her black and white cat, seemed annoyed by her prolonged absence. The cat opened her one eye to stare at Rose when she returned to the patio. She closed it again without disturbing her sleeping form.

"Craig, I have to go out again. I've a patient to attend."

Craig looked up. "Will you come back for lunch or head straight to the Mount Kenya Resort to meet the commissioner?"

"I'm not sure, probably the latter. Don't wait for me."

"Will you be back this evening?" Craig tried to keep his voice casual but he loosely crossed his hands on his lap.

"I hope so," Rose responded. "But it depends on what developments there are in the case. Kipto will look after you and you can rest after your busy weekend." Rose shifted her feet. "You'll be OK, won't you?"

"Of course," said Craig but his eyes didn't meet Roses'. She pecked him on the cheek and left, a band of guilt tightening around her chest.

Rose made two house calls. She checked the stitches on a bulldog she'd treated the previous Monday after it picked and lost a fight with a Doberman. Then she received a call from a neighbouring farmer so attended his cow, whose flank needed stitching after catching its belly on a fence post.

Rose drove through the nameless village which had sprung up on land around a bend in the road leading to the hotel. She felt guilty about leaving Craig but relieved to be returning to the hotel where Chris was staying.

She considered the village. Most of its population were people from the mountain who had either been displaced, so their land could be returned to forest, or had felt they needed to seek work and an education for their children closer to Nanyuki.

Each time Rose drove through it, another ramshackle wooden structure was being built. The irony this morning was that six foot lengths of offcuts—the uneven side pieces left when timber is sawn into planks— were being hammered into place to create an enclosure around the newly pronounced "Ready Timber Yard". Rose had no idea who owned the land on which the buildings were being constructed, and she doubted the occupiers knew or cared.

Her thoughts drifted back to Craig and Chris. She loved them both. Chris's withdrawal from her life had been gradual, but she'd been helpless to prevent it, and she was determined not lose him again.

But how could she rebuild their relationship without undermining Craig? What had caused Craig to push his son away again? Uncertainty and insecurity, but it was not concern for himself. Rose knew Craig worried about her, especially as his own health was failing.

Rose realised Craig was crudely seeking Chris's help and assurance that he would look after her when he was gone. She knew Craig felt Chris had a duty and a responsibility to care for her, but did he?

Rose had read articles about the problem of an ageing populating in the UK, and there were various debates. Did adult children have an ethical responsibility to ensure their parents were safe, secure and getting the attention they needed? How should this fit in with the adult children's own busy lives? Should elderly parents be moved to assisted living with guaranteed care? Was this the family or the state's responsibility?

Rose shivered. She wanted to end her days peacefully at home, not surrounded by other helpless geriatrics. She thought of the Africans and their acceptance that able family members support their vulnerable and less capable relatives.

In Kenya, she could employ empathetic and considerate staff to nurse her through old age and illness, if she could afford to pay them. Money. That was what it came down to for her and Craig. They had few savings, but the money Rose earned from her veterinary work wasn't enough to cover expensive private healthcare plans. Any treatment they needed would continue to be provided by the local Cottage Hospital.

Rose thought to the Bible. It clearly stated that families should support the aged but then, she thought cynically, the church wouldn't want the cost or responsibility.

She sighed deeply. Hopefully these were future concerns. The immediate issue was bringing Chris and Craig together in a functioning relationship. Both men would need to compromise. Would Craig be satisfied if Chris promised—

was promise too strong a word?—to be responsible for Rose in the event of Craig's death?

Would Craig respect that Chris had chosen to spend his life over four thousand miles away? Distance was less of an issue now as communication was easier by email and the various methods young people had for speaking face-to-face over their phones. The family would need to learn to communicate on a regular basis.

Guiltily, she remembered she had not emailed her daughter Heather last week. As regularly as individual circumstances allow, she conceded.

Rose was still musing as she completed the security checks and drove through the hotel gates. Her attention was drawn to a young man performing various martial art turning and pushing movements on a small lawn area behind the hotel. She realised it was Hugo.

As she parked her Defender, Rose thought gratefully that at least she could discuss matters with Chris without worrying Craig. Her family was one more conundrum she needed to resolve before the start of the summit.

CHAPTER FORTY-SIX

R ose was still in a reflective mood as she entered the hotel. She learnt from a receptionist that Commissioner Akida had not yet arrived. Picking up a "Welcome to the Giant's Club Summit" pack from a table in the hall, she seated herself in the corner of the Bongo Bar, but realised she'd forgotten her glasses.

She retraced her steps and hailed the hotel valet before he parked her Defender, and collected her glasses from the passenger seat. She ordered tea and a strawberry chicken salad before settling once again in the Bongo Bar. Opening her pack, she extracted a coloured leaflet of graphs and statistics which made disturbing reading.

Since 1900, the number of elephants in Africa had dropped from twelve million to three hundred and fifty thousand. A ninety-seven per cent reduction. In Kenya, the elephant population had declined by ninety per cent since 1970, and there were estimated to be only twenty-six thousand elephants left.

Rose was aware of other guests drifting into the bar, but she continued to read. The situation with the ivory trade seemed complicated. An international ban on ivory came into effect, in 1989, after President Daniel Moi burnt twelve tons of it. This seemed to work, as elephant populations increased. But then in the mid-1990s, some African countries were allowed to trade again, which stimulated demand for ivory, particularly in Asia, and poaching escalated.

Kenya retained the ban on ivory trading, and for a time its elephant population continued to recover, but then poaching increased and reached a height between 2007 and 2010. In 2010 ninety-two kilograms of raw ivory were confiscated at Jomo Kenyatta International Airport in Nairobi.

Rose was digesting this information when voices reached her from a nearby table. She looked up to see four men: Thabiti, Hugo, Freddie and Gabe.

Rose heard Freddie's strong deep voice ask, "Thabiti, was it your mother who was murdered last month?"

"Freddie, don't be so insensitive." The voice was higher pitched. Gabe's, Rose thought, trying but failing to read the material on the table in front of her.

"Yes," Thabiti stammered. Rose could feel his recently improved self-esteem evaporate.

"Leave the boy alone. Thabiti, you don't need to talk about it." The voice was calm and strong, lacking Freddie's edge. Rose glanced up. She was surprised to see Hugo speaking. His voice had seemed quiet and brittle until now.

"Sorry," Freddie drawled. "Must be the journalist part of me kicking in." He didn't sound very sorry, thought Rose. "What about you, Hugo? Did you leave your parents in the UK?" Freddie sounded in a dangerous mood today, like a hawk circling mice.

"No, my adoptive mum died last summer and my dad three years earlier." The waiter approached with her salad and Rose hid behind him, trying to remain anonymous.

She bowed her head to eat whist surreptitiously watching the men at the nearby table.

"I'm sorry." Rose just made out Thabiti's words. "Did you know your real parents?" Good question, thought Rose.

She watched as Hugo lifted his arms, imitating his

previous martial art movements on the lawn. "No. All I know is that I was abandoned as a baby with a small silver token."

Freddie's investigative nose sniffed again. "Ever thought of trying to trace them?"

Hugo swung round to him with both arms raised and poised. Freddie leant back. "I did, but it didn't work out."

"I never knew my mum." The shrill-voiced Gabe joined the conversation. "I was brought up by my gran. She told me my mum died in childbirth, but I'm not sure I believed her. I always imagined my mother as a glamorous lady running away to Africa or Asia to marry a handsome prince. I waited for her to invite me to join her. That was my boyhood dream as I stared out the window of our terraced house in Bournemouth at the identical houses opposite ours. I think it fuelled my passion for Africa. The wide open spaces, animals and romance."

"Oh please," scoffed Freddie.

"Why, what's your tale?" Hugo asked.

"None to tell. My parents live amicably, if not happily, in a large house in Karen with their every need attended to by an army of African staff."

CHAPTER FORTY-SEVEN

An efficient-looking African lady marched into the Bongo Bar followed by a wavy-haired European woman whose face was flushed as she clutched several files and a briefcase. The African lady removed her glasses and announced, "Gabriel Baker."

Her interest piqued, Rose watched Hugo nudge Gabe. "Gabriel, that's me." With another shove from Hugo, he was launched to his feet in front of the women.

"You told us you needed to speak with the representative from Peak Book Press when she arrived. This is Ms Wallace." The African lady indicated with the flick of her glasses.

The wavy-haired woman reached out a hand for Gabe to shake and dropped her files. Flustered, she bent to gather them. The African lady turned on her heels, glasses aloft.

"Gabe," Hugo stage whispered. "Remember 'joint ownership' and 'contributory copyright infringement'." Gabe appeared to repeat the words in his head before helping the lady with her files. They left the Bongo Bar.

Freddie stood up. "I need to make some calls. Catch you later."

"I've a meeting with the dragon who escorted Gabe's visitor," said Hugo. "She's bound to change the summit agenda again." He stood and turned to Thabiti. "I'll run through it with you later. Ignore Freddie, he's been hunting for a fight all morning."

As Hugo left, Thabiti turned towards Rose and said, "Enjoy your lunch?" He grinned and moved across to join her. "I spotted you trying hard not to listen to our conversation." Thabiti picked up a menu.

Rose coughed as she looked at the table. "It was an interesting discussion. You finally have your answer from Hugo about his parents." She lifted her head. "What's happened to him? He's rather forthright and confident today."

"I know, he's been like it all morning. It's as if he's found the answer to a question he's been debating." Thabiti put the menu back on the table. "I've done the research you asked for. Let me order lunch and I'll run through it."

Rose placed her empty salad bowl on an adjacent table and tidied up the summit papers. Thabiti returned, unlocking his phone. "All the information is easy to access and is on my phone, which is easier than lugging my laptop around."

He sat next to Rose. "Nicki's active on Facebook, and so are her two sons. The oldest is at St Randolph's School in the UK, sitting his GCSEs this year. The youngest is in his final year at Pembroke House and has a place at his brother's school in September."

Rose drummed her fingers. "Pembroke's school fees are substantially more than we used to pay, and UK school fees will be higher still."

"Yes, St. Randolph's fees are eleven thousand pounds a term, and that excludes extras and flights. With Pembroke's fees, Nicki has to find over fifty thousand pounds a year in school fees."

Rose whistled. "That'll be more than her salary." She considered the information. "The boys might have bursaries or scholarships, but she'll still have to find a substantial amount of money. What about her other costs?"

"She's living in a guest cottage in Burguret, south of Nanyuki, and as she eats at the hotel when working, I guess her day-to day-living costs aren't high." Thabiti scrolled through his phone.

"Anything about debts?" Rose asked.

"Not that I've been able to find."

Constable Wachira appeared at the door and Rose waved to her. Breathlessly, the constable said, "Commissioner Akida's entering Nanyuki, so he'll soon be here."

"Good, good," said Rose distractedly. "Did you find out if any guests were staying when the cleaners' key, or any other keys, went missing?"

The constable perched on a stool. "There was a party of American guests and Mrs O'Conner was their tour guide."

Rose sat back. "Interesting. Anyone else?"

"Not according to the hotel records," said the constable.

Kenneth crossed to their table carrying Thabiti's burger and fries. "Thanks, Kenneth. This Bongo Burger is the best." Rose looked away whilst Constable Wachira gulped.

"Kenneth," Rose began. "How well do you know Nicki, the tour guide for the American groups?"

"Not well. She keeps to herself, but her guests usually stay in the east wing, so I often bump into her. Sometimes she asks me to open rooms for her to check or leave information. She's always distributing pieces of paper to her group."

"Have you ever seen her leave rooms you've not let her into?" Rose asked.

"No, but she does have a habit of unexpectedly appearing in corridors."

CHAPTER FORTY-EIGHT

R ose and Constable Wachira left Thabiti happily devouring his Bongo burger. Commissioner Akida arrived and joined them in the incident suite, but he was not his usual polished self. He wore a Khaki coloured short-sleeved jacket with gold buttons and a peaked hat, but his uniform was creased and his face drawn.

"Mama Rose, I am so grateful for your assistance with this case and for supervising Constable Wachira," said the commissioner. Rose watched the constable over the commissioner's shoulder. She was impersonating Thabiti eating his burger.

"Commissioner, we both know the constable is a capable policewoman, which I suspect is why you chose her for this case when more senior officers were available." Bang on target. The commissioner looked at his feet and the constable beamed. "How were your meetings in Nairobi?" Rose asked.

"Complicated by Davina Dijan's death." The commissioner lowered his voice despite only the three of them being in the room. "The heads of state are as nervous as a herd of impalas scenting a lion. I suspect one of them has already used the murder as an excuse to cancel his visit."

The commissioner took a small penknife out of his pocket

and twiddled it between his fingers. "I am under a great deal of pressure to solve this case promptly."

"It might not be that easy, Commissioner," said Rose. "Constable Wachira has summarised our findings, and I suggest we work through them and any information gathered this morning."

Constable Wachira pulled over the flip chart and rearranged chairs in front of it. Rose felt it could be a long meeting, so she switched the kettle on. Commissioner Akida wandered through to the bedroom where the two women joined him.

Constable Wachira began. "Robert Dijan discovered his wife's body at ten o'clock on Friday evening. She was propped up in a sitting position on the bed, and had been stabbed through the neck. The pathologist confirmed this wound was fatal when the victim removed the weapon, causing her to bleed to death."

"This is the post-mortem we had to pay for?" asked the commissioner through gritted teeth.

"Yes," said Constable Wachira, and the commissioner grunted. "A small knife was found on the floor by the bed. The pathologist confirmed the weapon could have created the wound if used with sufficient force."

"We're looking for a man then?" The commissioner's eyes narrowed.

"Not necessarily," said Rose. "I believe a woman in a rage using the momentum of a downward thrust could have caused the fatal wound."

"Very good," said the commissioner, looking around and preparing to leave.

"One minute, sir," said the constable. "We need to show you possible hiding places."

"For what?" asked the commissioner. He began spinning his knife.

"For the murderer, sir. I will explain the reason shortly, but please follow me."

They entered the bathroom and Constable Wachira demonstrated how someone could hide unseen on the shelf in the shower.

When they returned to the living room, Rose made herself a cup of tea and one for the commissioner, with plenty of sugar. Constable Wachira searched the mini bar in vain for a Diet Coke so instead she chose a Stoney Ginger Beer, known locally as Stoney Tangawizi. She returned to the flip chart and cleared her throat as her audience of two took their seats.

"Commissioner, the most difficult part of this case has been establishing how the killer entered Davina's bedroom or, in one case, how he returned."

"Entered, returned? I don't understand," said the commissioner. He found a small piece of wood in a pocket and absent-mindedly began whittling with his penknife.

"Why don't you draw a diagram for the commissioner?" suggested Rose. "It will be useful for all of us to reconsider Friday night's events."

Constable Wachira lifted pages until she found a blank sheet. She sketched out the corridor, including the corner which restricted lines of sight, the suite and the secretary's bedroom. She added stick people to represent the American group and the lift engineers and wrote "restaurant" at the bottom.

Rose and the constable walked the commissioner through the timeline, and the constable added three more stick people to her sketch, to represent Robert and Davina Dijan, and Ethan, the secretary.

"So you see, sir, after the Dijans and Ethan returned to their rooms, only Kenneth, the steward, was seen entering and leaving the suite by the living room door."

"By the American witnesses?" the commissioner asked.

"Yes. The engineers saw a mzungu leave, but no one enter through the bedroom door."

The commissioner turned his carving. "I can see why you

concluded somebody was hiding in the room, and that they entered before everyone returned from supper."

Rose said, "Unless the secretary is our killer, but he had to find a way to return to the suite unobserved, as the Americans saw him leave later to alert Manager Bundi."

"If the killer was hiding in the bathroom, as you suggest, how did he or she get in without a key?" asked the commissioner.

"Keycard, sir," said the constable. "A piece of plastic with a magnetic strip on the back."

The commissioner grunted again.

Constable Wachira continued, "The very question we raised last night, and I've been following up this morning. The hotel confirmed that I returned all the keycards issued to the Dijans and their secretary, and that no other keycards were issued for these rooms. No communal cards have gone missing. Well, not this week at least."

The commissioner looked interested.

Rose explained. "Towards the end of last year, a cleaner was sacked after losing her keycard."

"And one guest, present on Friday, was staying at the hotel when it happened," said the constable.

"Excellent." The commissioner looked at the strange shape he had carved. "Who is he?"

"She, sir. Nicki O'Conner. She escorts groups of American guests to the hotel from Nairobi and on to Lake Elementaita."

"Let's arrest her." The commissioner's voice was loud.

"We can't, sir, she left with her party this morning," the constable said before examining her shoes.

"What!" The commissioner jumped to his feet. "You let our main suspect leave?" He confronted the young constable, who stepped back.

"Commissioner," said Rose softly. "We had no evidence on which to hold Nicki this morning. After further investigation, I think she is guilty, but not of the murder."

Two heads turned towards Rose.

CHAPTER FORTY-NINE

Rose read the piece of paper Joan, the American lady, had given her before leaving the hotel. She had been thorough and must have known a number of visitors on past tours.

There were no reports of missing belongings from stays at the Maasai Mara or the Kenyan Coast, but various items vanished when the group stayed in Nairobi, at Lake Elementaita, or at the Mount Kenya Resort and Spa. The list went back to December, and Rose noted the frequency of disappearances increasing as she moved forward along the timeline.

"What do you think the tour guide is guilty of?" Commissioner Akida asked. He was standing with his back to Constable Wachira, his arms folded across his chest, staring at Rose. His penknife and wooden carving were absent.

"Theft," said Rose, removing her glasses.

The commissioner's arms dropped to his side. "What theft?"

"Please, Commissioner, sit down and I'll explain," said Rose. The commissioner strode to his chair, still scrutinising Rose.

"The reason I'm here, staying at the hotel, is because

Manager Bundi asked me to look into possible robberies," explained Rose.

The commissioner bunched up his arms and chest. "Robbery is a police matter."

Rose put a hand on the commissioner's arm, which appeared to puncture his indignation, as he sank back into his chair. "I know, but the items stolen were numerous and varied," Rose said. "The majority had little or no monetary value, and the Manager didn't want to waste the police's time."

Rose lied with the fingers on her right hand crossed. She needed the commissioner to remain calm and focused. "We've cleared up most of them. Do you know how many of the hotel guests, generally those staying in the most expensive rooms, feel it's acceptable to remove hotel property? They take towels, pillows, even crockery."

The commissioner narrowed his eyes and asked, "What does the hotel do?"

"Nothing at present, but I'll suggest to Manager Bundi that he speak to you. Perhaps you can provide guidance? It's a delicate matter, considering the positions and professions of many of the guests," said Rose.

The commissioner sat up, straightening his jacket. "Of course, I'd be happy to provide assistance to this important establishment." Rose wondered if the commissioner would request a complimentary room whilst he undertook those discussions.

"So," said Rose,. "That left a small number of valuable items. Whilst I've been staying at the hotel, a phone and an iPad have disappeared. The iPad only vanished this morning. Both were taken from members of an American Tour party. Another gentleman, in the same group, thought some money had been taken from his room in Nairobi, but he couldn't be certain."

The commissioner said, "I suppose he exchanged a large

amount of dollars and was given a pile of one thousand shilling notes, which he wasn't sure what to do with."

"Exactly," said Rose. "He wasn't used to our money and couldn't tell if the pile of notes had diminished. Manager Bundi and Kenneth agree the thefts are usually at weekends, which is the busiest time for the hotel, but it's also when the American groups stay."

Constable Wachira stepped closer and asked, "Why would Mrs O'Conner risk her job by stealing from her guests?"

Rose looked up and sighed. "Desperation. Thabiti and I were discussing his research on Nicki just before you joined us in the Bongo Bar. Her husband ran off, and she is trying to educate her two boys and the cost is huge."

"Now I remember," said the constable. "She passed us at lunchtime on Sunday speaking on her phone. She needed money for something."

"A cast, so I guess her youngest son, at school in Kenya, has been injured. I think it's why she took a huge risk and stole the iPad this morning."

"We need to send someone to Lake Elementaita to arrest her," said the commissioner.

"Yes…" Rose said. "I'd really like someone to search her bags. I know that sounds underhanded, but if we can find the keycards she uses for the different hotels…" The commissioner's eyes widened.

Rose explained, "I believe she has a master key for each of the hotels she visits, and uses them to access the guests' rooms. I hope she will also have the missing phone and iPad, as I would like to return them to their owners. I presume Lake Elementaita falls under the Gilgil police's jurisdiction?"

The commissioner shook his head. "For something like this, it would be Nakuru." The edge of his mouth curled. "I'd rather not involve that bunch."

Rose looked at Constable Wachira whose hand was half raised. "Perhaps I could call Sam. I think he's at Soysambu, Lord Delamere's estate, which borders the lake."

"Your friend Sam?" The commissioner's brow wrinkled. "Is that the big smooth-talker?"

Rose jumped in. "Yes, he helped me with a few points during Aisha's investigation." Technically this was true, although it had been a personal issue rather than her friend's case. Constable Wachira smiled as she looked warmly at Rose.

"Go ahead, give him a call," said the commissioner.

As Constable Wachira left the room, the commissioner said, "Well done, Mama Rose. But if you are right and the tour guide is a thief and not a killer, where does that leave Davina Dijan's case?"

"I think there are three suspects. A journalist called Freddie Shaw, a research student called Gabriel Baker and…"

Constable Wachira returned. "Ethan, the secretary."

"Possibly," said Rose.

The commissioner leant forward, "Why possibly?"

Rose said, "Because I think one of our suspects is Davina's son."

CHAPTER FIFTY

C onstable Wachira's eyes bulged as she stepped closer to Rose. The commissioner stood and began pacing the room.

"Son? Mama Rose, what are you talking about? Davina Dijan has no children. I've read her file," said the commissioner.

"I don't think either of her husbands were the father, but the pathologist told Constable Wachira she had given birth," said Rose.

The commissioner completed a circuit and stopped in front of Rose. He said, "That opens up many possibilities. The child could have died, it could be a girl or..."

"It could be a boy. I believe Davina gave birth to a son before she was married." Rose was convinced, as she felt the case had too many holes, but a grown up son with a grievance started to plug some of them.

Constable Wachira consulted her notes. "Davina was twenty-nine when she married her first husband. He was a surgeon in London."

"So working on the presumption she gave birth before she was married, the youngest her son could be is ...?" Rose asked.

Constable Wachira did the maths. "Twenty."

Rose pursed her lips. "So theoretically her son could be Freddie, or Gabe, or Ethan or Hugo. I can confirm Aisha was Thabiti's mother."

"I've seen another young man in the hotel, but I can't remember if he was here Friday night. Has the most penetrating blue eyes and…"

"Too old," said Rose. "And he didn't arrive until Saturday morning."

"How do you know?" asked the constable, pressing her lips together.

"I saw Chloe greet him at reception," said Rose. She was relieved that Constable Wachira appeared satisfied with her answer and walked across to the flip chart. She turned to the page with the timeline and names and wrote "Hugo ?" next to it. "We have more interviewing to do." She said, capping her pen.

There was a loud knock on the door. Constable Wachira quickly pulled the front cover over the flip chart. She opened the door, flattening herself against the wall as Robert Dijan strode in with Ethan in his wake.

"Commissioner, you've finally arrived to take responsibility for the case?" said Robert.

The commissioner's eyes narrowed. "Presidents and national security take priority." Both men gathered themselves up like male waterbucks preparing to fight.

"Mr Dijan," Rose attempted to intervene. "You've arrived at an opportune moment. I have a few points which need clarifying, now the commissioner is here."

"Oh yes?" said Robert, turning to Rose. She remained seated but held his gaze. "Where were you when your wife was killed?"

Robert sucked in his cheeks. "I've already told you. In here, at the desk reading."

"I don't believe you. Nor do I believe you were in the

bathroom when Kenneth walked though this room to reach the bedroom where your wife was reading."

Robert Dijan was rigid and the cords on his neck stood out. Rose spotted Commissioner Akida open his mouth to begin speaking. She caught his eye and imperceptibly shook her head.

A clear steady voice behind Rose said, "Robert, do you remember? You had a few questions in respect of the documents you were reading. You came through to my room to discuss them." Ethan walked forward and stood next to Robert.

"Of course, now I remember." Robert placed his arm round Ethan's shoulder and laughed. "Bright boy. Don't know what I'd do without him." Rose noted perspiration on Robert's brow. She felt Ethan's stare and turned to him. For several seconds their eyes locked as they reached an unspoken agreement. Rose nodded and broke the spell.

Ethan turned to Robert. "I believe you came to talk to the commissioner about leaving?"

"Thank you for reminding me." Ethan walked away and was once again positioned behind Rose's chair. She remained aware of his presence.

Robert turned to the commissioner. "I, we, have an important meeting in Nairobi on Wednesday. It is in the national interest, as you would say, so when can we leave? I presume we have been cleared of any involvement with my wife's death?"

Rose shook her head at the commissioner's enquiring glance. "Not yet," he replied. "As you know, I only arrived a short time ago, and I'm still reviewing the case with my... colleagues."

"But I must leave by Tuesday night, Wednesday morning at the latest," said Robert. His voice was high-pitched as he pleaded. Rose nodded.

"I hope that will be possible. Yes, it should be. Now if you don't mind, we still have much work to do."

Ethan said, "Of course, Commissioner. Thank you." He guided Robert out of the suite.

"Why didn't you question Ethan about his whereabouts? About a possible motive?" whispered Constable Wachira.

"I don't believe he was involved."

"Why not?" the constable asked, tilting her head.

"He couldn't get back into the suite or his room after the lift engineers saw our culprit leave by the bedroom door. Also, he has red hair."

The commissioner laughed. "Mama Rose, I'm not sure what you will say next. What does his hair colour have to do with his guilt or innocence?"

"Red hair is a recessive genetic trait which has to be inherited from both parents. We have no idea who fathered Davina's child, but she is unlikely to carry the red hair trait," said Rose.

"Why?" asked Constable Wachira. She pulled her hair scrunchy tight.

Rose explained. "Davina had a dark complexion, of Mediterranean origin. Red hair is far less common amongst southern Europeans than their northern counterparts."

Constable Wachira nodded. "So it's not impossible Ethan could be Davina's son, but it is unlikely." She tilted her head left, then right. "And we haven't found another motive for him to kill Mrs Dijan." Rose believed she knew one, but telling the constable would only complicate the situation. She would speak with Robert and Ethan separately.

"So then there were three," said the commissioner.

CHAPTER FIFTY-ONE

The commissioner left the suite, claiming he needed some air.

"How was Sam?" Rose asked Constable Wachira.

"My call was opportune as he finished his work on Soysambu today. He knows the manager of the hotel where Mrs O'Conner is staying and will try to persuade him to hand over her room key. If successful, he'll search her room for us."

The commissioner returned and brought Freddie with him. "This gentleman started asking me questions in the hotel lobby. I discovered his name is Freddie Shaw and I think we have some questions for him. I asked him to accompany me," said the commissioner.

Freddie sat down and crossed one black-jeaned leg over the other. He leant back, resting his elbows on the chair arms.

"Into the lion's den," Freddie said and smiled. He looked at the commissioner, the constable and finally at Rose before lifting an eyebrow. "Well?"

Constable Wachira regarded the commissioner, but he had turned to look out of the veiled window.

"Freddie, we are trying to clear up a few points from Friday night and wondered if you could help us?" Rose asked as she realised neither the commissioner nor the constable were willing to begin the interview.

"Of course." Freddie re-crossed his legs and faced Rose, who had taken the other chair. "What would you like to know?"

"Firstly, your movements on Friday evening from seven o'clock," Rose said.

Freddie rubbed his chin. "Gabe and I had a drink in the Bongo Bar which led to an early supper, in the bar, not the restaurant. I had an article to complete about the conference, but Gabe was in a state. He was wound up about this book of Davina's, claiming it is based on his research and he wrote part of it. Apparently Davina promised they'd be joint authors, but he's not even mentioned in the acknowledgments."

Rose asked, "Did he tell you what he intended to do about it?"

Freddie sighed. "He didn't have a plan. Not at first, anyway. He calmed down a little whilst eating, and I suppose he became introspective and quiet. I was jotting down notes so didn't take much notice. I left around half eight, as I had to start writing."

Commissioner Akida turned from the window. "Where did you go?"

"Back to my room. It's in the east wing on the ground floor," said Freddie, leaning back and looking up at the commissioner.

"Did you see anyone?" the commissioner asked.

"Not that I recall."

Rose asked, "What about Hugo? Did you see him on Friday evening?"

Freddie rubbed his chin again. "Yes, he sat down with us in the Bongo Bar. He was also stressed, but when Gabe kicked off, he left." Freddie pulled his chin. "I think he wanted to talk to me but didn't get a chance."

"How well do you know Hugo?" Rose asked.

"Not that well." Freddie rested his arms on those of the chair again. "We've met at a number of government, NGO and charity events. Him doing his technical bit and me trying to find an interesting slant for a story."

Constable Wachira completed her notes and asked, "Did you stay in your room for the rest of the evening?"

"Yes. No! I went down to the bar for a Tusker. It was just before nine, according to the clock outside reception. I returned to my room." Freddie pulled his ear. "Gabe was coming down the stairs from the first floor."

CHAPTER FIFTY-TWO

After Freddie's interview, the commissioner despatched Constable Wachira to locate and escort Gabriel Baker to the incident suite.

"This case spins in circles," said the commissioner. He rocked back and forth on the soles of his polished black shoes, with his hands clasped in front of him.

Rose agreed, "I noticed that. Everyone we speak to gives us a small amount of information leading us in a particular direction, but they neglect to tell us something which would point elsewhere. Sometimes I think they're being deliberately obstructive."

"Let us see what Gabriel Baker has to say. Whether he can confirm Freddie Shaw's account. And we need to discover why he was on the first floor."

The Gabriel who sauntered into the suite was not the agitated Gabe Rose had encountered in the Bongo Bar.

"Sorry for the delay, sir. I couldn't find Mr Baker." Constable Wachira was flushed and out of breath.

"I was with the hotel barber." Gabe had been transformed. He was clean-shaven and his hair, which had previously been constrained in a ponytail, hung glossy and wavy onto his shoulders. Rose suspected he'd even had his eyebrows threaded as they were red around the edges.

"Mr Baker. We have spoken with a number of guests to ascertain their movements on Friday evening. What were you were doing from seven o'clock?" asked Commissioner Akida. Both men remained standing.

Gabriel shrugged his shoulders. "I was in the Bongo Bar."

"Alone?" asked the commissioner.

"For a bit. Hugo and Freddie joined me around quarter to eight, but Hugo walked out soon after. He didn't even stay for a drink. Freddie and I had a bite of supper, but he left around eight-thirty claiming he had work to do. I left about fifteen minutes later." Gabriel smiled and looked at the commissioner and Constable Wachira.

"Did you intentionally follow Robert and Davina Dijan upstairs?" asked Rose.

Gabriel's veneer cracked. His face paled and his shoulders slumped forward. He stammered, "Follow them? Why would I do that?"

"You did leave the bar as Robert Dijan escorted his wife to their suite, and your room is in the same wing, but on the ground floor."

"Yes, that's true." Gabriel's eyes opened wide as if alert to danger.

"And you were seen descending from the first floor around nine," Rose continued. Her voice was steady and matter of fact.

"I was? Who by?" Gabe was flustered.

"That's not important," said Commissioner Akida. "But what you were doing on the first floor is."

Gabe looked at each occupant in the room and flopped into the chair where Freddie had previously languished. "Just when I thought everything was sorted." He held his head in his hands and took a deep breath.

"I did visit Davina. She was in charge of my research

placement after all. Though that's not what this is about, or at least it is, but not directly."

He took another deep breath as if preparing to dive into deep water. "I was furious. I helped Davina write a book based on my research. It was exciting working with her. She was infectious, so when she claimed to be 'busy', I agreed to write the final third of the book."

Gabe looked at Rose and said, "But you know what happened? Davina stole all the glory, claiming to be the sole author of the book."

Gabe stood up and began pacing. "I was on my own in the Bongo Bar when I spotted Davina and Robert walk past. I did follow them, but hid behind some sofas at the end of the corridor when Robert left the room. I ducked down again as the steward followed, carrying the remains of someone's room service meal."

Gabe took several deep breaths. "I knocked on the door to this room, but nobody answered." Gabe moved across and opened the door to the bedroom. "So I knocked on the bedroom door. I was probably shouting, too. Davina opened the door wearing skimpy nightwear with a loosely tied, silk dressing gown, as serene as a crowned crane bird. She might even have been flirting, but I wasn't interested."

Gabe looked into the bedroom. "She half lay, half sat on the bed, propped up against the headboard and patted the space next to her, but I refused to sit down. I told her I wanted to be acknowledged as co-author of the book, as was my right. Do you know she laughed at me? Told me nobody wanted to read what a third-rate student from a mediocre UK university had to say about wildlife in Kenya. She was the expert and people wanted to hear what she had to say."

Gabe returned to the empty chair and sat down. "I'm not sure what else I said to her, but finally she lost it. She threw a book at me and I'm embarrassed to say I scuttled away from the room, down the stairs and hid in my room. Davina was alive, well and… magnificent when I left her. But she still cheated me." Gabriel blew into his hands.

As his composure returned, Gabriel said, "I didn't kill her. With Davina alive, my case was easier to argue. Now she's dead I've been pitching to closed ears and, despite my threats to sue under copyright infringement, the publishers refuse to acknowledge me as a co-author."

"But what about the new look?" asked Rose.

"They've conceded that my research will be credited, allowing me to finish my Masters, which is a huge relief as I won't have to start again with a new topic. I'm also involved with the book launch, which is exciting, but it was on condition I smartened myself up." Colour returned to Gabriel's face and he stroked his new hair style.

Rose smiled. "You look great." Gabriel beamed at her. Rose thought for a minute and said, "Gaia Conservancy will need a new managing director, and I think you should apply." Gabriel appeared about to protest but Rose held up a hand.

"Not only can you display knowledge of conservation through your work, but you also know many of the employees. Didn't you say you'd travelled round the conservancy speaking with those who worked on the ground?"

Gabriel nodded. "If you put your evidence of embezzlement, and payments to ghost workers, into a clear concise document, and show plans to stop future fraud, I think you stand a good chance of securing the job."

"Wow, do you really think so?" Gabriel asked.

"Why not? But you need to maintain the new image and start praising Davina and the conservancy. Posthumously, she will be the darling of the summit. And I would go back to the publishers and say you agree not to mention your writing involvement again as long as they acknowledge your work with five per cent of the sales revenue. You might not get it, but it's worth a try."

Gabriel jumped to his feet and pulled Rose to hers as he

shook her hand. The enthusiasm shone from his eyes and glowing skin.

"I am not sure we are finished," said Commissioner Akida.

"What else would you like to know?" Gabriel asked, turning to face him.

"You said Davina was alive when you left. Did you see or hear anyone else?"

Gabriel shivered. "As I left Davina's bedroom and opened the door, it was dark in the corridor. I didn't see anyone, but I did feel a lurking presence."

CHAPTER FIFTY-THREE

Rose needed a break from the incident suite, so she accompanied Gabriel downstairs.

"Thank you for what you said. I'd love to run Gaia Conservancy, but I didn't think I'd stand a chance," said Gabriel.

"You might not. I've no idea who else wants the job." Rose lowered her voice. "Proof of the conservancy being cheated out of money will be vital. If you're feeling bold and confident, contact Blake Holiday in America."

"The man who donated to the conservancy but demanded his money back after sending over an accountant?" asked Gabriel.

"Yes. Tell him Davina is dead and apologise for any past misunderstandings about his donation. You could invite him to the conservancy and say you'd be delighted to run through the finances with his accountant. With him on your side, your prospect of getting the job is much improved."

In the corridor, between the stairs and the Bongo Bar, Ms Wallace was arranging a book display. She had a number of titles on view, but Davina's book was the most prominent. A large picture of the dead woman was displayed alongside glossy green covers. Gabriel picked up a copy and handed it to Rose.

"Have this, and read what all the fuss is about," said Gabriel.

"You can't take that," said Ms Wallace.

"Watch me." Gabriel picked a pen up from the table, took Rose's book, and wrote on the first page before handing it back.

Rose left Gabriel with Ms Wallace and ordered a cup of tea in the Bongo Bar. She sank onto a chair on the outdoor patio, absorbing the fresh air and mellow afternoon sunshine. Fishing her glasses out of her bag, she flicked though the book. There were two blocks of photos which interested Rose more than the text. The first were of various elephants including Tim, who lived in Amboseli National Park and was famous for his long tusks.

The second section mainly comprised images of Davina. Rose turned a page and stopped. Her attention was drawn to a photo of a young Davina leaning against Freddie in a dusty landscape. That couldn't be right, Davina was nearly twenty years older than Freddie and the age difference in the photo was the opposite way around. She peered at the caption. "Davina with George Shaw, Ivory Impact Initiative, Kenya, 1988." Rose whistled.

"So this is you in sleuthing mode?" Rose jumped, dropping the book. Chris knelt, picked it up and placed it on the table as Rose's tea arrived.

"Would you like some?" Rose asked, recovering.

"Coffee please, no milk," Chris told the waiter. Rose waited. She leant back, closing her eyes.

Chris said, "I'm sorry about yesterday. Dad may mean well, but he goes about it the wrong way. My home is in London, at least for the moment." He leant over and took Rose's hand. "I will be there for you, although I suspect you'll outlive us all through sheer willpower and determination."

Rose opened her eyes. "My time will come, as it will for all of us. We mustn't waste what we have." She stared at Chris. "Particularly with needless family squabbles and misunderstandings." Her eyes softened. "What have you been doing today?"

"Checks and run-throughs for the summit," answered Chris. "I've been testing emergency escape and evacuation procedures and routes."

"Won't the top delegates have helicopters?"

"Only the heads of state or their representative." Chris's coffee arrived. "Asante," he said to the waiter.

"I think I'll return home tonight. Are you free for lunch tomorrow?" Rose asked.

Chris ran a hand through his hair. "I should be. I'm away tonight, having supper with Major Dan and his wife, and I'll be staying at theirs."

Rose wrinkled her nose and remembered. "Do you mean Chloe?"

"Yes. The major was company commander during our last tour of Afghanistan."

"Did he leave the army after that?" asked Rose.

"Many of us did," replied Chris. "It was a bloody tour. Literally. Whether we really did need to make progress, or whether generals in headquarters wanted glory, I'm not sure, but good men were killed. Friends." Chris's voice was beginning to crack. His eyes looked distant as he stared at the mountain. He gulped, rolled his shoulders and returned to Rose. "Funny that the major, Corporal Magori and I all ended up here."

Rose squinted. "Corporal Magori?"

"Yes, he works here as a steward, and I've seen him serving behind the bar." Chris looked back into the Bongo Bar.

"Do you mean Kenneth?" Rose asked.

"Yes that's right, Kenneth Magori." Chris turned back to Rose. "I can't see him at the moment."

"You know he's here with his son?" Rose said.

Chris hesitated. "Yes, Darren." Chris was rigid.

"So the newspaper was correct, Kenneth has kidnapped his son," said Rose.

Chris sagged and exhaled loudly. "His girlfriend was a cow and he doted on Darren. Have you any idea what it's like returning home after an Op tour, especially one as challenging as ours? Nobody understands what you've been through. To them life continues as usual."

"I don't think that's entirely true." Rose shook her head. "I'm sure the wives and girlfriends have their own issues when their men are away. Craig and I were worried about you and we didn't have young children to cope with."

Chris caught Rose's eye. "Well Corporal Magori's girlfriend coped by moving in with another man and taking Darren with her. They tried to stop Kenneth seeing his son, but still forced him to hand over a good portion of his operational allowance. I can't blame him for what he did, and Darren seems happy enough." Chris tugged his shirt collar.

Rose looked down at her clasped hands. She twiddled her thumbs. "The game's up. The police know. They haven't had a chance to confront Kenneth yet, as they're trying to clear up Davina's death, but they soon will."

CHAPTER FIFTY-FOUR

Constable Wachira appeared on the grass terrace below Rose. She waved and walked towards the hotel building.

"Catch you later," said Chris, as he slid back into the Bongo Bar.

Constable Wachira smiled at Rose. "Ready? Just one more interview today. I found Hugo. He's in the incident suite with the commissioner."

Wearily, Rose stood and followed the constable. In the incident suite Hugo seemed to be alone. He had pulled back the voile curtains covering the window and was staring out into the grounds and the mountain beyond. Rose heard the commissioner's voice emanating from the bedroom. He sounded agitated and as there were no other voices, she presumed he was on the phone.

"Tea, Mama Rose?" asked the constable. Despite having recently finished a cup on the patio, Rose accepted. She needed to get through this final interview.

The commissioner appeared. He was flushed and slammed the bedroom door shut. He planted his legs wide apart and said, "Young man. It has been a long and trying day. Answer our questions truthfully and succinctly and we shall soon be finished."

Hugo moved away from the window and hoisted himself onto the desk by the wall casually swinging his legs. He looked at the commissioner and said, "I'm not sure what you want to know? If this is about Davina Dijan's death, then the first time I met her was at the conference. It wasn't a warm introduction. Rather disappointing as she shouted and made a fuss about a mistake which she had created."

"Why?" asked the commissioner. "What happened?"

"I was working on the technical aspects of the conference. My temporary assistant loaded Mrs Dijan's presentation and it appeared on the conference screen, only it was the wrong presentation. She stormed off the stage and began berating us until we were able to persuade her to find the right one. Such arrogant behaviour." Hugo looked down at his feet, slowly shaking his head.

Rose said, "Hugo's right. I witnessed the episode."

The commissioner grunted and returned to Hugo. "When was the next time you saw Davina?"

"In the restaurant. Rose and her husband, Craig, kindly invited me to join their party for supper."

"But you didn't stay with us for long," said Rose.

Hugo leaned back, gripping the far edge of the desk. "No, I was tired and Mrs Dijan's behaviour was exhausting, and embarrassing." Rose noticed a vein pulsing on the side of Hugo's neck.

"Where did you go?" The commissioner was slowly rocking backwards and forwards on the soles of his feet.

"I saw Freddie Shaw in the bar. We've met at a few events since I started working in Nairobi, so I joined him, but his friend Gabe was upset and angry. I now understand why, and completely sympathise with Gabe, but at the time it was too much. I left them and returned to my room."

"What were you doing there?" The commissioner continued his questioning.

"I worked on some material from the conference and had

an early night. The day had been emotionally draining." Hugo maintained eye contact with the commissioner.

Rose wondered why Hugo had found the conference stressful. He was young, she knew he was fit, and he must be used to fixing technical problems or dealing with agitated event managers or speakers, all part of his job. At the conference both Hugo and Thabiti had appeared relaxed, and it was only at supper that Hugo became agitated and upset.

The commissioner asked, "Did you see anyone else?"

Hugo shook his head.

"Hugo," Rose said, her voice steady but casual. "I couldn't help overhearing…" The commissioner raised an eyebrow. "…You telling Thabiti, Gabriel and Freddie that you were adopted, but your adoptive parents had died. I'm sorry. Were you close?"

Hugo smiled and his eyes lit up. "They were good people. Unable to conceive themselves, and in their mid and late forties, they adopted me. Dad worked hard, but Mum was kind and gentle and always had time for me."

"Did you know you were adopted?" Rose continued watching Hugo closely.

"Oh, yes, they were very open about it. Praised God for answering their prayers and bringing them a child to care for. We'd play a game imagining who my real mum was. It was down to earth, not the fairy tale Gabe had of his own mother."

The commissioner looked at Rose, his eyes narrowed and his brow wrinkled. Rose shook her head and continued. "Did you try and trace her? Your real mother that is?"

"Yes. When I was eighteen, my mum encouraged me to apply for my original birth certificate. Then at least I had it and could ignore or act on it as I wanted. My real mother was named, but not my father. It meant nothing to me, so I filed it away." Hugo began picking at a nail on his hand.

"So you've not wanted to know more about your real mum? Have you tried to trace her?"

"Why?" Hugo jumped down from the desk and glared at Rose. "If I have or haven't, it's none of your business." He turned to the commissioner. "If you have nothing else to ask about Mrs Dijan's death, I'm leaving." Hugo spat the words out.

He turned away from them and moved towards the window. Rose could see his back move as Hugo composed himself with deep breaths. When he turned to them his face was passive and he even smiled.

Opening his arms in a conciliatory gesture, he said, "I'm sorry. I think most adopted children get prickly around the subject of their birth parents. The truth is I did try and find my real mother, but the only ladies I discovered who shared her name were either younger than me or in their eighties. I guess my mum moved on, got married or moved away." Hugo shrugged, but his bright eyes caught Rose's.

CHAPTER FIFTY-FIVE

R ose remained seated whilst the commissioner leant against the empty chair.

Constable Wachira stood beside her flip chart, turned to a clean page and said, "So we have our four prime suspects. Despite Mama Rose providing Mr Baker with career advice to apply for the managing director position at Gaia Conservancy, I still think he is the most likely culprit. He admits to being in Davina's room and we only have his word that she was alive when he left."

"And Kenneth's," said Rose. "As long as nobody is lying about times, which is quite possible, Gabriel visited Davina before Kenneth made her coffee. Gabriel couldn't have returned without being seen."

The young constable's shoulders slumped.

"I believe the handsome journalist was involved. I see him as a charmer, a lady's man," said the commissioner.

"Like his father," said Rose. She removed Davina's book from her bag and turned to the page she'd marked. She held it up in front of the commissioner. "This is Davina's new book and this is a photo of her with a man I believe is Freddie's father."

The commissioner snatched the book from Rose and

moved towards the window. Constable Wachira followed him. The commissioner rubbed his eyes but the constable's sparkled as she asked, "Do you think he is the father of Davina's child?"

"Yes, I do," said Rose. She couldn't help smiling at the reaction her discovery had caused.

"You don't think...?"

"No, constable, I don't believe Freddie is Davina's child. But I'm sure Davina took great delight in seducing and having an affair with the son of the man who did the same to her."

"A man as proud, confident and self-assured as Freddie Shaw might be unhappy to find out he has been used as a means to revenge his father," said the commissioner.

"Quite," said Rose.

"So do you think he killed Mrs Dijan?" asked the constable.

"I suggest we lie like crocodiles at the edge of the bank and wait. Eventually a clue, a revelation, or a slip of the tongue will reveal our culprit. I don't think we can achieve much more today, so if you don't mind, I'm going home to Craig. I shall be back bright and early in the morning."

"Tuesday," mused the commissioner. "I don't have the patience of a crocodile. If we don't solve the case tomorrow, I will be out of a job."

CHAPTER FIFTY-SIX

R ose felt refreshed on Tuesday morning after spending a night at home. There had been limited room on the bed as she and Craig were joined by Potto, her terrier, and Izzy, her cat. Potto had stretched out between them, whilst Izzy had curled up at Rose's feet, meowing whenever she moved.

As Rose and Craig enjoyed breakfast at the dining table on their outdoor patio, she noted the closeness of the humid air and suspected a thunderstorm was brewing. They discussed the interviews with Gabriel, Freddie and Hugo, but Craig had no illuminating ideas.

Rose poured a second cup of tea and leaned back.

"Are you joining the commissioner at the hotel for more investigating this morning?" asked Craig. He cleared a space at the table and smoothed out a crossword puzzle.

"I am, but I'm not in a rush. I don't have any more questions to ask and constantly analysing the case will only cause it to go stale. At the moment, patience, contemplation and awareness of the wider environment are required."

Rose sipped from her tea and listened to the birds chattering in the garden. Further away a dove coo-cooed in a low tone. "I'm not sure the commissioner would agree, though, as he's under pressure to solve the case as quickly as possible."

Kipto rushed in, gathering plates and bowls together as if she were sweeping them straight off the table.

"Steady on," said Craig.

"Visitors here," replied Kipto, carrying a precarious pile of crockery and cutlery into the house.

Craig and Rose looked up as Sam strode round the corner accompanied by a pale-faced Nicki O'Conner. Craig shuffled his chair back, attempting to stand. As he unbalanced and wobbled, Nicki rushed forward, settling him back into his seat.

"Thank you," said Craig. "I'm not sure if you remember me? I knew your parents when we were all in Kericho."

"Of course, Mr Hardie. You managed Msitu Tea Estate." Nicki tentatively pulled out a spare chair and perched on the edge. Her hands shook.

Craig covered one with his own. "How are you? I hear you're having a tough time."

Nicki covered Craig's hand with her free one. She trembled and tears started roll down her face. "It's been so hard but I've tried to cope. I took a tour manager's job even though I work most weekends and don't get to see the boys. It's not enough though, as my bills keep mounting." Nicki examined the table.

"Even so, stealing, and from your own clients, is not the answer." Craig was firm but gentle.

"I know." Nicki looked up. "It was just supposed to be the one time. I saw a pile of notes sitting on a chest of drawers. It was so easy to remove a few, and the client would never notice. Americans are confused by the huge piles of shillings they exchange their dollars for. After that it became easier to take a pair of shoes or a silver bracelet. I knew it was wrong, but the clients didn't miss the money, and they could claim the other items on insurance." Nicki gulped.

"But a phone and an iPad this weekend?" asked Rose.

Nicki released Craig's hands and turned to Rose. She wiped her nose on her sleeve and sniffed. "Yes, it's got out of hand. In a way it's a relief to be caught. What will happen to me now?"

Rose looked up at Sam standing beside Craig's chair. He shrugged. "I'm not sure," she said. "The police's priority is to arrest Davina Dijan's killer, but we're a long way from identifying who that is."

"That was on Friday evening, wasn't it?" Nicki sniffed again.

"Yes, she was stabbed in her room on the first floor of the east wing," said Rose.

Nicki chewed a nail. "I was on the first floor handing out itineraries, but the only person I saw was a young fair-haired mzungu."

"What time was that?" Rose leant forward.

Nicki rocked her head to the left. "I escorted my group to the restaurant, but I didn't join them. I checked the guests' rooms and left an itinerary in each."

She moved her head to the right. "I started on the ground floor, so when I saw him on the first floor it must have been about eight. He was standing by a wall light in the corridor and looked to be fiddling with it."

Rose slapped the table. "Thank you." She looked up at Craig. "You see? Patience and attention to detail will solve this case." She turned back to Nicki. "That's really helpful. I'm a step closer to solving the case." She sat up and looked at the others. "I need to return to the hotel. What about you, Sam?"

"I've some people to meet and things to do in Nanyuki this morning. Should Nicki come with you?" Sam asked.

Rose thought. "I think it best she keeps out of the commissioner's way at the moment. I suggest a meeting with Manager Bundi before the police."

"Nicki can keep me company this morning." Craig smiled

warmly. Slowly Nicki smiled back. "I shall enjoy catching up with news of your family and reminiscing about our days in Kericho."

Rose stood. "I shall prepare myself for the final round of this case to discover the murderer's identity."

CHAPTER FIFTY-SEVEN

Rose bashed the dashboard of her Defender with her fist, but the grills continued to blow out tepid air. She wound down the window, but the air outside was full of static. She looked towards the mountain as clouds gathered and knew Batian peak would soon be obscured. Rose tingled, feeling the charge in her own body. She sought the final clue, the spark to ignite the solution to the case.

Rose parked under the porticoed hotel entrance, handed her keys to a hotel valet lounging against the wall, and weaved through the busy reception area. All three desks were occupied by hotel staff booking in single people, couples and groups of guests. As Rose entered the main hotel area, she was confronted by Robert Dijan and an enormous bunch of flowers.

Robert spoke to the flowers. "What should I do with them?" He rubbed the back of his neck.

The flowers answered, "Ask Ms Wallace if she would like them to brighten up her book table."

Intrigued, Rose approached Robert. "Good morning. Lovely flowers."

Ethan's red-head appeared from behind the bunch. "I know, but it's rather embarrassing. Davina's half-brother sent them to wish Davina good luck at the summit and book launch. I don't think anyone's told him she's dead." Rose looked at Robert who seemed unsure what to do. He pulled at one shirt sleeve and then the other.

"Can I take them for you?" Rose asked. "I've met Ms Wallace. I'll see if I can find her, but if not, I'll ask one of the hotel staff to arrange them in a vase."

"That would be great." Ethan thrust the bunch into Rose's arms, smiling slowly in relief.

Rose noted yellow and red variegated roses, white lilies and red alstroemeria. "What lovely vibrant colours."

Ethan sighed. "It adds to the irony that Edwardo couldn't choose them. He's never seen a red rose in his life as he's colour-blind."

Rose felt her heart race. She nearly dropped the flowers.

"Are you OK?" Ethan asked.

"Yes, sorry. You said Edwardo was Davina's half-brother. Which parent did they have in common?"

Ethan shrugged. "Same mother, different father," said Robert.

"Of course," said Rose to herself. She believed she now knew the killer's identity.

CHAPTER FIFTY-EIGHT

Ethan placed an arm around Robert's shoulder and led him away like a lost child. Rose felt self-conscious standing by the hotel reception with a large bouquet of flowers.

A black Land Cruiser pulled up at the entrance door and three men and a woman climbed out. They were casually dressed, but clutched briefcases and carried bulging bags. They joined the melee in reception. Rose turned away from the entrance, her mind spinning. The intense aroma of lilies caused her further disorientation.

A wavy haired lady strode past. "Ms Wallace," called Rose. The woman turned towards her and frowned. "Ms Wallace. Robert Dijan asked me to give you these flowers. They were a gift for his wife, so he considered it most appropriate to display them alongside her books."

Ms Wallace's face lit up. "How wonderful and thoughtful." Rose was relieved to hand over the bouquet. "I'll organise a vase immediately."

One task completed, thought Rose. Now, the second, more difficult, one. She looked about, seeking inspiration for her next move. Along the corridor, past the entrance to the Bongo Bar, she thought she spotted Hugo and Thabiti entering the conference area. Impulsively, she followed them.

Tentatively, Rose pushed open one of the double doors to the conference hall and peered inside. Hugo and Thabiti stood beside their table at the back of the hall. There was less equipment on it, but still a number of wires and two black boxes, one with numerous dials.

Hugo looked up. "Hi, Rose, are you looking for Thabiti?"

Rose was unsure how to proceed, now that she was in the same room as Hugo. She had been hasty following him rather than waiting and looking for Commissioner Akida. "Thabiti, can I have a quick word?" she asked.

The two men spoke briefly to each other before Thabiti approached Rose. "I'll be back in two minutes, I just need to fetch another cable."

"But..." Rose started, but Thabiti had vanished. She felt a presence at her side and her mouth became dry. She turned to Hugo. "It doesn't matter." Her voice quivered. "I don't want to disturb you when you're busy. I'll find Thabiti later."

"I'll come with you." Hugo pushed through one of the doors, holding it open for Rose to follow.

"Thank you," she muttered.

"Not that way, Rose, through here." Hugo gestured towards a fire escape door. His eyes glinted and his body pulsated with energy. Rose dashed towards the door leading into the hotel, but Hugo was quicker. He stood in front of her. "Come, Rose, you and I need to have a chat in the grounds, away from onlookers."

Rose remembered Hugo's muscled physique as he gripped her arm and propelled her towards and through the fire door. He marched her round the side of the hotel and along a path which wound between lawns and flowerbeds.

They didn't stop until they reached the bench where she had met Joel. Bougainvillaea bushes screened them from potential rescuers. Only when Hugo had dragged Rose onto the bench beside him did he release his grip.

"What gave me away?" asked Hugo.

"Sorry. What do you mean?" Rose's voice was brittle.

"Come on." Hugo smiled. "You're oozing fear. The way you entered the conference room and your reaction towards me. You've never been uncomfortable in my presence before." His fingers wandered up the back of the bench.

"Hugo, why have you brought me here?" Rose gathered her strength, turning towards her abductor, her head held high.

"I think you're the only one who knows, who's worked it out, but I can't have you telling that pompous policeman." Hugo's voice was icy calm. Rose heard her heartbeat thumping in her ears as she realised Hugo meant to kill her, to silence her.

He was right. Although the police had Hugo on their suspect list, they didn't know about the colour blindness which linked Hugo to Davina and her family. Without that knowledge, they would never identify Hugo as Davina's murderer.

"Why so quiet?" Hugo touched Rose's arm. She flinched. "There's no need to be scared of me." Rose's skin felt clammy and her brain fast-forwarded through a slideshow in her mind. Enough!

"How did you find out Davina was your mother?" Rose asked. Her voice still shook.

"How did you?" Hugo countered. He leaned towards Rose and she felt his breath on her cheek.

Rose leant back away from Hugo. "Colour blindness." She kept her answer short, striving to maintain Hugo's interest. She needed time. Enough for someone to find them. Perhaps Joel would wander down. No, the lunch shift had started.

"My glasses." Hugo laughed. The image of a horror movie came to Rose as her captor laughed manically before the backdrop of a stormy sky. "I could have thumped Thabiti for his eagerness to show you, but still, I don't think my mother was colour-blind, so how did you know?"

"Women are usually carriers for the type of colour blindness you have. Red-Green isn't it?" Rose's hands gripped the front of the bench.

"Yes, so?" Hugo shrugged.

"But their male relatives, sons, fathers, brothers may develop the condition." She paused, continuing to lengthen the conversation.

Hugo drummed his fingers. "Davina's father died. She has a half-brother but he's in the UK."

"Today he sent flowers for Davina. Nobody told him she was dead."

"Get to the point. What have flowers to do with this?" The drumming intensified.

"Ethan, her husband's secretary, let slip that Davina's half-brother is colour-blind."

Hugo sat back. "Is he? I didn't know that. How very clever of you, Rose." He laughed again. "A simple flower nearly caused my downfall."

Afraid the conversation would end, Rose leant forward and asked, "How did you find out about Davina?"

"It was pure chance. I did get my birth certificate and looked for women possessing the same name as my birth mother, but it was a dead end. One day I was flipping through a magazine at the dentist and saw Davina's picture. She appeared to be looking straight out of the page at me. I scanned the article and stopped when I saw my mother's maiden name. From then it was just a matter of using Google to join the pixels. When my adoptive mother died, I decided to approach Davina, so I applied for a job in Nairobi. That gave me the money, contacts and, as it turned out, opportunity to meet her."

Hugo looked up at the darkening sky. "Thabiti will be wondering where I am. Sorry Rose, I have to get back, but I can't leave you here."

CHAPTER FIFTY-NINE

Hugo gripped Rose's arm again, but she used all her self-control to keep her body relaxed. She asked, "But why kill your mother?"

Her words seemed to press a buzzer as Hugo jumped up. He kicked the ground with his toe and roared. "So arrogant. So selfish. No remorse." Himself or Davina? Rose hoped someone had heard, but the wind was strengthening as the storm clouds gathered. The branches of the tree above them shook.

Rose took a deep breath and in a gentle voice she asked, "What happened?"

Hugo marched in front of the bench. "I discovered she was speaking at the conference and summit, so I asked for this assignment. I was worried another team would take over when my colleague was hospitalised, which is why I recruited Thabiti."

He stopped and addressed Rose. "I was so excited and proud. My mother, an authority on conservation, was addressing the packed conference room." He clasped his hands in front of him. "It all went wrong. She made the mistake, yet she was yelling at me as if it was all my fault. I was so disappointed. It felt as if someone had used a large nail to pop my balloon."

Hugo began pacing again. "In the relaxed atmosphere of the hotel and over sundowners with you, I calmed down. I thought giving the presentation must have stressed Davina out, and it was why she acted as she did. But in the restaurant, she was worse. Self-centred with no consideration for others."

"So you left the restaurant. Then you left the Bongo Bar, but you didn't go straight to your room, did you?" Rose said.

Hugo examined the Bougainvillea bush and snapped off a red flower. "No, I found my legs leading me towards Davina's room. I'd followed her after the morning conference session, wanting to confront her, but Gabe appeared and they entered her suite."

He stripped the petals from the flower. "There was nowhere to hide outside her room, so I removed some light bulbs, hoping to create some shadows in which to conceal myself. The lady looking after the American tourists might have seen me as she was skulking around in the corridor. I'm not sure what her game was." Hugo tossed the remains of the flower away.

"Nicki did see you, at least your features, but she didn't know who you were." Rose shifted her hands to the back of the bench.

"How do you know that? I checked. She left with the American party and it was clear she hadn't said anything to you." A tree leaf blew about in the wind.

"She's been returned to Nanyuki to help with another matter." Rose ran her fingers along the smooth edge of her seat.

"I was considering my next move when Davina's living room door opened. The red-haired man stepped out and walked away down the corridor without seeing me. I grabbed the door before it closed and went in to explore the suite. There were towels drying in the bathroom, so as the Dijans had already showered, the shower seemed as good a place to hide as any."

"Then it was a matter of waiting?" Rose asked.

"I sat on the ledge in the shower for a while, thinking about my childhood. I couldn't complain as my parents had been fair, even generous when they could afford to be. My bum became numb, so I walked around the bathroom. I had to dash back into the shower when I heard the Dijans return. After Davina washed her face, I opened the shower door, but I heard the steward speaking and boiling the kettle. Eventually, I peered out the bathroom door and saw Davina propped up on the bed reading."

"How did she react when she saw you?" The wind brushed Rose's hair and the temperature dropped another degree.

"She was surprised at first, but then indignant. She recognised me from the conference and scolded me for embarrassing her in front of her audience." Hugo spat out the last words.

"I'd hoped for a civilised reunion in which I could joyfully introduce myself. Instead I had to shout to make myself heard. My words finally silenced her." Hugo grinned as he began boring a hole in the ground with the toe of his trainer.

"You should have seen her jaw drop. 'What do you mean you're my son? I don't have any children.' 'But you had a baby boy, didn't you?' I responded. 'Did you care for and nurture him? Hold him when he fell over and grazed his knees? Soothe him when the other children bullied him because he couldn't name colours?'

She put her book down then and appeared interested in me for the first time. She asked if I was colour-blind. It felt like a sterile research enquiry. She didn't appear to care about me at all." Hugo screwed up his mouth and shook his head.

"I produced the small cutlery set which had been left with me as a baby. Just for an instant I thought I saw compassion, even sadness in her eyes, but they re-focused on me and hardened. I believe she made the decision to disown me all over again. She became cool, matter-of-fact, and said she was sorry I'd been led to believe she was my mother, but it wasn't true. She coldly told me her baby had died. Then she announced she was tired and dismissed me." Hugo sighed and sat on the bench.

"That was it," he said. "She showed not a gram of remorse or a tear of regret. I was dismissed. Something in my head snapped. I lunged at her with the little knife and struck her in the neck. I jumped back and for an instant our eyes locked. Then I ran. Through the door, down the stairs and out into the hotel gardens. I returned to my room through the back of the hotel about an hour later and slept deeply." Hugo looked up as the tree branches whipped the air.

"Next morning I realised what I'd done, but I was surprised how calm I felt. My mind moved forward to the week ahead and the summit. I had literally waited all my life to meet my mother and now I had, it was over and I could get on with my future. The moment I struck her replayed in my mind for a while but it doesn't anymore." Hugo sat back.

"Will you feel remorse about my death?" Rose felt cold.

Hugo considered her with his chin resting in his hand. "Perhaps. You're clearly a far better person than she was. Not so high profile, but I feel the community will grieve more over your death. But you're no baby elephant. The life of every matriarch eventually comes to an end."

CHAPTER SIXTY

In the distance, the angry sky thundered.

"Good," said Hugo. "Nobody will venture into the garden in this weather, and they won't hear you cry or scream, so don't bother."

Hugo's eyes were blank as he grabbed Rose. Partially unbalanced, she seized the wooden seat with one hand. Hugo tugged and Rose felt her grasp slipping. The wood was generally smooth, offering little grip. Rose winced as a splinter pierced her palm, but she refused to let go. Hugo gave a final tug on her free arm and her hand slipped over the bench. She fell to her knees, but Hugo continued unimpeded.

He dragged her down a small slope. Rose looked up and saw stone paving surrounding a small pond. Gathering her strength, she twisted onto her back, grabbing at her ensnared hand as she did. Silently she screamed. All that effort, but she had not managed to escape. Hugo grasped her free arm and pulled her backwards towards the pond.

"I suppose there's no point telling you this will be easier if you don't struggle, as you'll fight me anyway. You're stronger than you look."

With a quick movement, Hugo flipped Rose onto her front and knelt down with one knee pressed into the small of her back, pinning her to the ground. Rose's head smashed onto the stone lip of the pond. Blood seeped into her eye. She yanked one hand free, wiping her face. She thrust it towards Hugo, but he was waiting to capture it.

Rose heard him say in an amused tone, "Perfect. Now it'll look as if you tripped and hit your head, causing you to fall into the pond and drown."

Swiftly, he released the weight on her back. Rose tried to roll over again, but he grabbed her waist and hoisted her forward. Her head landed in the water. Writhing, she fought to lift it out. Her eyes scanned the water's surface. An ibis pulled its long pointed beak from the water and lifted its dark grey body in fright, flying upwards to the call of 'hadada.'

This is my end, thought Rose, as her face was forced into the water. Shutting her eyes and holding her breath, she jerked her head, but it remained submerged. She gyrated her whole body, but it was trapped. Still, she forced her legs to kick back at the weight holding her down. Twisting her arms to loosen her grip. Rolling her body to dislodge her captor. All useless.

A fire ignited inside her chest. She had to quench it. Water. Air. A deep, deep breath. No air. Another breath. Her head spun. She convulsed, unsure which way was up or down or round and round. The pressure was greater. Her head would pop. A breath. She seemed to be floating over the surface of the water.

CHAPTER SIXTY-ONE

Rose thought she'd opened her eyes, but all she saw was angry blackness. Her insides heaved and she was yanked onto her side as she retched, loudly and uncaring. Rolling back, she screwed her eyes against the blistering pain inside her throat and stomach. She turned her head and coughed. Hands gently but forcefully propelled her into a sitting position. Still, she gagged and a hand patted her on the back.

"Mama Rose. How can I help?" Thabiti's voice. She waved her arm at him before using it to cover her mouth as she bent over coughing. Finally she drew breath and lay back down on the cool grass. She felt water on her face. Panicking, she opened her eyes as heavy raindrops pounded her body. Thabiti helped her sit up again and held her. She felt a calmness spread through her body.

"No you don't." Rose heard Chris's voice and looked up. He propelled an irate Hugo in front of him. Hugo writhed and twisted, attempting to escape Chris's grip. Rose realised how strong her son must be to restrain Hugo. "Thabiti! Your belt. Quickly, before I lose him again."

Thabiti gently relinquished his hold on Rose and stood to remove his beaded leather belt. The two men fought Hugo until they secured his hands behind his back. All three were dripping from every angle of their clothes and bodies as the rain drenched them.

Hugo attempted to escape up the slope, but his feet slid underneath him and he crashed to the floor. Whether it knocked the wind from his lungs, or the will from his mind, Rose was uncertain, but he lay still. Hugo no longer fought Chris when he hauled him back to his feet. "Inside, everyone. Before we catch our death out here in this storm," said Chris.

Thabiti supported Rose as she slipped up the bank to firmer footing on the gravel path. Chris did the same for the unresponsive Hugo.

"Quick, quick," they heard Chloe call. The rain distorted Rose's vision, but she made out a figure dancing by the glass door to the Bongo Bar. Chloe grabbed Rose from Thabiti and propelled her through the bar, down the corridor and into a disabled toilet. Several towels backed with striped kikoi cotton were strewn across the floor.

Chloe peeled Rose's shirt from her body and tugged it free of her arms. She rubbed vigorously with a towel before draping Rose in a large grey-T shirt. Next, Chloe pushed Rose onto the closed toilet seat, wrestling her trousers off before rubbing her legs. Rose was pulled to her feet and handed a spare towel to wrap around her waist. Finally catching her breath, and standing in a puddle of water,

Rose said, "Thank you, Chloe, very efficient." It was all she could think to say.

"I'll clear up in a minute." Rose stepped over her saturated clothes into a pair of soft white flip-flop slippers with the hotel's elephant crest staring back at her.

Chloe said, "What you need is a steaming cup of tea."

CHAPTER SIXTY-TWO

Rose sat alone in the Bongo Bar, dishevelled and shivering, but safe. Outside, thunder rolled around the hotel and occasionally the sky lit up with a streak of lightning. Rose clasped her hands around her cup of Kericho gold tea and sipped appreciatively.

As well as her makeshift kikoi towel skirt and over-sized T-shirt, the waiter had wrapped a shuka around her shoulders. She had hoped Kenneth would be on duty, but when she asked the bar man, he averted his gaze, ignoring her question. Strange. Rose would speak to Manager Bundi later… or tomorrow.

A chattering group entered the bar. Rose looked around, realising how busy the room actually was. It must be nearly lunchtime, and the new guests who'd checked in this morning would be hungry.

She rested her hand on the table and winced. Lifting it, she spotted a small purple bruise with a red centre. She felt a small slither of wood protruding from it and tried to latch onto it with her teeth but failed. Chloe sat down beside her and took her hand.

"Nasty. I should have tweezers in my bag if I can remember where I left it," Chloe said. She stood as the bar man waved a kanga-trimmed reed basket. Returning with it, Chloe rummaged through a small tan-coloured bag.

"Chloe, I haven't thanked you properly for helping me or for providing my new outfit." Rose looked down at herself and grinned.

Chloe laughed. "You do look quite a sight. I think the other hotel guests are used to improvised kikoi skirts and shuka wraps at the beach, not in upcountry hotels." Chloe found a pair of stainless steel tweezers in her bag. "OK, let me see if I can remove that nasty splinter."

She held Rose's hand, palm upwards under a ceiling spotlight and began her work. The end of the splinter came away, but Chloe was not satisfied and she continued probing.

"There she is. That's the woman."

Rose looked over Chloe's shoulder. Manager Bundi stood beside a plump African woman, wearing a hotel shirt, who glared and pointed at her. Rose caught the manager's eyes, which widened. He strode towards her.

"Nearly there," the bent figure of Chloe said. Pain shot through Rose's hand. Her reflex action was to pull it away, but Chloe held firm.

"This woman is wearing the T-shirt and one of the towels." The plump lady turned to Manager Bundi, her double chin and ample chest thrust forward.

The manager shuffled back a step. "I'm sure there's a reasonable explanation?"

Chloe placed Rose's hand on the table. She lifted her head in satisfaction, holding aloft her tweezers which clasped a small splinter of wood. "All done," she said to Rose.

Aware they had company, Chloe turned to the plump lady. "Hi, I'm so sorry to run out on you earlier, but I had to help Mama Rose. She was saturated and we don't want her catching pneumonia, do we?" Chloe smiled widely. "Did you prepare my bill?" She rested her head on her shoulder.

"See," said Manager Bundi, wringing his hands. "Just a misunderstanding." He bowed to Chloe and dragged the plump lady away, but she turned her head and glared at Chloe.

"How to win friends and influence people," commented Rose.

Chloe laughed. "I can't blame the woman. I rushed into her little shop next to reception, grabbed a handful of towels and the T-shirt you're wearing and raced out. I heard her shout at me as I locked myself into the disabled toilet. The slippers I found down here, so I hope they're OK?"

"Everything's fine," said Rose. "Although my neck is itching." Chloe pulled the shuka aside and peered at Rose's neck.

"Oops, it's the T-shirt's price tag." Chloe tugged firmly and removed the plastic ends.

"Ma," Chris rushed forward and knelt in front of Rose. "What were you thinking?" He hugged her.

Rose sidestepped the question. "How did you find me?" she asked.

"You disappeared!" Thabiti joined the group. "I returned to the conference room, but you and Hugo had vanished. I couldn't understand it as I was only away a few minutes and I hadn't met you walking along the corridor."

Thabiti sat on a stool. "I noticed the fire door was ajar, but there was no sign of you outside. I retraced my steps back into the hotel which was when I spotted Chris." Thabiti gestured to Chris who took up the story.

"Thabiti grabbed me and began babbling about how you'd been abducted by Hugo, that he couldn't find you and it was all his fault for leaving you. When I finally calmed him down we returned to the conference room. I agreed you'd probably left though the fire escape door so we started our search outside, first in the hotel yard and then in the garden. But the grounds are huge and we weren't sure where to look."

"I spotted an ibis take flight," Thabiti said raising his chin.

"With no other options, we raced through the grounds

towards its take-off point... and found Hugo forcing your head into a pond." Chris cleared his throat noisily and wiped an eye with his finger.

Thabiti continued excitedly, "Chris shoulder-barged him out of the way, and I grabbed you before you fell into the pond. I was scared stiff. Your face was white and I couldn't tell if you were breathing. It was a huge relief when you opened your eyes."

"And Hugo?" Rose asked.

"He kicked me in the shoulder attempting to escape," said Chris. "I grabbed his legs and hauled him back. He was... manic."

Chloe shook her head. "I don't understand. Hugo seemed a pleasant lad. Are you saying he murdered Davina and was attempting to kill you?" She addressed Rose.

Rose shivered. "I think I need a hot shower and some presentable clothes, not that these haven't done the job." She patted Chloe's leg, but avoided her eyes.

Thabiti sniffed the air. "I'm hungry, it must be lunchtime." He spotted a waiter carrying a burger and sandwich.

"Nothing new there, but can someone explain what is going on?" said Chloe.

"That's something I'd like to know as well." Commissioner Akida loomed over the table.

CHAPTER SIXTY-THREE

R ose was seated next to Commissioner Akida on the restaurant terrace. Constable Wachira sat beside him, and Thabiti and Chris were opposite.

Chloe strode across the terrace and joined them. "You look more comfortable, Rose. Your old self." Rose had soaked herself under the shower, seeking to eliminate any lingering fear of water on her face. It hadn't really worked and she suspected she would be plagued with nightmares of drowning.

She felt far happier and more comfortable in a fresh pair of trousers and a blue striped blouse. She was grateful to Manager Bundi for allowing her to keep the cottage and she was relieved she'd left her bag of clothes in it.

"Before we get into complicated explanations, can we choose our starters from the buffet?" asked Thabiti.

Rose smiled. "Of course, Thabiti, off you go."

"Ma, can I fetch you something?" Chris asked.

Rose was about to protest, but realising she didn't have the energy to leave her seat, she accepted her son's kind offer. "A small bowl of soup and a roll would be lovely." She smiled at Chris. A waiter took their drinks orders and Chloe insisted on buying a bottle of something sparkling to celebrate Rose's survival.

The commissioner waited for Thabiti to return. He approached the table with a plate piled with food. "Have you gone straight to main course?" Chloe asked.

"No, this is my starter," he mumbled through a half-chewed bread roll.

Commissioner Akida cleared his throat. "Now we are all here." He looked across at Thabiti, who raised his eyebrows. "Perhaps Mama Rose could explain what has been happening this morning and why she believes Hugo killed Davina Dijan?"

Rose buttered her roll. She needed time to gather her strength and her thoughts. "The two main issues with this case have been access to the scene and motive. The lift engineers were sure they spotted a mzungu leave Davina's bedroom. This meant our prime suspects, Robert Dijan and Kenneth, the steward, could not be the culprits."

The waiter appeared with their drinks. Dramatically, he uncorked the prosecco, pouring glasses for the ladies, the men preferring beer.

Rose also asked him to pour her a glass of water, which she sipped before continuing. "At this point, Constable Wachira and I reassessed the case. I thought there were three possible suspects: Freddie the journalist and jilted lover; Gabriel the aggrieved research assistant, who'd been erased from Davina's book deal; and Hugo, because he and the other two were of an age to be Davina's illegitimate son."

Chloe spluttered into her prosecco. "Rewind. What illegitimate son?"

"Constable Wachira?" Rose looked at the young policewoman, who put down her fork and explained.

"The pathologist told us Mrs Dijan had given birth. There was no record of a child with either husband, so we presumed it happened when she was younger, before she was married. All three men were in the right age bracket to be that child." Constable Wachira looked back at Rose, who'd managed to eat some soup.

"In Davina's new book, we discovered a photo of a young Davina looking very comfortable with Freddie's father. I thought it a strong possibility he could have fathered her child. It would rule out Freddie as the son, but give him a strong motive." Rose bit into her buttered bread roll.

Chloe frowned. "You said Freddie was the jilted lover. But his father had an affair with Davina years ago. Father and son. Wow!"

"Exactly," said Rose. "But a witness this morning told me they'd seen a light-haired man in the corridor, which ruled out Freddie."

Constable Wachira leaned towards Rose. "I didn't know that."

"Sorry, I know I should have told you, and what I discovered next, rather than going after Hugo myself." Rose smiled apologetically.

"I still don't understand how you determined Hugo was guilty," said the commissioner.

"I learnt, thanks to Thabiti, that Hugo was red-green colour blind. It's a genetic condition which a mother carries, but rarely suffers from, and which she can pass to her son. Today Davina received a beautiful bouquet of flowers from her half-brother, on her mother's side. Robert Dijan's secretary joked the brother was colour-blind and the final piece of the puzzle clicked into place."

Rose drank more water. "I think I would have come and told you, Constable, but I saw Hugo and Thabiti in the corridor and I felt compelled to follow them."

Thabiti looked dejected. "So when Hugo asked me to fetch a wire, it was just an excuse to get rid of me."

"I think so," agreed Rose. "We all thought Hugo pleasant and harmless, but I had noticed how strong he was after you and he went for your bike ride, Thabiti. I also saw him practising some martial art in the garden. I guess he used it to keep himself grounded and his anger in check. As Chris and Thabiti witnessed, when unleashed, he became deranged."

"Did he admit to murdering Davina?" the commissioner asked.

"Yes, he'd discovered she was his birth mother. I believe he placed her on such a high pedestal that the real article was a disappointment, particularly after her petulant behaviour on Friday. When he told her he was her son, she dismissed him. He believed she was abandoning him all over again, which was his breaking point. His suppressed rage bubbled up and he stabbed her and fled. As we know, if she hadn't removed the knife, she'd probably have survived."

"And he was attempting to kill you?" the commissioner frowned.

"To keep me quiet. He guessed correctly I was the only one who knew he was the murderer. But I think he developed a taste for killing and would have eliminated anyone who got in his way. He was unable to control his rage after being rejected a second time."

CHAPTER SIXTY-FOUR

Rose felt some strength returning to her body as she looked out of the window of the Bongo Bar at the sodden grounds. She had finished her soup and explanation of the morning's events and picked away at a chicken salad whilst her companions engaged in lively discussions.

Although she felt exhausted, and wanted nothing more than to lie down and sleep, she knew she had some loose ends to tie up, and time was pressing.

Commissioner Akida and Constable Wachira had returned to Nanyuki police station to question Hugo. He had been escorted earlier by a burley policewoman and her colleague who the commissioner had summoned.

Chloe, Thabiti and Chris had been summoned to a pre-summit meeting. Rose sipped yet another cup of Kericho Gold tea as she considered her next move. The decision was made for her as Sam and Nicki entered the bar.

"Rose, are you OK?" Nicki rushed to Rose's side, sitting on an empty chair. Sam loomed over them.

"Fine now, but it was rather frightening at the time. I was very lucky Chris and Thabiti found me in time," Rose said. She looked up at Sam. "Did Constable Wachira call you?"

The big man nodded. "She also told me she and the

commissioner were returning to Nanyuki, so I thought it safe to bring Nicki with me to the hotel."

Rose heard a buzzing noise. Sam pulled a mobile phone from his trouser pocket and answered it. "Ladies, I'm needed," he said and left.

"What now?" asked Nicki, biting her nail.

"A visit to Manager Bundi's office. Let's get it over and done with, or I'll find I've sat here all afternoon," answered Rose.

As they left the Bongo Bar, Manager Bundi scuttled past them. Rose called out, but he continued without hearing her. They found him in his office searching under a mound of paper. "Where did I put it?"

Rose knocked on the partially open door. "Manager Bundi, may we have a word?"

The rotund man looked up, clutching a bunch of papers. "If you must know, now's not a great time. Kenneth's walked out. He's cleared his room and vanished with his son." Rose pursed her lips. Had Chris anything to do with Kenneth's vanishing act?

Rose opened the door for Nicki, but paused, watching her. Nicki's eyes opened questioningly. "I might have a remedy for you. One that may provide a solution to our other business," she told Manager Bundi.

"Really?" The busy man looked up again.

"Yes, Nicki here could step in for Kenneth." The chubby man wiped his forehead and sat behind his desk. Rose and Nicki dragged chairs in front of it and sat down.

Rose nudged Nicki. "Yes, that's right, I'd be happy to help out. There are no American tours this weekend because of the summit." She looked down. "I doubt there'll be any more tours for me."

The manager's eyes narrowed. "Why? What's happened?"

Nicki continued to examine the cracked linoleum floor. Rose took a deep breath. "Nicki is very sorry, she knows it was wrong, but she was desperate. She's the one whose been stealing from the Americans whilst they've stayed here."

Manager Bundi spluttered, but Rose ploughed on. "I could hand her over to the police, but I'm sure you'll agree it won't do much good, and it's more likely to harm the hotel's reputation. There'll be a public investigation, a high-profile court case, and the police and legal system will make the hotel pay all the costs. I can't see anyone gaining if Nicki is handed over."

Manager Bundi leaned back. "I understand they are busy with Davina Dijan's killer and that you triggered this morning's events." He raised his hands in front of him, tapping the ends of his fingers together. "I owe you, Mama Rose. Thanks to you, the summit's going ahead, but it's why I'm in such a panic now. I have to send mountains of forms, schedules and planning information."

Rose and Nicki remained silent.

"I agree." Manager Bundi sat up. "No good will come from handing Nicki to the police and I need an experienced pair of hands. Mind you, the merest whiff of anything missing and I'll drive you to the police station myself."

Nicki slumped in her chair. "Thank you."

"Don't thank me yet, you will be working long and hard over the next few days. It's going to be exhausting." He opened a drawer, removing an envelope and from it two plastic keycards. Holding them in front of Nicki he said, "These are for the east wing, ground and first floors. You will be in charge of both for the next week."

Rose refrained from mentioning Nicki already had a keycard to the first floor. Manager Bundi continued. "Come with me. I'll explain your duties."

The dumpy hotel manager departed swiftly. After giving Rose a brief hug, Nicki ran to catch him up. Rose left the office, closed the door behind her and leant against it. Her next discussion would need to be more delicate.

CHAPTER SIXTY-FIVE

Rose was surprised to discover Robert and Ethan had been given a cottage near her own after Davina's death. She declined the golf cart driver's offer of a lift, deciding to walk to their cottage to clear her head and stimulate her body.

The morning's rain had been ferocious rather than cleansing. It had bounced off surfaces, cascaded down inclines in rivulets and gouged out the earth, leaving behind muddy channels.

Rose stepped over a makeshift stream as she approached the cottage. Robert answered the door. His damp hair indicated he had recently freshened up, and his vibrancy, missing for the past few days, shone through.

"Rose, isn't it? I'm so pleased you've found us so I can thank you in person. Come in." His smile was modest but warm.

The cottage was larger than Rose's, with two bedrooms leading from the living room. She spotted Ethan packing a suitcase in one. Robert called through to him.

Rose sat in the indicated chair, whilst Robert lounged on the sofa, his arm wrapped over the back. Ethan appeared less relaxed perched next to Robert.

"Again, thank you, Rose, for identifying my wife's killer and I'm so sorry it caused you much personal pain and distress. I don't think the police would have reached the same conclusion, not for a while at least. Why did you suspect Hugo?"

Rose explained about Davina's missing child, the flowers and colour blindness.

Robert scratched his chin. "So Hugo really is Davina's son?"

"It appears so," said Rose.

"And he felt abandoned by her, cheated?" said Robert. "He's not the first. Many people, myself included, realised too late that we were merely a means to Davina's personal ends."

He sighed. "Don't get me wrong. She was magnetic and achieved considerable success with the conservancy, with conservation in general, but at the expense of people and their feelings." Robert stared into the corner of the room.

"And what of your feelings?" Rose opened her hands to both men. Ethan glanced sharply back at Robert who smiled slowly and languidly.

"I see nothing gets past you." Robert placed his hand on Ethan's leg. "I haven't always been aware of my true feelings. Too busy with my work, I guess. Then Davina swept me away with her passion and energy and we married. But she got bored and went in search of new conquests. I was lost. Ethan had recently joined the company, and he was so empathetic and understanding. I came to rely on him, first as my secretary, and secondly as my confidant... and lover. Is that so terrible?"

"Not to me. I don't like to judge others, especially those who are not harming other people, but your relationship is illegal under Kenyan law. You need to be careful." Rose walked to the door. "I wish you happiness together in the future." The two men stood with arms wrapped around each other.

"If you ever need anything… just call." Robert held out a simple white business card. "My personal contact details."

Rose took the card. "Thank you. I might just take you up on that."

CHAPTER SIXTY-SIX

Rose fought her way through a group of guests disembarking from a bus at the hotel entrance. She strode through the reception and spotted Chris conferring with a group of people which included a man carrying a large TV camera and another holding a sound boom. She hovered until Chris spotted her. He excused himself and walked over.

"Mum! Are you OK? I'm in the middle of something right now." He glanced back at his colleagues.

"Did you warn Kenneth?" she asked.

He looked like the small boy she'd scolded for climbing trees to steal honey out of their neighbours' suspended beehives. He drew his shoulders up, tucked in his elbows and stared at the floor.

"Well?"

Chris's shoulders slumped. "Corporal Magori's a good man and Darren's his whole life. He'll care for the boy way better than the boy's mother. If Kenneth was caught, not only would he be sent to jail, but he'd lose his son and miss him growing up. He would do anything for that boy."

"It's not the point. What he's doing is illegal and the commissioner knows. After the summit, he'll realise Kenneth has vanished and start searching for him. No doubt he'll want to speak to me."

"Well, I'll be long gone, so blame me if you have to," said Chris.

Rose felt a breath catch in her throat. She managed to whisper, "You're leaving so soon? I hoped you might stay on for a week or so."

"Sorry, not this time. I've another contract starting on Wednesday which I've to prepare for."

"Will we see you before you go? You have to clear things up with your father," Rose implored. A shadow passed over Chris's eyes.

"I'll see. I'm tied up until Saturday morning. Now I must go." He pecked Rose on the cheek and re-joined the group of people as they ambled towards the conference room. Rose felt tired and alone. Her phone rang in her pocket.

"Dr Farrukh?"

Rose dashed through reception, barging guests out of the way. She jumped on a waiting golf cart beside the driver just as a tall African man was about to deposit a large suitcase.

"Cottage 25. Be quick," she instructed at the driver. "Sorry," she shouted back at the disgruntled man who'd dropped his case.

Rose asked the driver to wait as she raced into the cottage. She threw her clothes and toiletries into her overnight bag, grabbed her car keys from the bedside table and hoisted her tote bag over her shoulder. At reception she handed her keys to a valet. She cut off a new guest as he asked for a morning wake-up call and said to the receptionist. "Tell Manager Bundi I had to leave. It's an emergency."

Rose sped down the hill in her Defender, away from the Mount Kenya Resort and Spa towards home.

CHAPTER SIXTY-SEVEN

When Rose arrived home, a hysterical Kipto dashed out of the kitchen door, throwing herself at Rose.

"Mama, quick quick." Rose's heart slammed into her chest as she was swept into the bedroom where she froze. The scene was calm. Craig lay on the bed whilst Samwell, who helped Rose with her animals, gently rearranged his bedding.

Dr Farrukh—the female side of the marriage and the Doctors Farrukh business partnership—wore a stethoscope. She wrapped a large blue Velcro cuff above Craig's elbow under which she secured the end of the stethoscope. Lifting a stopwatch in one hand, she pumped a rubber ball, attached to a tube, in the other. Rose watched as Craig's blood pressure was assessed.

Dr Farrukh undid the cuff and removed the stethoscope's ear tips. "One hundred and forty-five over ninety-five. Your blood pressure is high. It could be a contributory factor or your body's response to the incident. I will need to check it again tomorrow. For now, rest."

Samwell bent over Craig, helping him get comfortable. Rose thought Craig whispered something to Samwell before he left the room. She sat on the side of the bed as the doctor packed her bag. Clasping Craig's hand, she said, "I'm back. So sorry I wasn't here for you earlier."

Craig looked back lovingly and croaked. "Sorry to be so much trouble, old bean." He leaned back and closed his eyes as Samwell returned with a glass of water.

Out on the patio, Kipto fussed with tea. She'd even produced a packet of stale digestive biscuits.

"What happened, doctor? How bad is he?" Rose asked.

Doctor Farrukh stirred her tea slowly. "He's lucky, it was a warning. If his high blood pressure persists, together with his polio complications, he's a target for a full-blown stroke."

Rose rubbed her neck. "What was it this time?"

"It's commonly known as a mini-stroke. Similar signs to a full stroke, but milder. A temporary interruption of blood supply to the brain. Your man Samwell was solid. Apparently, the house girl found Craig slumped to one side in his chair. His speech was slurred and confused. She panicked, but did have the presence of mind to find the number for the Cottage Hospital."

"Good. It's written clearly at the top of the kanga chalk board by the kitchen door," said Rose.

"I came straight over. Samwell was instructed over the phone by my registrar. He made Craig comfortable and gave him some aspirin. He helped prevent it escalating into a full blown stroke," Dr Farrukh told Rose.

"So what now?" she asked.

"Rest and a course of aspirin. If his blood pressure does not improve, he needs to take beta blockers. I can't prescribe daily exercise, as the secondary polio complications restrict his movement."

"And cause pain, though he refuses to admit it." Rose pursed her lips.

Dr Farrukh stood. "I don't see any point admitting him to the hospital if you can cope with him at home. Samwell seems a good man, not the brightest, but diligent and strong. If he can help Craig wash, dress and sit out here on the patio in the fresh air, it will do far more good than him being bed bound in a hospital ward. I'll check on him in the morning."

Dr Farrukh's phone alerted her to another patient requiring urgent attention. After she left, Rose looked in on Craig, who was either asleep or resting peacefully, with Samwell silent beside him. Rose didn't disturb either of them.

She ran a bath in the guest cottage where she decided she would sleep for the time being, so as not to disturb Craig. She even added some bubble bath from a small faded bottle collected from a hotel or lodge some time past. She allowed the water to lap over her exhausted body. Life was never simple. As soon as one issue was dealt with, another erupted.

This was the beginning of the end for Craig, she admitted to herself. It might be years—she hoped it would be—or months. Whichever it was, she would have to balance her veterinarian duties with spending time at home with Craig. They must enjoy whatever time was left together.

Samwell was a surprise. If he could manoeuvre Craig, she might be able to take them out in Craig's old Subaru. They could visit old friends and have picnics at their favourite places. The thought cheered Rose.

CHAPTER SIXTY-EIGHT

Rose ate breakfast alone out on the patio on Wednesday morning. She had not slept well. Nightmares of Craig's face trapped under water haunted her.

So did the return of the screaming woman, though the voice no longer had an echo quality to it. There was substance to the voice, and to the woman, which Rose recognised but could not place. She felt the woman to be strong and courageous, but terrified.

Dr Farrukh strode round the corner of the house, her ear pressed to her mobile phone. She listened for a minute then said, "I'll be with you shortly." Barely taking a breath, she addressed Rose. "How is our patient this morning?" The doctor placed her medical bag on the floor.

"Surprisingly bright, but I'd expect nothing less. He'll hide any pain or discomfort from me as long as possible," said Rose.

Dr Farrukh assessed Rose and tilted her head. "I expect you would do the same should the situation be reversed. What has he had to eat or drink?"

"Only water yesterday." Rose gestured for Dr Farrukh to sit, but she shook her head. "Tea with some honey and mashed banana on toast this morning."

Dr Farrukh lifted her chin and smiled. "Excellent. I shall check on him now." The doctor picked up her bag and entered the house. She did not invite Rose to join her and Rose felt it best to give the doctor and Craig space and privacy. That's what she would want in these circumstances.

A deep cough startled Rose, and she jumped out of her introspection. "Commissioner Akida!"

"Habari, Mama Rose." The commissioner's voice was hearty and bright, but his smile distorted to a frown as he examined Rose. "I take it all is not good with you this morning." He pulled out a chair and sat across the table from her.

Rose felt cold and wrapped her hands around her cup. "Sorry, Commissioner. I'm not great company today."

The commissioner stilled. "Where is Craig?"

"In bed."

He audibly released a breath and reached for the tin of instant coffee and flask of hot water. He busied himself making coffee.

"Craig suffered a minor stroke yesterday. The doctor's here checking on him." On cue, Dr Farrukh stepped onto the patio.

She nodded curtly to the commissioner and addressed Rose. "His colour has returned. His heart and chest are fine, but his blood pressure remains high so I have prescribed beta blockers. If he feels up to it, I recommend he sit out here for an hour this afternoon. I'm an advocate for fresh air wherever possible. I'll check on him again tomorrow."

The doctor left. Rose reached for the hot water and noticed her hand trembling.

"Is that good news?" the commissioner asked, rubbing his jaw.

Rose took a long deep breath and looked directly at the commissioner. "Yes. It's just the realisation that Craig's days are numbered." She sipped her tea and the commissioner waited. "Still, he's reached seventy, which is an achievement.

We've been through the good and the bad, the hard years and moments of pure joy."

Rose shook herself. Now was not the time to slip into self-absorption. After another sip of tea, she once again looked at the commissioner and asked, "What news do you bring?"

"Hugo admitted killing his mother. He told us it wasn't planned, but a terrible rage overwhelmed him and he acted without fully realising what he was doing."

"Do you believe him?" Rose asked.

"I'm not sure. But his attempt to kill you was not an act of rage. It appears calculated once he realised what you knew. He reminds me of a spotted hyena. Many people incorrectly believe they are scavengers when they are really skilled predators. Once they target their prey, they stalk, kill and completely consume it."

Rose shivered. "Hugo seemed so pleasant. He helped Thabiti."

"You were the one who pointed out his immense self-control. Actually, he needed Thabiti's help to remain working at the conference and summit."

The commissioner leaned back and looked out over the garden to the mountain. "I expect it will soon be out of my hands. I believe Hugo will use temporary insanity as his defence. Being a British citizen, it will be easier to send him back to the UK for 'treatment' rather than pay for a potentially expensive trial. I doubt Robert Dijan will object. It would suit me."

"I think you're right," said Rose. "Robert Dijan is unlikely to pay towards any investigation or court fees. I think he views Hugo as someone else Davina let down. As her son, the primary person. Poor Hugo."

"Mama Rose. You always seem to have sympathy for the criminals you catch." The commissioner drained his coffee. He picked up the instant coffee tin, but replaced it.

"They are worthy of our sympathy. Aisha's killer's actions were rooted in a childhood misunderstanding. Hugo's through a sense of rejection. No mother should treat her son like that. There is something I read that an Italian footballer said. Mario Balotelli. He'd been fostered at a young age. Yes, I remember. 'They say abandonment is a wound that never heals. I say only that an abandoned child never forgets.'"

CHAPTER SIXTY-NINE

The next few days were quiet for Rose. She attended a lame horse from whose foot she extracted a small nail. She left the owner instructions to draw out infection by placing the horse's foot in a tub of hot water, containing Epsom salts, twice a day for fifteen to twenty minutes.

The water would soften the foot, encouraging any abscesses to burst, whilst the Epsom salt drew out infected pus.

She had the privilege of massaging a cow's rectum to stimulate its uterus. The action worked, as the heifer expelled the retained placenta it had carried around for three days.

Dr Emma also asked her to assist with the extraction of a pug's infected tooth. She didn't believe Dr Lucy needed her help, but that it was her way of checking up on Rose's well-being.

Rose was pleased to leave the house and help her colleague. She also did a spot of shopping in town, but met few people she knew. Apparently, most farmers were staying at home, expecting Nanyuki to be busy during the summit.

Thabiti sent WhatsApp messages, including a photograph of Elizabeth Hurley at Ol Pejeta Conservancy meeting Ringo, a six-month-old white Rhino. Thabiti appeared quite taken with the British actress. He said the summit was a huge success.

There had been speeches by the Presidents of Gabon, Uganda and Kenya. Heather Higginbottom, American Deputy Head of State, delivered a message from President Obama. Rose hoped success translated into action to stop poaching and re-establish elephant populations.

Dr Farrukh returned every day and appeared satisfied, but not delighted, with Craig's recovery. His appetite was returning, together with some of his strength, but his blood pressure remained high. Samwell helped Craig out of bed and to his chair in the living room, where he enjoyed watching horse racing from South Africa, or to join Rose on the patio. She wrote out his crossword answers though doubted her spelling was correct. Still, it was a great way to maintain Craig's brain activity.

Today was Saturday. Rose lounged on her oversized cedar sofa on the patio. Thabiti had called to say he'd finished at the summit. He would join her and Craig to watch TV coverage of President Kenyatta setting fire to a hundred and five tons of ivory. She knew Craig would be grateful for company other than hers. He'd enjoyed Thabiti's regular morning visits before the conference, and Thabiti could talk him through the summit. Rose had not told Thabiti about Craig's stroke.

There was still a hollow feeling inside Rose. Chris had not called or messaged her. She wondered if she should try to contact him about his father's illness, but had no idea when he was due to fly home. Their relationship was still fragile. She hoped he would want to visit his ill father, but was worried about disturbing him or upsetting his plans. She bit at a jagged fingernail.

A white bundle of fluff sped around the corner, signalling Thabiti's arrival. Pixel, Thabiti's rescue dog, resembled a miniature sheep. She jumped onto the sofa, attempting to lick Rose's face. Rose sat up. "Well done, Pixel. You've finally managed to jump onto the sofa, but you don't get to lick me as a reward." Rose's terrier, Potto, who also tried to lick Rose's face, had taken to sleeping on Craig's bed, either as company or to keep a watchful eye over him.

An unseen Thabiti called "Pixel" and the fluffy dog sped back round the corner. She soon returned, accompanied not only by Thabiti, but also by Chris. Rose stood, swaying.

Chris rushed over. "Mum. You OK?"

They sat together on the sofa, whilst Thabiti entered the house.

"I'm so relived you've come. I wasn't sure if I should try to find you or if you had already left. Your father's not well. He had a mini-stroke on Tuesday."

"Oh, Mum." Chris wrapped his arms around Rose. She felt his strength as her own crumbled, and she started sobbing. Chris just held her. After several minutes, the tears receded, leaving Rose weary but cleansed. The pressure of the past week had built up like a large boil inside her, which had burst, releasing a torrent of frustration and worry.

Thabiti stuck his head round the living room door and quietly asked Chris to join him. Rose hugged her knees for reassurance. She watched a group of small red-cheeked cordon-bleu birds swirl around her stone bird table before landing. They pecked at the remains of toast and fruit Kipto had put out from breakfast.

Mount Kenya rose majestically. Looking upon its snow-topped peak, glimmering in the morning sunshine, Rose felt refreshed and invigorated. There was something about the mountain, its solidness, permanency and man's dependency upon it. The mountain brought water, which in turn bred life. To die under the watchful gaze of the mountain; there could be worse endings.

"Mama Rose," Thabiti called. "It's starting."

Sighing, Rose left the peace and serenity of the natural world to witness its destruction on the TV. She sat on a dining room chair next to Craig, taking his hand. The landmark burning of huge amounts of confiscated elephant tusks and rhino horns was a monumental event. The spokesman told them there were eleven pyres. To Rose, it represented mounds of dead animals lying in the muddy earth.

"I hope they can start the fires. It looks rather damp in Nairobi," said Thabiti.

"There was a lot of excitement at the summit about this final event," said Chris. "It sends a strong message against the illegal trade in wildlife, highlighting that animals are worth more alive than dead. Personally, I think retaining the ivory in a museum for all to see is more of a statement than a grand burning."

"I agree," said Rose. "I've seen photos of the giant elephant statue in Botswana, though the ivory used is from animals that died of natural causes."

"I understand President Khama of Botswana boycotted the summit this week because he did not believe the ivory should be destroyed," said Chris.

"Ivory destroyed or exhibited. It doesn't detract from the summit's aim to create a plan to preserve the future of elephants and their environments," said Craig.

Thabiti remained with Craig, watching and listening to the commentary from the event in Nairobi. Chris and Rose returned to the patio. Kipto brought fresh tea and coffee for them. She fussed over Chris, who she'd always indulged as a child.

"Will you be all right?" Chris asked his mother.

"Of course. Your father's already much brighter this morning. Did you two speak?" Rose held her breath.

"Yes." Chris said and Rose exhaled. "I told him my work and my life in London are important, but don't stop me thinking about you. We agreed communication is getting easier and I can call via WhatsApp or Skype."

"Even just a short message or photo would be appreciated," said Rose.

"I know. I realise that now. Let's see how it goes before I make other plans."

"Heather's coming over this summer, though I don't think the family are joining her. Maybe you could travel with her." Rose hoped she had not overstepped an indistinct line.

"I'll think about it."

CHAPTER SEVENTY

On Tuesday morning, Rose returned to the Mount Kenya Resort and Spa. Joel had asked her to join him in a meeting with Manager Bundi.

The upturned oil barrels remained outside the front gate, but the security guard waved her through without taking down her details or handing her a vehicle pass.

She parked by the stables and checked the two horses within them. A syce was tacking them up. Rose watched him force a bridle over the head of one horse. The bridle was too small, but the syce did not appear to notice.

Rose opened the door and marched into the stable. "Come, look at the way the bit pulls up in the horse's mouth. This bridle is too tight. See all you need to do is lengthen these two cheek pieces to make it comfortable." Rose demonstrated lengthening leather straps on either side of the horse's head.

She watched the remaining horses and ponies grazing quietly in an adjacent paddock before walking towards the hotel. It seemed peaceful after the previous week's activity.

In the small garden area at the back of the hotel, gardeners swept leaves and pruned bushes. Just over a week ago she had watched Hugo practice his martial art moves.

Inside the hotel, a single receptionist greeted her. She continued along the corridor towards the hotel kitchen. Joel looked tired with dark circles around his bloodshot eyes.

"Habari, Mama Rose. Asante for coming today," Joel said. He closed the dishwasher and pressed a button.

"You look tired."

Joel chuckled. "I'm exhausted. Last week was full on and now the head chef and his deputy are both on leave. I'm in charge, which is proving challenging even though we only have a handful of guests. Nicki's been a great help. She fetches and carries and even helped cook breakfast this morning when one of the other chefs slept in."

"What about Wanje?" asked Rose.

Joel picked up a plastic bottle and sprayed the chrome counter. "He's learning. I had to be out front this morning to cook eggs, omelettes and pancakes. When I popped into the kitchen for more pancake mixture, Nicki was showing him how to cook bacon and sausages." Joel began rubbing the top with a cloth.

"Any sign of Kenneth?"

"No. He has completely vanished." Joel scrunched his mouth. "I couldn't understand it, but that pretty policewoman was here today looking for him. She told me Kenneth kidnapped Darren from the UK."

"He did. A difficult situation, and one I can't entirely blame him for. What did Constable Wachira say?" Rose moved into the middle of the kitchen so Joel could continue his cleaning.

"There was nothing to indicate where he'd gone. She said she'd report back, but couldn't see the point chasing someone who clearly didn't want to be found."

Joel paused and straightened up. "She also told me the man you caught for killing Divina Dijan has been sent back to the UK." Joel sprayed another length of countertop and began wiping it.

"I heard he might be," said Rose. "I think he'll end up in a medical institution rather than prison. Commissioner Akida will be pleased to hand him over, as it will save him time and expense."

Joel finished wiping the stainless steel counter and rinsed his cloth. Washing his hands, he said, "Shall we see Manager Bundi?"

If Rose had thought Joel looked tired, then Manager Bundi was a walking rotund zombie. As they entered his office, the chubby manager popped a small white pill out of its sealed packet and washed it down with bottled water. "Headache," he said, tapping the side of his head. He leaned back in his chair, yawning.

Rose tried to lighten the atmosphere. "Was last week a success?"

"Yes. Though as exhausting as I expected." He yawned again and smiled. "It was great to see the hotel so full and vibrant. We promoted a special offer to delegates. If they return within three months, they qualify for a discounted full or half board rate. We've already taken a dozen bookings."

"Congratulations," said Rose. She coughed. "Joel asked me to join him to discuss waste food and other items thrown away which might benefit the local community."

The manager tapped the ends of his fingers.

Joel hesitated, then launched in. "To prevent stealing and waste, and to help people, I thought we could set up a programme to distribute food to those most in need."

"I agree," said Manager Bundi. He stood and walked over to a drawer from which he extracted a folder. "These are letters I've received in the last year requesting help from the hotel. There are a number of individual families, but I think it better to begin with schools, orphanages or other organisations. Where one delivery can help a larger number of people. You have to understand, though, it's not just delivering the items, you have to monitor their use and distribution."

"Yes," said Rose. "I've known orphanages where the staff stole donated food. They even took blankets given for the children's beds."

"Precisely," said Manager Bundi. "That's why I recommend starting with just one or two recipients. If they are using the donations fairly, add another organisation to the distribution list. Report back to me at the beginning of June and we'll discuss your progress."

"Can I use a hotel vehicle?"

The manager scratched his head. "Something else that is open to abuse. Until our next meeting you can, but write down when and where you went and the distance travelled."

"Thank you." Joel stood and waited for Rose.

She said, "Joel, good luck. Let me know if you need my help. I still have a couple of things to discuss with Manager Bundi."

Joel closed the door behind him. "Firstly," said Rose, "A clinic to teach the syces and staff how to correctly tack up the horses."

"Horses again." Manager Bundi groaned, rubbing the back of his neck.

Rose continued. "I won't abide animal cruelty and what I witnessed this morning is close to it. Ill-fitting tack hurts the horses. It will also lead to increased vets bills, from me, and unusable horses. So what do you think?"

Manager Bundi held his hands up in surrender. "Whatever you think necessary. Go ahead and organise it with Nicki."

Rose sat up. "How is she doing?"

Manager Bundi brightened. "She's a godsend. Not sure how I'd have managed without her. Indeed, unless the Belmont Group send a replacement manager by tomorrow lunchtime, I'm handing the reins over to her. I need a break, I can barely think straight at the moment."

"No trouble with thefts during the conference?"

Rose sat back realising she'd lit a fuse. The Manager's face reddened and he stood up and leant forward, his hands propped on the top of his desk for support. "Not from Nicki. But can you believe it? A minister and his wife absconded on Friday night with one of my best king-size mattresses!"

CHAPTER SEVENTY-ONE

C hloe shrieked with joy as she watched a procession of over a dozen orphan elephants. They followed two green-coated keepers out of the bush of Nairobi National Park into the muddy roped off area in front of her. The young elephants marched along in single file with the smallest grabbing the tail of his older friend in front of him.

Peeling off, each chose a keeper who held an oversized milk bottle. It was made from a two litre plastic soda bottle with an extra-large teat attached to the opening. One warden teased his charge by walking away from the young elephant. It followed, tapping him on the back with its trunk.

A group of school children, wearing light blue skirts or shorts with bright red jumpers, squealed in delight. Rose reflected that it was over two weeks since she had helped rescue the young elephant from Mount Kenya. She wondered which of the elephants in front of her she had treated. They all looked well and happy as they rolled on the floor or drank water from large metal barrels.

Sister Lucy, who ran the orphanage at Rose's Church, had persuaded her and Chloe to join them on the trip to Nairobi to visit the rescued elephant. Rose suspected Sister Lucy had persuaded Chloe to pay for the matatu which transported the children.

The youngsters danced around, pointing at the elephants. They had been so excited about the trip and had all drawn pictures of "their elephant" which Sister Lucy would present to the Sheldrick Wildlife Trust.

The orphanage had been given the honour of naming the elephant rescued from Mount Kenya, and once again Rose suspected Sister Lucy had something to do with obtaining this privilege. The children had chosen the name Francis, after the patron saint for the environment and animals.

Rose looked around the large crowd who smiled and chattered animatedly to each other. Most were tourists capturing the spectacle on camera or video with their phones. Rose knew this event, which took place each morning, raised essential funds for the elephant orphanage. Smaller groups of people also visited in the evening on the understanding they would adopt an orphan elephant or rhino.

Chloe and Rose walked behind the skipping children. They were being given a special tour of the elephant orphanage. Stopping in front of a tall wooden stable, they peered through the open door into the straw-covered interior. A small elephant wearing a brightly coloured red and green blanket drank milk out of a bottle held by a keeper.

"Is this your elephant?" asked Chloe.

Rose enquired from the keeper in Kiswahili. "He said this elephant arrived two weeks ago from up north. It has an injured side." The warden lifted the edge of the blanket and Rose squinted at the wound. The keeper spoke to her. She straightened up. "He said it's healing well. Good. But the young elephant is still unsettled and grieving for its mother and the herd. They have it under constant observation which is why it's not out with the rest of the orphans."

A young boy stepped through the door. Sister Lucy held him back as the elephant shrank against the wall. The keeper made soothing sounds.

"These are the lucky ones," Rose said. "The Sheldrick Trust will love, nurture and teach these elephants and eventually they'll be returned to the wild. As John F. Kennedy said, 'children are the world's most valuable resource and its best hope for the future.'"

"It's a shame Thabiti couldn't join us. He'd love to have seen the elephant," said Chloe. "I must take a photo for him."

"I'm delighted he's found something to do. Working at Mr Obado's garage on his Rhino Charge team's vehicle will be great experience."

"If the Rhino Charge event is not too far from Nanyuki, shall we go and support him?" asked Chloe.

"As long as you promise me there'll be no dead bodies," said Rose.

"Come on. You love a good mystery. Next stop the Rhino Charge."

Dear Reader

I hope you enjoyed Tusk Justice. I loved watching the characters interact at the Mount Kenya Resort and Spa. Many of them were introduced in Fowl Murder, book 1 in the Kenya Kanga Mystery series, and some, like Constable Wachira, wanted more prominent roles in this story.

But I wondered what became of Kenneth, and his son Darren, who disappeared from the hotel? If you would also like to know what happened to them visit https://dl.bookfunnel.com/iyiv5eal3z.

When you request Kenneth's epilogue, you will be signing up to receive updates from me. I don't send spam and you can unsubscribe at any time.

If you enjoyed Tusk Justice please leave a review on the platform you bought it from, and any others you are willing and able to post on. Reviews will help bring Tusk Justice to the attention of other readers. A couple of lines highlighting what you like most, such as characters, setting, plot etc. are sufficient.

At the end of Tusk Justice, Chloe and Rose discussed the Rhino Charge event which Thabiti will be competing in. It is an off-road 4x4 fund-raising event and part of Kenya's annual sporting calendar. It is also central to the next book in the series, Rhino Charge, which takes its name from the event.

Craig is too ill to attend, so Chloe joins Rose in Kenya's iconic Maasai Mara Game reserve. To buy Rhino Charge visit https://books2read.com/RhinoCharge, or read the extract at the end of this book. I hope you will join me for another enthralling tale, with a large cast of fascinating characters including Sam, Mama Rose's Guardian angel from Fowl Murder, and Marina, who we met briefly in Tusk Justice. Will she and Thabiti become more than just good friends?

Best wishes

Victoria Tait

To Find Out About Kenneth and Darren visit
https://dl.bookfunnel.com/iyiv5eal3z

Rhino Charge: A Gripping Cozy Murder Mystery
(A Kenya Kanga Mystery Book 3)

A treacherous race to stop an extinction. A mysterious death linked to the past. Can a silver-haired sleuth unearth the clues in time to save a life?

'Mama Rose' Hardie has always fought to conserve Kenya's precious wildlife. Officiating at an off-road fundraising race in the famous Maasai Mara game reserve, she's shocked when a vehicle crash claims the life of a colleague. And worse still, this was no accident…

When a good friend is accused of plotting a deadly sabotage, the clever amateur detective vows to clear his name. But with motives between teams reaching deep into an unfortunate past, the determined woman must work fast to track down the wily killer.

Can Rose catch the culprit before more lives are endangered?

Rhino Charge is the thrilling third tale in the Kenya Kanga cozy mystery series. If you like sharp heroines, suspenseful reveals, and iconic African settings, then you'll love Victoria Tait's breathtaking story.

Buy *Rhino Charge* to set a trap for a callous murderer today!

To Buy Rhino Charge Visit
https://books2read.com/RhinoCharge

RHINO CHARGE - EXERT

Chapter 1

Rose squashed her clothes into her brown canvas bag and forced the zip closed.

"All packed," she exclaimed to her husband Craig, who was propped up in bed. Rose Hardie, fondly known as 'Mama Rose' by the local community, was a tall, thin, sprightly woman despite being sixty-five years old.

Her husband Craig, who was in his early seventies, was almost bed-bound. He had caught polio as a child and now a secondary complication was paralysing the left side of his body. Recently, he'd also suffered a mini-stroke.

"Now you're sure you'll be OK?" Rose asked. "I shall be away nearly a week."

"Stop fussing, woman. You've left me plenty of times before and I've survived." Craig's jaw set into a thin line. She had spent time away in the past, but that was before he had fallen ill.

Craig continued, "I have Kipto to look after me, and she'll make sure Samwell helps me out onto the patio for fresh air, or into the living room so I can watch horse racing from South Africa."

At the sound of her name, Kipto, their house girl of

unknown age, entered, closely followed by a fluffy white dog which resembled a small sheep.

Kipto turned to the dog and flapped her arms. "Shoo. Is this dog always hungry?" she asked. "It not stop following me."

"Its owner, Thabiti, is the hungry one," responded Rose. "I think she's scared of being alone again. She was abandoned in a locked house before Dr Emma rescued her." Pixel, the dog, jumped onto the bed and started sniffing Rose's bag. Potto, Rose's black and tan terrier, growled as it lay beside Craig's feet.

"I'm ready." She walked around the bed and pecked Craig on the top of his balding head. "It won't be the same at the Rhino Charge this year without you. Do you know, we've never missed a Charge since it started in 1989." Rose looked down as Craig smiled weakly at her. They both knew he was unlikely to attend another.

"Just keep out of trouble," Craig told her.

Rose parked her battered, red Land Rover Defender in a free space beside Mr Obado's garage in the centre of Nanyuki, a small market town, three hours' drive north of Nairobi, the capital of Kenya. A crowd of people gathered outside the garage and watched a blue 4x4 car being loaded onto a long flat-bed trailer. The vehicle started life as a Range Rover, but it had been stripped down to its skeleton and rebuilt into a robust off-road machine capable of travelling across rough terrain.

Rose stood next to a young African man with cropped hair and a neat beard and moustache.

"Thabiti, am I OK on your side?" the driver shouted as he drove onto the trailer's ramp.

"Plenty of room," the young man called back.

A well-dressed, attractive blonde-haired lady joined them.

"Morning, Chloe," Rose greeted the new arrival.

Chloe pressed her hands together and exclaimed, "So this is the car you've been hiding. It's a beast."

Thabiti grinned. "This event is not called the Rhino Charge for nothing. The vehicles have to be strong enough to navigate sandy slopes, rocky ground, and force their way through bushes, just as a real Rhino would."

Chloe slipped on a large pair of sunglasses. "I've never really understood the fascination between men and cars, but I am looking forward to spending a week in the Maasai Mara. I can't wait to see all the wildlife."

Rose turned to her and said, "We'll be working, so I'm not sure how much time we'll get for safaris."

Chloe's mouth drooped.

At that moment Rose's mobile phone rang. The voice on the other end said, "Hi, Rose. Are you busy?"

Rose's heart sank. The caller was Dr Emma, who was technically her boss. Rose called herself a community vet, but when the Kenyan authorities altered the veterinary regulations, she became a veterinary paraprofessional, working under the only qualified vet in Nanyuki, Dr Emma. "Why? What's happened?"

"I've had a call from Ol Pejeta Conservancy. Ringo, the orphan rhino, is unwell."

"Just a minute," Rose said into the phone. She lifted her head. "Dr Emma needs my help at Ol Pejeta."

"But we'll miss our lift," cried Chloe.

"You go. I'll see if I can find someone else travelling to the Mara."

Chloe shook her head. "I'm not going alone."

Chapter 2

Rose steered her trusty Defender around another large pothole in the dirt track. Chloe and Dr Emma were squeezed together in the passenger seats beside her. Dr Emma was a diminutive figure, but she had a huge afro hairstyle and wore enormous, round, yellow-rimmed glasses.

"Why don't they mend this road?" Chloe wondered aloud. "I'm surprised it's in such poor condition considering the number of tourists who visit Ol Pejeta."

They arrived at the conservancy entrance and, after signing the visitor's book, were ushered through.

"It's so green after the recent rains," pronounced Dr Emma.

"Look, impala," cried Chloe.

Rose's two passengers bobbed up and down like excited school children. Sweeping plains opened out ahead of them, interspersed with denser areas of bushes and solitary acacia trees.

"This is fantastic." Dr Emma gazed out through the windscreen. "I don't get to visit Ol Pejeta very often. I just don't seem to have the time."

Rose turned off the track besides Morani's Restaurant and parked outside the Rhino caretakers' wooden hut.

A serious-looking African man wearing green trousers, shirt, and matching short-brimmed hat strode to meet them with his arm outstretched. "Habari. I'm Zachariah." He shook hands with each of them. "Follow me."

They entered a large wooden enclosure with a dirt floor. At the far end stood a tiny dejected rhino, with a drooping head and ears pinned back against his stocky neck.

This was Ringo, who had been abandoned by his mother when he was only two weeks old. The team at Ol Pejeta had done a wonderful job nursing him back to health from his severely malnourished state. At an outreach day for the Giant's Club Summit, earlier in April, he had been the star attraction.

"He's so sweet," cried Chloe. "Why's he called Ringo?"

Zachariah answered, "After the famous musician who raises money for wildlife conservation, and has spoken out against rhino poaching. I think his band was called the bugs."

266

Chloe wrinkled the corner of her mouth but Rose laughed. "I think he means Ringo Starr from The Beatles."

Chloe jumped as they heard a grunting noise and something hit the wooden partition against which she leant.

"It's OK, Sudan," soothed Zachariah. An enormous rhino on the far side of the fence stamped a foot. "He's really taken to Ringo. We were worried about his health as he's getting old, until this little one arrived and he perked up."

"What are you feeding Ringo?" asked Dr Emma.

Zachariah replied, "A mixture of lactose, porridge oats, glucose and salt. We usually feed him five or six times a day, but he won't touch it now."

"What about his usual routine?"

"Normally he is bright and loves his daily runs with one of the caretakers. He's less keen on his mud-wallowing lessons, but now he refuses to leave this enclosure."

Rose said, "It's notoriously difficult raising young rhino. Is someone always with him?"

"Yes, and one of us always sleeps next to him at night."

Rose nodded. "Even so, it's not the same as having a mother. However hard you try, you can't replicate the care or education she should be giving him." She laid a hand on Zachariah's arm. "We'll do our best for him."

Rose knelt beside the small rhino. She ran her fingers gently across his thick hide, but couldn't find any cuts, or anything caught in or sticking out of it. She placed a hand on his shoulder. "He doesn't feel too hot. Actually, I think we should put a blanket on him."

Zachariah placed a red and blue checked shuka over Ringo's small frame.

"Keep trying him with water. We don't want him getting dehydrated," directed Dr Emma. "If he still refuses to eat his normal food, try some milk formula. And if he continues like this, and there is no obvious cause, we will need to test his blood to see if he is fighting a virus, or lacking any vitamins or minerals."

Rose, Chloe and Dr Emma were subdued as they left the conservancy, and took little notice of the warthogs, rushing away from the noise of the car, with erect tails.

Do you want to find out what happened next?

To Buy Rhino Charge Visit
https://books2read.com/RhinoCharge

ABOUT THE AUTHOR

Victoria Tait is the author of the enchanting Kenya Kanga Mystery series. She's drawn on her 8 years experience living in rural Kenya, with her family, to write vivid and evocative descriptions. Her readers feel the heat, taste the dryness and smell the dust of Africa. Her elderly amateur sleuth, "Mama Rose" Hardie is Agatha Christie's Miss Marple reincarnated and living in Kenya.

Like all good military wives, Victoria follows the beat of the drum and has recently moved to war scarred Sarajevo in Bosnia. She has two fast growing teenage boys. She enjoys horse riding and mountain biking. Victoria is looking forward to the sun, sand and seafood of neighbouring Croatia when the world returns to normal.

You can find Victoria at VictoriaTait.com, or at Goodreads and Bookbub.

If you would like to email Victoria her address is victoria@victoriatait.com

COPYRIGHT

A Kanga Press Ebook

First published in 2020 by Kanga Press

Ebook first published in 2020 by Kanga Press Copyright Victoria Tait 2020

Book Cover Design by ebooklaunch.com

Editing Cassandra Dunn and Allie Douglas

❀ Created with Vellum

UNTITLED

UNTITLED

UNTITLED

Made in the USA
Las Vegas, NV
31 May 2023

72787077R00166